THE C
AND OTHER OCCULT FANTASIES

JANE DE LA VAUDÈRE (1857-1908) was baptized Jeanne Scrive and was married to Camille Gaston Crapez, who began styling himself Crapez de La Vaudère after inheriting the Château de La Vaudère from his mother. Her prolific literary work is very various but she was assimilated to the Decadent Movement firstly because of two scandalously scabrous Parisian novels, *Les Demi-Sexes* (1897) and *Les Andrognyes* (1903), and, more pertinently, because of a series of accounts of *moeurs antiques*, some of which—notably *Le Mystère de Kama* (1901)—set new standards of excess in their exotic eroticism and fascination with torture.

BRIAN STABLEFORD has been publishing fiction and non-fiction for fifty years. His fiction includes an eighteen-volume series of "tales of the biotech revolution" and a series of half a dozen metaphysical fantasies set in Paris in the 1840s, featuring Edgar Poe's Auguste Dupin. His most recent non-fiction projects are *New Atlantis: A Narrative History of British Scientific Romance* (Wildside Press, 2016) and *The Plurality of Imaginary Worlds: The Evolution of French* roman scientifique (Black Coat Press, 2016); in association with the latter he has translated approximately a hundred and fifty volumes of texts not previously available in English, similarly issued by Black Coat Press.

SNUGGLY BOOKS

JANE DE LA VAUDÈRE

THE DOUBLE STAR
AND OTHER OCCULT FANTASIES

TRANSLATED AND WITH AN INTRODUCTION BY
BRIAN STABLEFORD

THIS IS A SNUGGLY BOOK

ISBN: 978-1-943813-64-3

CONTENTS

INTRODUCTION

THIS is the second of six projected volumes translating fiction by Jane de La Vaudère (15 April 1857-26 July 1908). The other five volumes each contain two of her short novels. The first volume in the series, *The Demi-Sexes and The Androgynes*, contains translations of *Les Demi-Sexes*, originally published by Paul Ollendorff in 1897, and *Les Androgynes, roman passionel*, originally published by Albert Méricant in 1903. The third volume in the series, *The Mysteries of Kama and Brahma's Courtesans*, contains translations of *Le Mystère de Kama, roman magique indou* (Ernest Flammarion, 1901) and *Les Courtisanes de Brahma* (Flammarion, 1903). The fourth volume, *Three Flowers and the King of Siam's Amazon*, contains translations of *Trois fleurs de volupté, roman javanais* (Flammarion, 1900) and *L'Amazone du roi de Siam* (Flammarion, 1902). The fifth volume, *Syta's Harem and Pharaoh's Lover*, contains translations of *Le Harem de Syta, roman passionel* (Méricant, 1904) and *L'Amante du Pharaon, moeurs antiques* (Jules Tallandier, 1905). The sixth volume, *The Witch of Ecbatana and the Virgin of Israel*, contains translations *of La Sorcière d'Ecbatane, roman fantastique* (Flammarion, 1906) and *La Vierge d'Israel, roman de moeurs antiques* (Méricant 1906).

The stories contained in the present volume were mostly published in the early years of the author's career. "Le Centenaire d'Emmanuel" (tr. herein as "Emmanuel's Centenary") was originally published the *La Nouvelle Revue* in November 1892 before being reprinted in *L'Anarchiste* (Paul Ollendorff, 1893), along with "Une Vengéance" (tr. as "A Vengeance"), "L'Étoile double" (tr. as "The Double Star") and "Réincarnation" (tr. as "Reincarnation"). The first three stories were all reprinted in *La Mystérieuse* (Ernest Flammarion, 1901), the second retitled "Les Amants tragiques" and the third "Dans un étoile." "Une Vengéance" had also been reprinted in *Les Sataniques* (Ollendorff, 1897) as "Bérénice," and that collection also featured "Viviane," originally published as "Amour Astral" in *L'Univers illustré* 1890-91 in seven parts (tr. as "Astral Amour") and the novella "Yvaine," first published in *Gil Blas* as a thirteen-part feuilleton in November 1896.

Two of the other stories were first published in the weekly supplement of the newspaper *La Lanterne*, to which La Vaudère supplied a long series of unreprinted short stories in 1901-03. "Sapho" appeared in the 3 December 1901 issue and "Volupté rouge" (tr. as "Red Lust") in the 18 December 1902 issue. The final story was originally published as *Le Rêve de Mysès, roman d'amour de moeurs antiques* (Libraire d'art technique, 1908; tr. as "The Dream of Myses").

Jane de La Vaudère was baptized Jeanne Scrive; both her parents died when she was a child, and in the social class to which her family belonged, which might be described as the "upper bourgeoisie," the standard practice when a young girl was orphaned at an early age was to put her in a convent, where she would be educated until her teens, and then marry her off as soon as possible. That appears to be what happened to Jeanne Scrive and her elder sister Marie. It is necessary to say "appears" because almost nothing is known for sure about Jane de La Vaudère's personal life and death, all of it covered by an obscurity that remains virtually impenetrable save for the statements she made in a few newspaper interviews and a few objectively determinable facts.

In one such interview La Vaudère said that while in the convent of Notre-Dame de Sion she seriously considered remaining there permanently, the idea of living as a nun having a certain romantic attraction, but soon abandoned the idea. In fact, shortly after leaving the institution, when she apparently went to stay for a while with Marie, by then married to a military surgeon, she was married herself to Camille Gaston Crapez (1848-1912), who inherited the Château de La Vaudère in Parigné-l'Éveque (Sarthe) from his mother and styled himself thereafter Crapez de La Vaudère. The name with which she signed her books was not, therefore, as many sources report, a pseudonym, although she deleted the Crapez and anglicized her forename.

The Crapez de La Vaudères had one child, a son named Fernand, who apparently stayed with his father when his mother went to live in Paris, where she seems to have lived alone. Although she was never divorced, and her body was taken back to Parigné-L'Éveque for burial after her death in Paris, the separation appears to have been complete, no newspaper reports of her appearances at social events or interviews conducted at her home mention the presence of her husband. Nothing was reported about the circumstances of her death, and neither her husband nor her son appear to have been with her at the time; the unusual brevity of the death notices and the conspicuous absence of the customary post-mortem eulogies suggest a diplomatic silence, but we can only speculate as to what it was that was deliberately not being said about her sudden death at a relatively young age.

The circumstances of Jane de La Vaudère's early life evidently had a profound impact on her literary work, to which she turned a trifle late in her career. Before she began writing, in her thirties, she attempted to make a career as an artist, and exhibited at the Paris Salon; when she decided that her real vocation was literary she first began writing poetry, and then wrote for the stage. Her first collection of poetry, *Les Heures perdues* [The Lost Hours] (1889) appeared in the same year as the production of her one-act comedy *Le Modèle* [The Model]. Her verse is Romantic and might have seemed a trifle old-fashioned at the time of its publication; she was certainly not unaware of contemporary trends in Symbolist poetry, for she was a very voracious reader and her influences were eclectic. *Le Modèle* was the first of many frothy one-act comedies, often in verse and often performed with musical accompaniment—fifteen of them were collected in *Pour le*

Flirt! Saynètes modernes [approximately, Just For Fun, modern satirettes] (1905)—but she also wrote longer comedies and dramas.

She continued to write poetry and plays alongside her prose fiction, but there are very striking differences between her works in the three genres, and her prose work also shows sharp generic divisions. It is not unusual for writers to manifest seemingly different personalities in their prose fiction and work for the stage, especially if the latter mostly consists of vaudevilles written as pure entertainment while the former is more earnest and detailed, but in La Vaudère's case the difference is extreme, even in her contemporary Paris-set novels, which often feature female characters not unlike those routinely portrayed in her stage comedies—young socialites, actresses and artists' models—but is very markedly so in the remarkable series of exotic novels set in far-flung places and times that make up the last four volumes of the present series of translations.

La Vaudère's first novel, *Mortelle étreinte* [Mortal Embrace] (1891) is the story of a young orphan brought up in a convent who then goes to live with a relative, where she continues to live in virtual seclusion, in the psychological environment of her vivid imagination and the books she reads in abundance. She knows nothing about the real world and is utterly unready to cope with her own hectic emotions when she is first attracted to a man—a man who is also greatly attracted to her, but is, from every other viewpoint, quite unsuitable, and incapable of providing her with the existential anchorage and security that she needs and desires.

The basic features of that story-line were to recur again and again in the author's work, even in the most bizarre décor. Its melodramatic intensity is inevitably restrained in *Mortelle étreinte* by the conventions of the society in which it is set, but when it is removed to ancient India or ancient Babylon, in the author's accounts of *moeurs antiques*, such shackles no longer apply and the pitch of that intensity is turned up to a level unequaled in the work of any other writer of the era. The sensation of having been brought up in an artificial environment, with little or no parental guidance, and then thrust into a world equipped with hopes and expectations that are certain to be betrayed, is developed in story after story, in variants that are extraordinarily wide-ranging, often wildly exaggerated, and almost always brutally tragic.

It was not long before the appearance of her first novel that La Vaudère's shorter works of fiction began appearing in periodicals, often as short serials, "Amour Astral" being followed by two political fantasies, "Terka" (1891 in *Le Matin*; reprinted as "Nihiliste"), and "L'Anarchiste" (1892 in *Le Figaro*), both of which disapprove strongly of Anarchism—an opinion unfashionable at the time in Parisian literary circles, especially among the Symbolists. The references in her other early stories, however, especially those collected herein, reveal that she had become intensely interested in contemporary research in physiological psychology, especially hypnotism, and the possible connections between hypnotism and the magic and mysticism of the occult revival. Although the intensity of that interest declined over time, it continued to exert a strong influence on her more exotic works of fiction, several of whose plots have central supernatural elements, and it is still echoed in *Le Rêve de Mysès*.

La Vaudère probably attended spiritualist séances in the 1890s, led by curiosity rather than belief, but we can only speculate as to how closely she was acquainted with Camille Flammarion, the brother of her principal publisher, whose weekly salon played host to many of the most celebrated mediums of the day, as well as writers and unorthodox scientists, and often included experiments in automatic writing and drawing. "L'étoile double" is clearly based on Camille Flammarion's ideas, but La Vaudère had surely read his bestselling *Uranie* (1891) and might well have picked them up from there. The question is, however, of some interest because La Vaudère's fiction, which rarely stands up to rational analysis, often gives the impression of having been written in a self-induced alternative state of consciousness. One could say that about all fiction, of course, but La Vaudère's more exotic work seems to have been exceptionally disconnected from rational afterthought. All of her novels seem to have been made up as she went along, with relatively little advance planning, and often meander or change direction in response to her reading or her mood, routinely lacking continuity, consistency and coherency.

Her short stories tend to be more focused than her novels, usually progressing directly and smoothly to a predetermined ending, but they make extravagant use of dreams and hallucinations as a narrative device, and often seem hallucinatory themselves, even where their subject matter is far more pedestrian than the phantasmagorical "L'Étoile double." That story seems particularly significant in the context of her career, however, in its remarkable characterization of the heart-collecting Chimera, the latter term being the label that La Vaudère consistently gave to the generating impulse of her flights of fantasy.

The early short stories are also distinct from the novels in their customary use of a male first-person narrator, who necessarily sees the female characters from an angle markedly different from the disembodied quasi-objective narrative voice of the novels, which delves more elaborately into the typically-obsessive psychology of La Vaudère's heroines. The narrators of the early short stories are perhaps not all insane, but they are all male, and hence dubiously reliable in their judgments, even at their best. They do, however, share the same obsessive character-traits as her heroines, yielding readily to erotic obsessions that are usually disastrous for them. "Réincarnation" is exceptional among the author's works is depicting an erotic obsession pursed to a successful, albeit highly unorthodox, conclusion, although "Yvaine" is also an exception, in spite of the peculiar contrived ambiguity of its conclusion. "Le Centenaire d'Emmanuel," however, stands out even more within her canon as an exceedingly rare story in which the obsession has no erotic component, being purely artistic—although that does not prevent it from proving disastrous.

The two short stories from *La Lanterne* are representative of an entirely different phase in the author's career, most of the work she did for that periodical being flippant and anecdotal, in an ironic spirit much more similar to her one-act comedy plays than to her longer prose works. The two samples are particularly interesting in the context of her work because they reflect a particular fascination with black panthers, which seem to have acquired a significant symbolism in the author's mind—perhaps being, partially at least, a magnification of the pet cat featured in "L'Étoile double" as the Chimera's alter ego. Erotically-charged female black panthers play significant roles in *L'Amazone du roi de Siam* and *Les Courtisanes de Brahma*, and it is possible that the first of the posthumously-published novels bearing La Vaudère's signature, *Sapho, dompteuse* [Sapho, Animal Tamer] (1908) was written in the same period as those two novels and the two short stories included herein.

Le Rêve de Mysès belongs to yet another phase of the author's career, obviously affiliated the series of exotic novels featured in the subsequent volumes in the present series, and particularly to *L'Amante du Pharaon*, from which it reproduces several passages of background description as well as developing a similar central notion. The book, but not the story, also reflects another curious development in the author's career. Albert Méricant, its publisher—although he used a different label in this case—was a prolific publisher of erotica, and an ardent advocate, in particular, of the artistic credentials of nude photography. He published two periodicals of such photographs and numerous books—of which *Le Rêve de Mysès* is one and the extremely elusive *Les Prêtresses de Mylitta*, the last novel La Vaudère published during her lifetime, another—in which nude photographs are used as plates, each helpfully bearing a reference number in case the reader wanted to order larger prints.

Méricant's argument had an undeniable logic to it. If the Paris Salon was replete every year with nude paintings of prostitutes, which everyone accepted as "Art," why should photographs of the same prostitutes in the same poses be considered merely as "dirty postcard" fodder? That was, however, the prevailing prejudice, and the reputations of the various authors he recruited to his publicity—which included "Jean Bertheroy" (Berthe Le Barillier) and other leading exponents of the *roman de moeurs antiques*— might well have suffered in consequence. The presence of the nude photographs probably contributed to the fact that *La Rêve de Mysès* is such a rare book; the erotic illustrations included in the other novels by La Vaudère that Méricant published, mostly by the artist Charles Atamian, might also be a factor in their rarity. (The copy of *Le Harem de Syta* that is available for consultation on-line has been stripped of all its illustrative plates, and the copy of *Le Vierge d'Israel* that I bought for translation—the only one available at the time—is also missing all but two of its plates.) The story told in *La Rêve de Mysès* is relatively innocuous, as sentimental fantasies of necrophilia go, and although it has a good deal in common with some of the hallucinatory fantasies from the 1890s, it surely has the edge if they are viewed as Poesque horror stories.

The influence of Poe on La Vaudère's early fiction is clearly marked in the opening of "Une Vengéance," which is obviously derived from "The Fall of the House of Usher," and "Yvaine," which quotes and is seemingly inspired by "The Man of the Crowd." Her male narrators have a good deal in common with Poe's, and "Réincarnation" might well have been directly inspired by Poe as well. Although the short stories from *La Lanterne* clearly have other models, perhaps taking a considerable influence from another of the regular contributors to that newspaper's weekly supplement, Catulle Mendès, a Poesque fascination with what the American writer called "The Imp of the Perverse" seems to have been a constant feature in the artistry of La Vaudère's literary endeavor, the pattern of her career, and perhaps her life as well, if what seem to be echoes of her own sentiments in her work really are revealing. That element of her work made her a significant writer in the development of modern horror fiction, although she is not mentioned in any reference book on that subject. That must in part be due to the scattered nature of her publications in the genre—*Les Sataniques*, her only specialist collection, is exceedingly scarce—but the present volume might help to redress that omission.

The translations of "Le Centenaire d'Emmanuel," "Une Vengéance" and "L'Étoile double" were made from the copy of the Flammarion edition of *La Mystérieuse* reproduced in the Bibliothèque Nationale's *gallica* website. The translation of "Réincarnartion" was made from an undated print-on-demand reprint of the text of *L'Anarchiste* produced by General Books LLC. The translation of "Amour Astral" was made from the relevant issues of *L'Univers illustré* reproduced on *gallica*, the translation "Yvaine" from the relevant issues of *Gil Blas* and the translations of "Sapho" and "Volupté rouge" from the issues of *La Lanterne* reproduced on the same website. The translation of *Le Rêve de Mysès* was made from a copy of the Libraire d'art technique edition.

—Brian Stableford

THE DOUBLE STAR
AND OTHER OCCULT FANTASIES

EMMANUEL'S CENTENARY

WE are certainly reincarnated, and each of us has undoubtedly lived several previous existences. A human being dies every second, over the whole surface of the terrestrial globe. In ten centuries, more than thirty billion cadavers have been delivered to the earth and then returned to the general circulation in the form of water, gas, etc., and, little by little, have formed new beings, which the souls of the humans of old have come to inhabit. If the constituent elements of bodies drawn from nature are renewed, each of us bears within himself atoms that have previously belonged to other bodies.

The soul that animates us remains, in the same way as every molecule of nitrogen or oxygen, and all the souls that have lived still exist. They govern matter in order to organize the living form of human beings. Everything changes, is confounded and renewed, in the immutable law of amour that governs the world. However, the passage from one body to another is unconscious, and although abrupt reminiscences sometimes awake in us at the sight of a location that is familiar to us, even though we are examining it for the first time, the mists of our intelligence are still too dense for us to understand.

By virtue of a special grace, however, or an explicable punishment, memory has remained permanent in me and has maintained my conscious identity with certainty. I know that I was a great and illustrious poet in my previous incarnation and I rediscover all the impulses and all the ecstasies that rendered me famous among men. Perhaps those faculties are enlarged as well as being improved, for the tender poems that were once my glory now seem to me to be the conceptions of a child, brilliant but inexperienced. I know that I am in possession of a younger art, more vibrant and more equal; the thoughts that crowd within me, like bees in a hive, are only asking to take flight; but men go past me indifferently; I am poorly clad and do not always eat when I am hungry. Who, then, would recognize in me the great Emmanuel?

⁂

I have been wandering for three days in this city, which recalls such strange memories. It is the first time that I have come here, and yet everything is familiar to me. The back street that I am in at present is narrow, made of low, gray, damp constructions, which the sun scarcely illuminates. Profound cracks divide the walls, and the ground is sticky; in spite of the cold, a fetid moss is growing between the cobbles. A ray of sunlight makes its appearance; the lower part of the houses is fringed by a black shadow, and the sky, squeezed between the shaky balconies, looks like a blue stainless paving stone.

Yes, I remember; there is the gutter where I set paper boats afloat; there is the boundary-marker where I used to sit, with my feet in the mud and my head in the stars; there is the wall where I scribbled my first verses ninety-five years ago. But I have died since then, and no one would recognize my face, which is not that of old. I died thirty years ago, and my soul, after having wandered in space, descended to Earth again and was reincarnated. How and why does that happen? I cannot say. An intelligence superior to ours governs our destiny; at its whim, we go and we come until it pleases it to cut the light thread that attached us to life.

I have been rich, powerful, and idolized; triumphal arches then loomed up above my head, and the arms of the multitude made me a glorious throne. When I passed by, beautiful ladies threw me the flowers from their corsage and men acclaimed me like a monarch. When I died, the mourning was universal. Five hundred thousand people followed my hearse, and the procession of funereal emblems, wreaths and carts decked with flags lasted for an entire day. Balconies were veiled with crepe. Shops closed, and all France regretted me.

Today, no one knows me; my new works cannot find a publisher, while the old ones never have time for their beautiful yellow robes to crumple in the windows of bookshops. And I am jealous of them, those daughters of my youth, I scorn them, I hate them! What use has it been to me to acquire the experience of two lives if my purified talent, my more powerful genius, cannot vanquish routine and prejudice? Even when I read, in private, one of the beautiful burning strophes that have sprung from my soul in words of fire, at which I still quiver, the obliging friend that is listening to me shrugs his shoulders disdainfully and says to me: "After Emmanuel, you see, poetry is dead. Reread him, and try to inspire yourself with his divine tones."

If only I could shout at him: "Emmanuel is me! Do you not sense that the same breath animates us? That his verses—very beautiful, I agree—do not have the finish and splendor of mine? I am Emmanuel, but a younger, more vibrant, more complete Emmanuel, an Emmanuel no longer ignorant of anything, whom the tomb covered with its shadow in order to render him better and more robust."

No, I cannot shout that at him, because he would think me mad and abandon me. Now, I love that friend, who is all I have. Devoid of parents, a hearth and protection, I have grown up as I could, living on alms and devoting to labor the few sous picked up at hazard. Hunger has torn my entrails, cold has stiffened my limbs, murder has tempted my arms; but the bloody mud of reality soon disappeared, and if my thought sometimes dipped its wings therein, it was only to wipe them on the azure veils of the eternal fiction.

The true poet only has the mystical care of the imperishable, and his noble knighthood almost always dooms him to defeat. He sings his eternal canticle recklessly, disdaining to make himself understood to the prejudiced individuals who remain deaf to the humble and the resigned.

One day, when I had let myself fall on to a bench, succumbing to hunger and sadness, a young man who was slightly less poorly dressed than me came to offer me his mansard and his bread. I went with him, and since then, we no longer quit one another. He is the companion of my late nights and my despairs; I love him with all the strength of my poor bruised heart. Yes, I love him as much as one can love; but he does not know me, and his sarcasms add to my bitterness.

O genius, futile and cruel gift that doubles suffering and crucifies souls, hazard immortalizes you and hazard kills you. Who knows how many pure and vibrant strings are broken under the bow of poverty? Who knows how many sobs have resounded without awakening the indifferent echoes? The success that sometimes crowns us always has ironic laughter at the corners of its lips as it puts its dolorous roses on our heads, made of the flesh and blood of our unknown brethren.

Alas, what justice is there for human beings, light beings who move at the whim of the wind without opposing any more resistance than a wisp of straw? What is terrestrial glory? An illusion, like all the others, and immortality is a frightful lure. The genius once so idolized will be misunderstood or scorned by his most fervent defenders if it pleases the Master to open the doors of the tomb for him. I have returned, and I have been cast out!

Today, in order to renew my memories, I wanted to contemplate my first cradle, and draw a little consolation and strength from my former glory. My centenary is being celebrated: Emmanuel's centenary! The orators are preparing their speeches, and the populace is crowding in front of my dwelling. It is that old house with the disjointed steps and cracked walls, which a pious inscription identifies for the veneration of passers-by.

I try to cleave through the flood, but I am brutally thrust back on to the pavement and my hat rolls into the gutter. I dare not pick it up in its present condition.

"Let me pass, my friends," I say, softly. "I would like to go into that house."

"Why, then, should this *mossieur* want to see more than us? He doesn't look so good himself!"

I fall silent, ashamed, and the woman pushes me away scornfully.

Two hours pass. The old dwelling attracts me increasingly. It has been decorated with ivy and flags; the crowd jostles in the narrow corridor. It's the one to which my mother—the first, the one I knew—brought me back in the evening. I was afraid of the dark and I clung on hard to her hand.

O good mother, I shall go to pray on your tomb and perhaps you will recognize the child you cradled gently on your knees, singing as mothers sing, in a voice of love and caress. There is the window of my bedroom; it is higher and narrower than the others, and I climbed on to a chair to look out into the street on sunny days. They don't know that, these people who are going in and coming out, without even darting a glance over the poor redoubt. Legend says that it was in the big room downstairs that my childhood was spent, but I know that my parents, being too poor, rented that one to strangers, along with the furniture, for sixty francs a month.

The street empties; the suburbanites want to receive at the railway station the representatives of departmental scholarly societies and innumerable musical societies who are to take part in the festival. The Minister of Public Education is having lunch at the Prefecture with the artistes of the Comédie-Française, who have interpreted some of my works. Yesterday, the politician was being celebrated, today it's the poet, tomorrow it will be the family man and the religious man. Two archbishops will speak in his favor.

Everywhere there are lush literary lunches, and I don't have a slice of bread to put between my teeth. Hospitality here is very broad; every local personality has guests. Joyous fanfares file past under the windows. The official procession forms, and follows the delegations in order to render homage to my statue. God, how hungry I am! I want to take my place in the ranks, but I'm sent away indignantly. It's true that my clothes are worn and that my wan face can't inspire confidence.

Everyone, including the least young academicians, is traversing the city on foot. The majority of the delegates are wearing either crowns of laurel or bouquets of immortelles. The spectators utter frantic acclamations. Cold sweat runs down my forehead and trickles over my face; my eyes are dazzled; however, I want to see and struggle to the end. Perhaps someone will recognize the noble intelligence that is hidden within me.

"Emmanuel is not dead! Emmanuel! Emmanuel!"

My voice dominates the others; people look at me, jeering; a few hands reach out to seize me, but another spectator attracts attention. In the great square of the city where my statue stands, a marquee has been prepared for the minister and the principal members of the official cortege. The fanfare bursts forth in strident notes, and then all the united choirs intone a mighty hymn . . .

I fall on to a boundary-marker, exhausted, my legs trembling, my throat dry, and, as if in a dream, I hear a few speeches, after which numerous decorations of the Légion d'honneur are awarded to Emmanuel's friends and relatives. My grandniece passes close to me; she is very pretty in her bright cotton dress, and a great expression of pleasure is spread over her face. I want to retain her, but she looks at me fearfully, a cry expiring on her lips. I frighten her, alas. She doesn't recognize me either. Of all the anguishes that I've felt thus far, that one is perhaps the most dolorous. An infinite sadness inundates my heart, drowning the slightest fibers of my being; a few tears fall from my eyes. What! It's me, me, that is being acclaimed! No human being was ever more admired, and I'm dying like a pariah.

Now the cortege is heading for the hall where the solemn session is to be opened. Everywhere, there are accumulations of green plants, in spite of the cold, crowns of ivy and laurel dotted with golden flowers, and cartouches on which the titles of my principal works can be read.

The official personages climb on to the vast stage, the public invades the hall, and, pushed by the flood, I find myself in the front rows. It's a mob, an extraordinary human throng. Warm speeches are pronounced by the academicians, who are wearing, with a false modesty, the costume of green palms designed by David under the first Empire. The poets also have brought their tributes: an enthusiastic panegyric to my works.

And suddenly, full of inspiration and power, I stand up and cleave through the crowd with an irresistible force. I sense myself capable of braving all wrath, all insults; I am transfigured, invincible! My gaze has such radiance that the immortals jostle one another in an involuntary movement of recoil. The poem that one of them was reading falls to the floor.

I utter a cry of triumph, and, in a resounding voice, I pronounce the verses that rise from my heart to my lips; the golden rhymes flow like a dazzling river, the fortunate images, the divine visions, the reckless accents, the thunder of passions and murmurs of tenderness pass by turns through my strophes. Never, I believe, have I been as great, as emotional, or as sincere. I talk about my youth, my first voyages to the realm of the stars, my debuts in the art of charming human beings, my dreams, my projects, my ambitions, my despairs; the entire soul of Emmanuel vibrates in my tones; it seems impossible that anyone could fail to recognize it. I conclude with a line as explosive as a clarion call, in which the breath of the beyond has passed.

Tottering, I parade my wild gaze around me. Undoubtedly, the hall is about to crumble under the applause and the stamping of feet, and a thousand arms will reach out toward me in a surge of involuntary enthusiasm. It is finally the triumph of truth and justice . . .

I feel faint . . .

A glacial silence reigns in the auditorium. The academicians look at one another, and one of them, the baldest and the most decrepit, lets fall these simple words: "That man is mad!"

Immediately the most terrible vociferations are heard; I am dragged outside the hall, I am insulted; people spit in my face. And behind me, the fanfare plays a triumphal march in order to drown out my sobs and cries of distress.

O insensate and cowardly crowd! Do you even understand those verses that you are acclaiming, those verses by the defunct Emmanuel, since those of Emmanuel resuscitated only excite your scorn?

Scintillating gazes turn toward me, jeers pursue me, and as I stop, at the end of my strength, I am struck and trampled underfoot; soon, my hands and my face are streaming with blood, my garments are in tatters . . .

I lose consciousness.

When I come round I find myself lying outside a brightly lit café. Eight o'clock is chiming at the cathedral, and people are sitting down at table. Dishes are circulating, wine is running in floods. My stomach tightens dolorously; an intolerable pain reminds me that I haven't eaten since yesterday. I make an effort to get up, but my arm is dislocated and I fall back, groaning.

We have now reached the moment of the speeches; the most eminent among the guests stand up and, after having warmly celebrated by works and my merits, drink to my eternal glory. I feel my pockets, which contained a few coins this morning; they're empty. However, here comes a waiter carrying remains of meats and bottles; I make a new effort and, extending my imploring arms toward him, I say:

"A little bread, my friend. I'm injured and very weak; just a piece of bread, I beg you!"

The man considers me suspiciously.

"Another beggar," he says. "They ought to throw all those vagabonds in prison. You can't work, then, vermin?"

"My arm is dislocated; I'm in great pain."

"Go to the hospital then. A dislocated arm doesn't prevent you from walking. Here, this is for the journey."

He threw me a crust of bread and went away swearing. The stars were lighting up in the sky; a bitter wind was blowing over the large square, where my statue rose up, as white as a dead man in his shroud. I got up, with difficulty, not knowing where to spend the night, and drew away through the narrow alleyways and passages warmed by the comings and goings of the petty people, disinherited and ragged like me.

I stopped at intervals under porches in order to get my breath back, and my gaze wandered along the windows with closed shutters, where the gleam of a gas-lamp sometimes silhouetted a sculpted mascaron above a bulging balcony of flamboyant wrought iron. But the cold of the paving stones extracted me from my contemplation.

I set off again, my back in a ball in order to offer less purchase to the whips of the icy evening air. I wander at random, with the vague hope of finding a shelter, of interesting a passer-by in my fate. I linger outside the doors of cabarets, having noticed that every time customers go in or out, a little of the good warmth from inside reaches me.

On passing into a deserted quarter, a stray dog came to rub timidly against my legs; I stroked it a few times, and it attached itself to my heels with little joyful squeals and a quivering of its whole starveling carcass. Poor friend! It was the last I would encounter . . .

O solitude! Frightful solitude in destitution and despair! Are you not already the commencement of death?

At the contact of the sad animal, as scorned and vagabond as me, a little warmth returned to my heart, and a tear fell from my eye. I resumed my route, stopping mechanically from time to time in front of the window displays of rotisseries. Large pink flames shone inside, and birds on spits, streaming and gilded, gave off penetrating and salutary odors of nourishment. The papillae of my tongue quivered with desire; my companion, who also seemed to delight in the sight, raised its wild and shiny gaze in ardent supplication . . .

Soon, the shops would close, and I would no longer have the resource of doors flapping in the coming-and-going of clients. The air was becoming damp and icy; everything fell back into a mortuary silence, with the vague tremor of files of gas lamps burning like candles along the deserted sidewalks. A great frisson ran through my bones; even the bitterness of my destiny seemed to have drained away. What was the point of cursing and blaspheming? Isn't everything futile?

My soul in pain, my legs exhausted, and my stomach empty, I set forth again. The houses became increasingly scarce; soon there were no longer any and I found myself in the country.

Gray clouds were rolling in the sky under the pressure of the wind; the denuded trees were twisting in the darkness. I was now frightfully hungry, one of those hungers that cause wolves to attack men. Exhausted as I was, it was difficult to keep my legs moving, and, my head heavy, the blood buzzing in my temples and my eyes red, I talked aloud under the obsession of incoherent ideas. I felt faint, harassed by lassitude; there was a breaking sensation in my back, a stiffness in my knees, which I could no longer bend, and such a painful curling of my toes that I seemed to be walking over white-hot metal.

"My God! My God!" I murmured. My throat was torn by barking coughs, my bare chest was clawed all the way to the liver by the bite of obstinate fangs. I went on for a few more meters and then fell on to the bank, and a mortal agony commenced, sharp and atrocious, so terrible that, by means of a supreme effort, I got back on to my poor feet, already dead, and set off again into the shadows, a wretched rag agitated by torment.

"Oh, men! The insensates!" That cry vibrated ironically, and the echoes repeated it in the distance. I took my last poems from my pocket, copied out in large handwriting, as if in a dream, and I tore them up furiously and stamped on their debris on the muddy ground.

My chest was getting tighter, gasps were emerging from my throat and the clappers of bells were hammering my temples; around me there were tumultuous metallic impacts, the racket of a train traveling at top speed, and the sound of the sea submerging a world . . .

And the pain in my limbs, the pain in my belly and the pain in my heart rose to my head like a redoubtable intoxication, and gave birth in my head to thoughts of crime . . .

I fell down again and lost consciousness . . .

How long I remained like that I don't know. Warm breath on my face woke me up. The poor dog, lying next to me, warmed my body and attempted timid caresses in order to extract me from my torpor. I was astonished no longer to be suffering, to feel rested and less weak.

Rain was falling now, fine, compact and icy. I set forth to go back to Paris, to the home of my unfortunate companion, but I no longer had a very clear idea of distances. Paris was salvation, hope reconquered. Why, then, had I come to this place of distress? I remembered, and a burst of laughter vibrated in the night. Oh yes—glory! Emmanuel's centenary!

I knotted what remained of my handkerchief around my neck, in order to interrupt the icy water running down my back, but I soon felt that it was passing through the thin fabric of my garments and streaming over my bare chest. Again, intolerable bites were tearing my entrails, and iron pincers crushing my bones.

Then it seemed to me that death invaded me slowly, gently, like a frightful caress. Well, so much the better! What was the point of struggling? Isn't death the most enviable thing of all, since happiness and justice are encountered so rarely in this word, and are led by hazard?

What was the Emmanuel of old compared with the Emmanuel of today? An inspired buffoon, whom the true faith had never touched with its wing, who did not know the power of tears, the eloquence of cries of distress. He had sung of calm horizons, florid valleys and all the banal beauties of nature. I knew its accursed precipices, its bottomless abysms. Above my head, the roaring heavens were opening in cataracts, the woods bending over, gasping, hells were howling in the stampede of hideous larvae eternally twisted and deformed: everything existed, everything was vibrating, and everything was exploding with the irresistible force of dolor! Oh, what poems! What terribly beautiful songs would have emerged from my burning soul! What cries of the damned, what blasphemies and what prayers!

I felt big and strong; circles of light were passing before my dazzled eyes; I was beating the air with my hands as I walked, and my brain was bursting with enthusiasm. I was no longer in pain; divine visions were transfiguring me, great landscapes of light with copper foliage and ruby skies; the sand of the morning was fuming under my feet like the dust of a censer, flowers of fire were blooming in crosses, striping the sky with their immense calices, like the embers of precious stones.

Then the décor changed: a river of gold was now flowing at my feet and flamboyant eyes were gazing at me from the other bank, eyes without bodies, framed in a fog of blood. All the way to the horizon, the immense plain was bare, and blanched by innumerable bones. I heard a divine music, so bewitching that I felt myself dying deliciously. The voluptuous wave of the harmony flowed through my veins. I was warmed up, in spite of the rain that was soaking my garments.

While my miserable body went along the muddy road, tripping over stones, picking up all the mud of the ruts, my soul, its wings spread, was soaring in the blue immensity. And my voice rose, dominating the din of the tempest; it rose with the sonorities of a clarion, telling nature about my joy, my torments, the hell of my life and the sunshine of my dream. I talked, and I talked, and the great trees inclined with murmurs; the shrill clamors of the wind shook the echoes like the applause of a delirious audience.

Suddenly, like the curtains of a tabernacle lifting, the silver clouds, swirling in broad spirals, uncovered the monstrous, frightful sun, like a lake of flame.

Abruptly, I ceased to hear myself; everything became vague. The furies of nature weakened around me, an atrocious pain traversed my brain, and it seemed to me that I fell into nothingness.

[This strange story was told by a poor madman whom a cart had knocked down on a deserted road at first light. The driver, still half asleep, had not been able to retain his horses in time and the wheel of the cart had passed over the unfortunate's legs, breaking them above the knee. An amputation had to be carried out, but the patient was in such a state of exhaustion that he died a few hours later.]

A VENGEANCE

"LOVE is stronger than death," Solomon has said.

There is certainly a mysterious bond that attaches us to the person that we have loved the most, a bond that reveals itself during separation by presentiments, and is not always broken when one of the two has ceased to live.

One evening, as I was going home at eleven o'clock after a most suggestive spiritualist séance, I felt that I was under the influence of that hereditary spleen, the black obsession of which thwarts efforts of our will, and which is only explicable as the brush of the invisible wing of misfortune floating above us in the shadows.

While lighting a cigar in front of the mirror above my mantelpiece I perceived that I was mortally pale, and it seemed to me that a fluid, spectral visage was visible behind mine, like a reflection.

The idea of leaving Paris came to me immediately, and the name of a friend that I had not seen for years expired on my lips: "Georges d'Ambroise," I murmured. "But where is he to be found?"

Then a sort of anguish gripped me by the throat, and it seemed to me, on casting a new glance into the mirror, that the pale silhouette that I had remarked already was standing out distinctly beside my own image, and that the phantom in question had Georges' features

The next morning, my valet de chambre brought me a telegram, and it was almost without surprise that I learned that my friend was on the brink of death. I left immediately in order to receive

16

the final adieu of the man who had been the dearest and most faithful companion of my childhood.

The château in which he lived had, on one side, a view over an immense pond bordered by centenarian trees, and on the other, the most admirable landscape that one can imagine. It was a large, very ancient building of monastic and somber appearance. An entire curtain of tangled climbing plants covered a part of the walls and veiled the ogival windows, which seemed already to be open, as if regretfully, to life and sunlight.

Georges was very rich, and I was astonished that he had not restored his dwelling and taken full advantage of that admirable location. With a relatively minimal sum, marvels could have been worked. All along the avenue of plane trees that led to the main gate, I amused myself by imagining changes in the dispositions of the park and the English garden, presently invaded by brambles and long grass.

A great sadness emanated from the château, which, following the example of certain old mansions described by Edgar Poe, was surrounded by a special atmosphere, doubtless due to the nearby pond, whose troubled surface was covered with water lentils and nenuphars with large yellow flowers. Flocks of crows were passing overhead heavily, and the croaking of frogs was vibrating in the general melancholy.

The horizon was reddening over forests of distant oaks and wild pines, where the last evening breezes were taking flight, and the water, as motionless as a great fallen mirror, reflected the blood of the sky with a solemn horror.

How many dreams must have been broken there, in the sinister reality of death and destruction! I thought. *How many awakenings have hollowed out wrinkles and blanched hair! How many hours have chimed in solitude and abandonment!*

I was in that state of lassitude in which the sensitized nerves vibrate at the slightest excitation.

A leaf fell nearby; its furtive rustle made me shiver, and, incapable of taking another step, I sat down on the moss, my gaze turned sadly toward my friend's dwelling. Long cracks ran over the walls; the window panes, illuminated by the dying rays of the sun, were burning with an intense light on the upper floors, while sinister shadows were rising like a tide, drowning the lower part of the house, which seemed to be sinking slowly, like a ship-wrecked vessel.

Those sorts of visions, being mental rather than physical, fade rapidly. Undoubtedly, I was the victim of the intellectual depression to which we are mysteriously subject at certain moments of life, which is like a warning of the nullity of our efforts and ambitions. I resolved, if there was still time, to take Georges away from that unhealthy place, which must have favored the illness from which he was suffering; and, shaking off my torpor, I set out en route again.

When I arrived at the gate I saw a Newfoundland dog lying on the ground. Bloody foam was emerging from its mouth; it was no longer moving. I felt it; it was still warm, and had just been killed by a rifle shot to the heart.

Why that act of cruelty? I promised myself to demand an explanation from the first domestic I encountered.

The house, however, seemed deserted; the air of desolation spread over everything caused me to dread a catastrophic event, and, my mind full of disturbance, I went rapidly through the vestibule with sonorous flagstones. A stone stairway rose up in front of me; I took it, at hazard, not seeing anyone and not hearing any sound.

After having rapidly opened the doors of a dozen damp and dilapidated rooms on the first floor, I found myself in front of a door padded with black cloth, underneath which a faint light shone. I opened it, and the spectacle that struck my eyes will never leave my memory.

Livid and haggard, Georges was lying on a bed and trying to dive away sinister visions with trembling arms. A groan emerged from his mouth, his wide eyes, frightfully dilated, were directed toward a part of the room that the obscurity prevented me from examining.

"Georges, it's me," I said.

He turned toward me, and a weak smile was sketched on his face.

"It's you! Oh, what joy! I'm no longer alone. You'll install yourself by my side and no longer leave me!"

I drew nearer, and examined him more closely.

His fine hair, cut short, was gray at the temples; his high and prominent forehead was the color of wax. His nostrils were pinched, his lips drawn back. Without the extraordinary brightness of his eyes, he would have seemed already to belong to the tomb.

"You don't have anyone to care for you?" I asked.

At that question, an individual crouching beside the bed stood up slowly. It was a small, paltry negro with thick lips and an alarmed expression.

Georges indicated him with his hand. "I have Porto, but he's such a coward that he trembles at the slightest noise and runs away on the slightest pretext. My otherworldly head evidently seems to him to be disagreeable to contemplate when night falls."

Porto babbled a few unintelligible words, and, his master having dismissed him, he departed with an evident satisfaction.

"If you only have that Moor here," I said, "it's inexcusable that you didn't summon me sooner."

"I also have a housekeeper, but I'd prefer not to have anyone."

"I don't understand. In your condition, you need devotion and attentive care. Who, here, could help you in case of an aggravation of the illness?"

Georges put a finger over his lips. "There are things about which it's necessary not to talk," he said. "There are frightful secrets that ought to descend into the tomb."

"Secrets?"

He shivered, and laughed convulsively. "I don't know what I'm saying—I'm crazy. At least I'll sleep tranquil tonight. Clairon is dead."

"Clairon?"

"Yes, my dog. He was howling incessantly. I had him killed."

"Ah! The poor beast that I found bleeding on the threshold of your dwelling."

"Don't talk to me about him. Since a fatal date he's been torturing me with his horrible plaints; they've turned my hair white!"

"You could have shut him away, in order no longer to hear him, or made a gift of him to someone."

"I tried everything, but he came back under my windows incessantly. He was beaten, martyrized, deprived of nourishment—nothing worked. So I decided to employ radical means."

While my friend was talking I saw his gaze steer toward the same dark part of the room, and his dilated pupils were two black patches almost as large as the irises of his eyes. I tried to take account of what was attracting his attention in that fashion, but the room, which was very large, was plunged in darkness with the exception of the area where the bed was.

"If you want me to stay with you, my dear Georges," I said, jovially, "it would be better to brighten your abode, for the gloom is taking away any scant enthusiasm that I might have. Permit me, then, to light the candles of those candelabra I can see over there."

I got up, but he grabbed me by the arm, with terror.

"No, no, stay with me. I don't want to see more clearly. She's there, she's lying in wait for me. I'm afraid!"

He uttered a cry of anguish, and hid his face under the bedclothes.

I was beginning to feel painfully oppressed myself, and I almost regretted having come; Georges d'Ambroise was, however, a childhood friend. We had had an excellent relationship once, and it was only a few years ago that mysterious events had separated us.

I knew, vaguely, that an irresistible passion had disrupted his existence, and that, after having abducted a young woman from her husband, he had kept her jealously in solitude, surrounded by cares and amour. Why had I found him now abandoned, ill and desperate? That was what I sought in vain to know.

The adventure, in any case, had made very little noise. The parents of the young woman in question, very honorable, had tried to hush up the affair. Apart from two or three intimates, whom it had been necessary to take into confidence, and who had sworn to keep quiet, no one had suspected the liaison.

Georges was no longer moving. I might have thought that he was asleep if his eyes had not remained wide-open, and if the imperceptible tremor of his lips had ceased.

At about three o'clock in the morning, he lost consciousness, and I was so afraid of seeing him die in my arms that I uttered desperate appeals.

The door soon opened silently, and the grimacing face of the negro appeared in the shadow.

"Come here, Porto," I said. "Your master is no longer moving. What is it necessary to do?"

"Oh, nothing, Monsieur. That happens frequently. Don't worry about it—it's the statue that is tormenting him."

"What statue?"

"You don't know? You'll see her tomorrow; she's avenging herself. Oh, Monsieur, let me go! My cares are unnecessary, since you're watching over my master. His faint will cease with the light of dawn. What can a poor sick negro do, who is weaker than a child?"

Porto was almost kneeling, reaching out imploring hands toward me. Under the influence of fear, his face was contracted and wrinkled, and seemed very thin, like an apple dried up on the tree.

I felt ill at ease, and, picking up the lamp that was burning next to the bed, I advanced into the room, determined to explore every corner of it.

On the wall hung a Gobelins tapestry representing the triumph of Amphitrite, after Boucher. The ceiling, formed of blackened oak beams, bore the family escutcheon in the corners: silver with a sable band charges with four gold bezants, and a golden patriarchal cross in each quarter with the motto: *Una fidus unus dominus.*[1] The furniture, with tapestry in petit point or changing brocade, had rigid and outdated forms; a vague odor of mildew and pharmaceutical potions floated in the air. Porto, collapsed on the carpet, was hiding his face in his hands, uttering shrill moans that irritated my nerves frightfully.

I did not see anything abnormal in the vast room, and I was about to sit down again at the invalid's bedside when a sort of black veil, thrown over an object that I could not make out, attracted my attention. I lifted it up carefully and revealed a life-sized statue of a woman, in bright metal as shiny as silver.

Her arms were hanging down along her body, which was leaning forwards slightly, and the head was tilted over the left shoulder. I lifted the lamp in order to get a better view of the face, and found it singularly indicative, but with a frightful expression of anguish and horror. The body, entirely naked, fine and pure, had a bizarre, awkward stiffness, which was inexplicable in such a scrupulous work, for the slightest creases of the flesh, and even the pores of the skin, were rendered with an exaggerated fidelity.

I searched for the name of the strange sculptor who had executed the work, but I did not find it; the pedestal bore no date or signature.

"What is this statue?" I asked the negro, after taking a few steps back in order to see it more clearly in its ensemble.

"I don't know," he replied, in a halting voice. "It arrived of its own accord. Monsieur found it installed in his room one evening when he came back. It's since that moment that he's been ill."

"What are you telling me, my poor Porto? Fear has troubled your reason; your master must have bought the figure from a sculptor among his friends, but I don't understand the sentiment that guided his choice. It's an emblem of despair or remorse, and poor Georges' enfeebled mind certainly hasn't been strength-

---

1 "One faith, one Lord"—an inversion of two phrases in *Ephesians* 4:5.

22

ened by contemplating it. If you'll take my advice, we should take that ornament into another room, unless our strength is insufficient."

At that proposition, the black man got up as if moved by a spring, and fled, screeching. I took the lamp back to the place from which I had taken it, and remained plunged in singular thoughts. What did the terror of the master and the servant signify? Why the mystery? How could the sight of a statue disturb sensate individuals to that extent, and what remedy was it possible to bring to that state of affairs?

Georges remained immobile, but a slight coloration had returned to his cheeks, and his respiration had become regular again.

I tried to sleep a little, in order to recover, with the repose of the body, the full possession of my reason. As I closed my eyes, however, a sigh extracted me from the kind of vague torpor that precedes slumber. My friend had made a movement, and I soon heard him murmur: "Jean, don't leave me! Protect me! She's there, I sense her, I see her . . . oh, who will deliver me from her terrible specter?"

"Listen," I said to him, bitterly, "I don't understand your imaginings at all. What's the matter with you, and what danger is threatening you? Since my arrival here I've been floating in a fantastic world where my mind goes astray. I can care for the sick, but I'm impotent to cure the insane."

Georges started to weep.

"What will become of me if you abandon me? Your charity won't be exercised for long, in any case; I sense that I'm going. It isn't death that frightens me, but the terrible visions that are accompanying my slow agony. Yes, I should have confided in you earlier, liberated my heart from the secret that is oppressing it; I dared not, I had promised to keep quiet . . . the honor of a woman, you understand . . ."

"You can talk without fear. I know that a violent amour turned your life upside down, but I can't explain, at present, your solitude and your despair."

"How can one explain the inexplicable Yes, I'm mad. I'm suffering like a damned soul, and the idea of suicide is imposing itself upon me irresistibly. Anything rather than the frightful mystery against which I'm struggling with rage and despair! That statue . . . oh, the statue that is haunting me, martyrizing me and killing me! Where did it come from? What does it want? You, who can reason and understand, tell me what it wants. You can see that it's torturing me pitilessly and that I'm dying of dread and horror!"

"It would be simpler to get it out of this room, and if you wish, I'll liberate you from the sight of it."

I took a step toward the statue, but Georges sat up in his bed, his eyes glittering and his lips twisted.

"Take Berenice away from me!" he howled. "Never, you hear! I forbid you to do it! We'll descend into the tomb together. You believe me to be very weak or cowardly, then!"

He burst into frightful laughter, which made him fall back on the pillow, his face cadaverous and his eyes convulsed.

"Calm down," I begged. "I had no intention of irritating you."

After a brief interval, he came to his senses and, seizing me by the arm, he made me swear solemnly never to touch the somber image of his beloved, adding that he would kill himself before my eyes if I disobeyed him.

When he had received my oath, he went on: "Berenice is dead, you see, for, if she were alive, she wouldn't remain motionless beside my bed with her face eaten away and her eyelids empty."

"But it's only a statue!" I exclaimed. "A statue that doubtless bears no resemblance to your mistress. You're delirious, my poor friend!"

Georges shook his head.

"It's her, I tell you. They've murdered her. Do you think that an amour like ours could be extinguished without reason, like the vulgar caprices of society? We were bound to one another by the purest and most ardent sentiment; everything that exists down here was, for us, subordinate to that tenderness, and I'm dying of no longer sensing its wings flapping around me like a bird of paradise."

I took Georges' hand and squeezed it gently, not finding any words eloquent enough to ease his pain.

He continued in a strange voice that passed rapidly from trembling indecision to the abrupt, hollow-sounding enunciation that one observes in lunatics or opium smokers.

"When one has tasted those delights and one has lived in them, one cannot imagine that one can obtain any happiness and consolation elsewhere. It's like the juice of a fruit that poisons little by little, but whose savor is so sweet and so intoxicating that tasting it once is sufficient to create the desire to intoxicate oneself with it until death."

"Was she very beautiful, then, the woman you have lost?"

"She was more than beautiful. What can the regularity of the features and the harmony of the contours do for me, if the flame that sets the heart ablaze, charms the thought, bewitches and communicates the science of amour, is lacking in the work of God? Berenice was not a beautiful fragment of marble, pale and insensible; she incarnated woman, true, eternal and unique, the enlacing and tender creature, nervous and passionate, whose tears and kisses are as necessary to an intelligent man as the bread he eats and the air he breathes."

Georges let his head fall back on the pillow, and tears trickled slowly down his cheeks.

"She'll doubtless come back," I said, in order to put a little hope back into that ulcerated heart.

"She won't come back, because she hasn't left. Look, I'll tell you our story; perhaps you'll be able to help me discover the truth, for chagrin in taking away the faculty of judging things sanely.

"It doesn't matter where I met her. It was in Switzerland, Spain or Italy. When I saw her, it seemed that I only began to feel and think at that moment, so much had my previous existence been surrounded by mists. Like a butterfly emerging from its chrysalis, I perceived that the sun was shining and that the flowers were opening on their stems. A great breath of happiness swelled my chest; everything that had seemed dull and miserable to me became an enchantment. Thus, doubtless, on the threshold of paradise, the just feel themselves inundated with a boundless felicity, and stumble into heaven under the intoxication of its impressions.

"We loved one another from the first day, and as she was incapable of pretense and lies, she left her husband to go with me, begging me to hide her in a retreat unknown to everyone. She feared, with good reason, the fury of that man, to whom greedy parents had bound her without consulting her heart. He was powerfully rich, and the balance had inclined in his favor in spite of his notorious depravity, his crudity and the dread that he seemed to sow around him. Berenice was his companion for three years, and two children were born of that union, two poor children being raised distantly, whom the mother never saw, in spite of her prayers and tears. Nothing, therefore, attached her to that husband, except the word given before men and God. But divorce releases what humans have united, and God cannot want what is unjust and cruel.

"One evening, therefore, I came to wait for her beneath her windows, and she did not take long to appear, so carefully veiled that it would have been very difficult to recognize her.

"I threw a mantle over her shoulders, and we departed like two criminals, minds filled with anguish and souls exultant with joy. When we found ourselves alone in the railway carriage that was carrying us toward happiness, we hugged one another as if to choke one another, laughing and weeping with delight, lips dry and eyes sparkling with fever and amour. It's necessary to have known that ecstasy of two young people, recklessly infatuated, vibrant with desire and audacity, finally united after a thousand perils, to understand what we felt.

"Berenice's husband scarcely knew me, fortunately, and our flight had been so cleverly planned that we were able to hope that he would never pick up our trail. My fortune permitted me to live as I pleased, and I thought immediately that this old abandoned manor would be a charming nest for our tenderness.

"As soon as we arrived, I hired a housekeeper from the neighborhood and I sent for Porto, whom I had picked up as a child and had raised with sufficient solicitude for him to be grateful and devoted to me.

"Berenice passed for my wife, and as people only knew me by name in the region, no one worried about our antecedents. Things having been arranged for the best, it seemed to me that I would be able to live without dread, savoring in liberty the supreme happiness for which I had never dared to hope in my most ambitious visions.

"We had long excursions on horseback, we drew, we read, and above all—oh, above all!—we loved one another with the fervor of a first amour. Our lips never had enough of kisses, my arms never had enough of embraces. I didn't understand how one could weary of possession. My desires were reborn of their satisfaction, and when I went to sleep, holding against me the supple body that abandoned itself, slumber continued the interrupted ecstasy. We lived in a perfect community of thoughts and sentiments; Berenice read mine as I read hers, and our sole preoccupation was to anticipate one another's wishes. There was never the slightest friction, the slightest dissonance in that duet of two souls equally made to understand and cherish one another. I believe that the conception of human felicity cannot go beyond that, and when a passion is everything for us, and gives us the dose of enjoyment for which we can be ambitious, we have the plenitude of terrestrial happiness."

"Perhaps," I said, pensively. "But you would have wearied of that very happiness, and you would have broken those flowery chains."

"No! For Berenice was never consistent. Penetrating my most secret desires, she showed herself by turns joyful, ardent, tender or severe. She incarnated all the forms of amour, and the most capricious individual would have been satisfied. Even her physical appearance and her allure changed. Whether it was the effect of a new coiffure or a differently cut garment, her aspects were as varied as those of the sky and the sea."

"And how long did your enchantment last?"

"Two years! Two years that passed with a prodigious rapidity, although sown with memories as numerous as the stars of a summer night."

For a few moments, a singular suspicion had come to me on seeing the thin body, the corroded eyelids and the crazed eyes of Georges d'Ambroise. I thought that the woman about whom he was talking with so much exaltation had deliberately stolen his strength and drunk his life, accomplishing her accursed work with the perversity of certain beings dedicated to evil. Bewitching and libertine, she had lavished upon him, with the feline expertise of a succubus, the caresses that burn and devour, leaving him neurotic, devoid of energy, his marrow and his brain melted like lead in an alchemist's crucible.

If that were the case, all was not lost. Have we not arrived, thanks to the progress of science, at being able to combat and correct all the weaknesses and emaciations that depress plaintive humanity? Do we not have remedies for physiological poverty, whatever its causes, genesis and forms might be? Can we not put back on their feet those whom malady, excess and exhaustion have cast down and emptied? Has specialist attention not been paid to neuropathy, paralysis, ataxia and hypochondria?

As if he had penetrated my secret reflections, however, Georges suddenly reduced them to nullity at a stroke.

"Berenice was not the kind of woman you might think. Her heart was as tender and generous as her intelligence was keen. Very often, at the thought of her children, she shed abundant tears, desolate at never having hugged them in her arms and knowing nothing of their dear existence. Oh, if she had been able to reach them and carry them away, and always keep them as a pure safeguard, her happiness would have been cloudless."

"And Berenice's husband never discovered your hiding place?"

"We did not know what had become of him, and, as you can imagine, we did not try to find out, wanting, on the contrary for him always to remain ignorant of our fate. However, when I recall the details of my lover's disappearance, I cannot help associating it with the thought of that man. For what reasons would she have left me? We cherished one another as we had at the first moment; she was happy and desired nothing more. I believe, you see, that he lured her into a trap, abducted her, sequestered her or perhaps killed her. Otherwise, I would have received news of her one way or another."

"Has she been gone a long time?"

"Six months: six months of frightful tortures, laments and tears."

"How did it happen?"

"Oh, in a very strange fashion, as you'll see. We were sitting in this room; it was in March, it was cold and a big fire was crackling in the hearth. For two months Berenice had seemed to me to be taciturn. Previously so confident, and so sincere, she turned her head away when I questioned her, and did not reply. Her anxious gaze wandered at random; her ear attentive to the slightest sound, a shiver sometimes ran through her whole body, and an extreme pallor spread over her face.

"I was tormented, but could not succeed in penetrating the reasons for that singular condition. She was trying to read to me, but her feeble voice suddenly stopped, and the volume dropped from her tremulous hand.

"'You're tired, Berenice,' I said, 'and that novel doesn't interest you.'

"'That's true,' she said, eagerly, as if freed from a great weight. 'If you like, I'll get another from the library.'

"'Let me choose it instead; it's cold and I fear that you might catch cold.'

"But she insisted on going, in an imperative tone that was unfamiliar to me.

"'At least permit me to accompany you. I'll bring back the books that you designate to me, and I'll light the way through the long corridors.'

"'Porto will suffice for that task. Don't insist, I beg you,'

"Devoid of strength against her will, I summoned the negro, who appeared immediately, as if he had been lying in ambush behind the door. He took a candle and went out silently, followed by Berenice.

"A quarter of an hour went by, and, not hearing any noise, I went down to the library, which is directly below this room. It was deserted, the volumes had not even been disturbed, I searched the entire ground floor in vain; then I went back up to the first floor and visited all the rooms, calling out anxiously. The manor was dark and silent, no voice replied to my shouts.

"I went back downstairs and visited the outbuildings, the courtyards and the park, without being able to discover any trace of flight. What was she doing? Where could she be?

"I wept, I sobbed, making the echoes of my desperate appeals resound. Suddenly, Clairon began to howl in a lamentable and continuous fashion; I untied him and he set off like an arrow in the direction of the woods. There is a gamekeeper's cottage about two kilometers away; the dog seemed to be going there, barking more rapidly, his fur bristling, his muzzle to the ground, as if following a trail. We soon arrived, and I knocked on the shutters, which were closed. A sleepy voice answered, and the gamekeeper's wife, hastily putting a skirt on, came to open the door. Clairon was howling with furious obstinacy. Trembling, I asked whether Madame d'Ambroise was not in the house. But those people had not seen her; they seemed bewildered, and looked at me uncomprehendingly.

"I set off back to the château, in the hope that Berenice had returned during my absence, and was so penetrated by that idea that I started to run, without paying any more heed to Clairon, who had remained in the gamekeeper's hut, and was no longer barking.

"From a distance, I saw Porto standing on the threshold. 'Where's Madame!' I shouted at him, impetuously.

"'But I left her in the library a long time ago. Why didn't she go back upstairs?'

"The negro was blocking my path; I thrust him aside brutally, and ran through all the rooms, crying out and vociferating in despair and rage.

"The night passed thus. At the first light of dawn I set out into the country at random, sounding the bushes, parting the tall ferns and darting glances obscured by tears in all directions. At midday, I returned, exhausted and worn out; she had not reappeared.

"For a week I wandered the woods, interrogating the peasants, searching all the leafy coverts, all the fissures and all the ravines, more unhappy than the most wretched vagabond, more abandoned than a dog lost at the bottom of a precipice. I envied the quarryman who was pursuing his rude labor in the midday sun; I would have liked to bloody my hands, crush my bones, martyrize my body in order that I might only feel physical pain.

"Not one clue! Nothing! Porto 'had left her in the library,' he did not know what had become of her, and seemed desolate at her disappearance.

"I was still hopeful, however. We had no enemies and no murder had ever been committed in the vicinity. What motive could have guided a criminal? Theft? Berenice had no money on her. Her beauty, it is true, could have given birth to the desire of a greater crime, but I would have heard her cries, I would have followed her traces; dead or alive, I would have found her.

"And the torture of not knowing anything, of not being able to imagine anything, was added to my other sufferings. I enclosed myself in a grim silence; even the sight of the negro exasperated me. Should he not have remained with Berenice, to protect her and guide her? I was the master, after all; why had he disobeyed me by leaving the library?

"Porto made himself very small, only looking up at me tremulously, uttering moans at the slightest reproach.

"One evening, after having drunk a few glasses of Spanish wine, I felt very sleepy; my head was aching, and an extreme lassitude obliged me to lie down on the bed, where I did not take long to lose consciousness.

"Frightful visions haunted me then, without it being possible for me to shake off the torpor of my mind and my body. An intolerable weight crushed my chest and I made futile efforts to call for help.

"I don't know how long I remained like that, but it seemed to me to be a century.

"Finally, the mists that enveloped me suddenly vanished, and I sat up, seeking to recover my senses.

"A partly consumed log had rolled out of the grate, and a large oblique flame was illuminating the room. I felt all the hair on my head stand on end, and, voiceless and incapable of movement. I remained still, my eyes dilated by fear.

"Berenice was there, or rather, her deformed image, hideous and terrible. She was standing immobile beside my bed, and her body was shining with a livid light. I tried to cry out, but my contracted throat would only let out an agonized gasp. For an hour, I stayed there contemplating her, sensing my ideas collide confusedly in my head and the beats of my heart hammering my chest. I refused to admit what I was seeing

"In the end, however, it entered my soul, forcibly and victoriously; it was imprinted in fire on my quivering reason. She was dead—oh, yes, I could no longer doubt it!—and her lamentable specter had come back to the man she had cherished uniquely down here. Clairon had recognized her too, for he was howling in the courtyard as at the moment of the crime. I extended my arms toward her, and called to her softly in a voice steeped in tears.

"It seemed to me that her face contracted, that her lips parted in order to respond to me, but she remained in the same place and the desolate expression of her features chilled me to the bone. I spoke to her again; in spite of the fear that dominated me, I begged her to make me understand, by some manifestation, that she could hear me, that she felt compassion for me, that she still loved me. But she did not move, and I could no longer support the terrifying expression on her face. I got up and extended my hand toward her, closing my eyes in order not to faint.

"I encountered a rigid, icy body, steeped in the damp of the tomb. Unable to bear any more, I fell backwards . . .

"When I came to, Porto and the housekeeper, both paler than wax candles, were standing beside me. I told them briefly what had happened to me, glad to find myself with living beings. They looked at one another and whispered very quietly, as if the sound of their own voices would have frightened them. I started to laugh loudly, in the dread of feeling madness take hold of me.

"'It was a dream, wasn't it? No one came last night, you haven't seen anything?'

"The woman made the sign of the cross and Porto fell to his knees, putting his hands together. I looked at them irritatedly. 'Come on, speak! I won't tolerate anyone playing games with me! I want to know—enough grimaces!'

"The black pointed to a dark corner of the room, and I saw the hideous specter of Berenice, standing as I had seen it during the night by my side.

"In the courtyard, the dog was still moaning, and that profound plaint exasperated my anguish. Then I had an atrocious crisis of nerves, and since then, I've been passing on slowly. A few more steps and I'll have joined her, the dear, tender beloved. She's waiting for me elsewhere, on the lookout for me, and I can hear her encouraging me to die. Oh, it won't be long now!"

Georges d'Ambroise uttered a sigh, and a little foam flecked his lips. I handed him a potion prepared on the side table; he drank a few mouthfuls and, having taken my hand, shook it gently.

"I had you come, you see, so that you can bury me with her."

"What! With that statue?

"It's not a statue; it's her body, torn from the tomb, which can't repose there without me. Promise me that you'll accomplish my will . . ."

"So be it," I said, not wanting to exasperate his madness. "But we'll save you, I hope."

He shook his head.

"I can't live any longer; let my destiny be accomplished. In any case, I'll kill myself if death delays too long. Now, go and rest; the moment hasn't yet come."

All those emotions had exhausted me; I sensed my reason becoming obscured, and, my legs like jelly and my hands icy, I left the room in order to try to recover my self-possession and savor a moment's repose.

I threw myself down on a divan fully clothed, in an adjacent room, in order to be ready at the slightest sound, and did not take long to go to sleep. My slumber lasted for a long time, perhaps five or six hours, and I had some difficulty, when I awoke, in recalling the fantastic events that had disturbed me. As soon as the memory returned to me, I ran to Georges, who shook my hand and welcomed me with the pale smile that now seemed to be fixed on his lips.

That day went by tranquilly; the invalid saw nothing but his dear Berenice, and talked to her constantly about a thousand light and tender things, sometimes stopping as if to listen to replies.

Singular phenomena were happening within him now; he was confusing the imaginary and the real, no longer being conscious of his condition. A presence was floating in the air, a soul was calling to him, striving to become visible, to assimilate itself to his. He was seeing double, like an illuminate. A face leaned over his, a kiss closed his mouth at the moment when he was about to speak; affinities of feminine thoughts awoke in him, responding to what he said. There was a duplication of his self, such that he sensed the vertiginously subtle perfume of his beloved like a fluid mist; and at night, between waking and sleep, quiet breaths were heard shaking him like an electric current. The dead woman already possessed him, as the living one had, completely and exclusively.

In his rare moments of lucidity, he did not complain; his dolor was too profound to be exhaled in banal lamentations.

For those who judge superficially, mute pains do not exist, and great minds, following the opinion of the crowd, must feel the faculty of *really* being submissive to the torments or sensualities devolved to them weakening within them. The cerebral fibers affected by sensations of joy or chagrin appear to them to be relaxed, desensitized, and dead. They are, on the contrary, only sublimated, and are endowed with an almost unhealthy sensibility in certain privileged individuals. Other men seem to be gratified with better-conditioned properties of tenderness, franker, more serious passions, while the tranquility of their organism, still obscured by instinct, leads them to offer us mere overflows of animality as supreme expressions of sentiment. Their hearts and their brains, served by nervous centers buried in a habitual torpor, are renovated in more muted and less numerous vibrations. They hasten to dissipate their impressions in clamors, in order to give themselves an illusion, and to justify in advance the inertia into which they sense that they will fall back. They are called "men of character," when they are only incomplete and ineffectual individuals.

Georges was not one of those. After he had told me the story of his woes, he did not speak of them again, and yet, I could see clearly that he was dying slowly of them, having exhausted suffering to the lees, as a lamp goes out when it has used up all its oil.

One evening, he seemed to me to be transfigured; his speech was clear, his lips smiling, his eyes shining.

"You feel better, don't you?" I asked him, with solicitude.

"Yes," he said, "it's the end."

He put his hands together, uttered a profound sigh, and fell back on the pillow.

I approached; he was dead.

When he was ready for the coffin I thought of the bizarre wish that he had formulated, and which I had promised to accomplish; I therefore ordered two biers, one for Georges and the other for the statue, which had remained at the foot of his bed, lugubrious, in the light of candles that were slowly consumed. It was the last night; no one had wanted to keep vigil over the body and I had slumped into the armchair that I had so often occupied during Georges' illness.

Everything was calm. A great fire was burning in the hearth, for, although it was only September, the walls of the old dwelling were marbled by damp patches, and the wind was keening in the long corridors in a sinister fashion.

I contemplated the pale face of my friend, who seemed to be asleep, so much had his features recovered the suppleness and serenity of life. I thought about our youth, our games in the school playground. A host of distant events, previously forgotten, suddenly returned to my memory. Georges d'Ambroise was then the most cheerful, the most sincere and the most helpful of my comrades. We had promised one another an eternal amity, and but for that fatal amour, we would never have ceased to see one another.

How little it takes to disrupt a human existence! A few paces too many, I said to myself, had put him in the path of that woman. Was that chance or fatality? In sum, nothing is indifferent down here, since the most minimal circumstances sometimes decide our fate: a journey, an excursion, a distracted gaze or an unthinking word engages us, involuntarily, and all our efforts cannot untie what a banal event has united forever. That woman passing by indifferently in her dark costume might perhaps be the element necessary to our life; her eyes, which have scarcely turned toward us, might moisten with the most ardent tears of passion; her mouth, which is mute, might be glued to ours with cries and sobs. Yesterday we were nothing to one another, to-morrow we might no longer be able to do without one another; yesterday, a world separated us, tomorrow we might be indivisibly bound. What an abyss of joy and sadness! What strength and what fragility!

I remained immobile, buried in the mists of dream. The flight of the minutes, however, was heavy and dolorous. My thought, like a wounded bird, returned incessantly to its point of departure, its wing broken, agonized. The fit of spleen became painful, to the extent of malaise, of asphyxiation. I seemed to see the curtains hanging in front of the windows like shrouds agitating, and I shuddered at the slightest sound. The only things that could be heard, however, were the slow patter of the rain outside, the distant murmur of a waterfall and the monotonous moaning of the wind, which breaks at the corners of large edifices and falls into chimneys like a flock of bats.

I had been like that for a long time, avoiding sounding the black profundities of the room, when a slight scraping sound made me shiver. I turned round fearfully. It was Porto, whose grimacing head appeared in the gap of the door. I made him a sign to put some wood on the fire, because I was chilled to the bone. He threw a few logs into the hearth and disappeared with feverish haste. A large flame sprang up, illuminating the escutcheon of the Ambroise family above the high tapestries with fabulous characters.

I picked up a book at random and started to read, in order to ward off my inexplicable apprehensions. The few days that I had spent in that bizarre place had sufficed to take away the skepticism of which I habitually boasted; my nerves were vibrating terribly and the solitude was becoming intolerable to me. I could not focus my attention on the volume I was holding, only my eyes were following the characters aligned on the white page.

Unusual events acquire or lose their gravity in accordance with mental dispositions or the more or less strange circumstances in which one finds oneself. It sometimes happens that one is called upon to keep vigil over someone dear, and that duty, although dolorous, has nothing surprising about it; but if the existence that has just been extinguished has had a dramatic and mysterious past, and if sinister presentiments have enveloped us for some time, everything becomes fantastic and terrible, and there is perhaps no worse torture than that of terror. It is in isolation, above all, that the pale phantom comes to torment us. The weakest being, a dog that caresses us, a child who smiles at us, although neither could defend us, is a support for the heart, if not a weapon for the hand.

I remained motionless, the sweat of effort on my brow. I listened to the clock chiming the sad hours of the night, and at that sound, although so natural, I clung on to the arm of my chair with an inexpressible anguish. A rat sometimes made the woodwork creak, and I sat there, eyes staring, not daring to turn them away from the point at which I was gazing, in the fear that they might encounter, on turning round, some cause of real stupor. Then I was ashamed of my weakness and, standing up, I took a bottle that contained an energetic cordial and poured myself a few mouthfuls of it.

As I returned to my place, it seemed—pure illusion, certainly—that the statue of Berenice had changed position. The head tilted over the shoulder had straightened with an air of challenge, the hands had drawn away from the body slightly.

It might have been midnight, perhaps earlier, perhaps later, for I was no longer conscious of the time, but it seemed to me that I had been there for centuries; no similar anguish had ever gripped me.

I kept my eyes on the statue, trying to discover any movement, but I could not perceive the slightest one.

Suddenly, a sort of very low, very slight, groan struck my ears. I wanted to doubt it, to persuade myself that I was mistaken, and yet my mind was fully awake; I could distinctly hear the beating of my heart, and, stretching out my arm, I palpated Georges' dead hand lying on his icy bed. That contact made me feel ill, but I maintained my attention resolutely and obstinately fixed on the young woman.

A few minutes went by devoid of any incident. At length, it became evident that the breast had swelled and that an imperceptible tremor was agitating the lips.

Under the pressure of a horror and a terror for which human language has no expressions sufficiently energetic, I sensed my heartbeat stop, and my limbs stiffen in place. By means of a superhuman effort, however, I succeeded in getting up, and, picking up a candle, I held it up in front of Berenice's face in order to dissipate all illusion; but the symptoms that had struck me were renewed.

I fell back, shuddering, into the armchair I occupied next to Georges and abandoned myself to all the terrors of a troubled soul. This time, my confused imagination really believed that it had seen and heard, and I began to tremble with regard to myself, as if I had felt the claws of madness entering into my flesh.

Outside, the wind was blowing tempestuously; the candle flames were oscillating and taking on blue or green tints, more visible by virtue of the dying of the fire, which I dared not aliment, in the grate. Every object had become mobile, like the uncertain light that animated it. The doors swung, the hangings quivered, long moving shadows passed over the ceiling, and my friend, on his mortuary couch, seemed to be writhing like a damned soul prey to the torments of hell.

I felt that I was ready to fall ill, and was only preserved from fainting by the terror itself.

Suddenly, I thought I perceived a friction by my side and I turned my head, my neck stiff, holding my breath, my hand clasping the icy hand of the dead man. I inhaled the silence, still doubting, in an unspeakable agony of anguish; but nothing abnormal happened.

An hour went by like that; I was gradually falling back into my vague reveries when, once again, I had the perception of a slight sound coming from the back of the room. I listened, at the peak of horror; the sound became audible again; one might have thought that it was a sigh.

I ran to the statue and I saw the lips relax, uncovering a brilliant line of nacreous teeth. Stupefaction then struggled in my mind with the indescribable terror that had dominated it thus far. I sensed my vision blurring, my reason fleeing, and I uttered a shrill cry. However, I tried yet again to persuade myself that I was the victim of a hallucination. Closing my eyes, in order not to see anything any longer, I ceased all movement, and remained nailed to my seat, desperately engulfed in a whirlwind of violent emotions, which froze the blood in my veins and penetrated me with an icy chill.

Soon, a strident crack resounded, similar to the breaking of a metal rod, and it seemed evident to me that Berenice had moved again. She was inclining, leaning over more and more, her entire body reaching for the mortuary bed. She seemed to want to launch herself, by means of a supreme effort, and to project herself forward; and I recoiled all the way to the door, ready to flee and to abandon that frightful chamber.

I was already turning the handle when the same metallic tearing sound that I had heard rang out again, and the statue, all of a piece, rolled at my feet.

I was considering it dully, stupidly, when something strange happened. As if the body were duplicated, a sort of silver armor plating, which had enveloped it tightly, split and came away. Then, I perceived, at the extreme of amazement, the human remains that it had covered faithfully. It was a woman's body, and I had no doubt that it was that of the idolized mistress of my poor friend.

I dared not touch the blackened, corroded remains, as hideous as those that have lain in a coffin for a long time. Bowled over by that strange event, it seemed to me that Berenice was still agitating in all the convulsions and horrors of agony, in spite of the evident state of decomposition of her body.

I made vain efforts to understand. Certainly, there had been a murder, but why had that monstrous figure of flesh and metal been brought into that chamber of dolor? Was it to maintain the obsession of the dead man, the distress of the maddening horror and anguish of the nightmare? Was it, in sum, a vengeance? Porto's disturbance and hesitations came back to mind.

Perhaps he had known more than he wanted to admit. Did not his very silence prove his culpability?

I resolved to clarify the matter immediately, and I rang for the negro, who was always ready to come down at the slightest appeal.

In fact, he did not take long to appear.

I had placed myself in such a fashion as to hide the debris of the so-called statue, in order to be able to reveal it suddenly, and extract from his terror the confession that I would doubtless be unable to obtain in any other way.

"Porto," I said, "have you always been faithful to your master?"

He looked at me with anxiety. "Oh, yes, Monsieur."

"He picked you up, cared for you, and raised you; you therefore owe him the greatest gratitude."

"I would have myself killed for him."

"Are you sure of always having served him with devotion and affection?"

"I have done everything that a poor servant can do and I do not believe that the slightest reproach could be addressed to me."

"Come on, you ought to tell me what his unhealthy sensibility would have prevented me from hearing. It is inadmissible that Madame Berenice could have disappeared thus, without you having seen or heard anything. I shall not scold you; be sincere—that will be better, I assure you."

He stammered, grimacing, seeking to read in my expression what I was implying.

"I don't know anything, Monsieur, I swear to you! I don't know anything more than I've told you."

Seeing that mildness was futile, I suddenly unmasked Berenice's cadaver, and, seizing the black man, who was howling with anguish, I made him fall to his knees.

"Will you talk now, clown? I know your crime, and your reckoning is due!"

He was shaking like a leaf, his large eyes rolling desperately in their orbits.

"It wasn't me who killed her!" he moaned.

"Who, then?"

"Mercy! You won't do me any harm? Will you have pity on me if I tell you everything?"

"Speak first—we'll see afterwards."

"Well, it was her husband, who strangled her in the wood."

"And you assisted him, no doubt?"

"Oh, no—I came back to the château right away."

"Wretch!" I murmured, kicking that human larva, who was struggling. "Did he give you a lot of money for that?"

"Alas! How, otherwise, would I have been able to betray such a good master?"

"But Berenice never went out? By what fatality did she fall into the power of that man?"

"He used cunning. He had been wandering in the vicinity for a long time, only waiting for an opportunity. I don't know how, by virtue of research, he had been able to discover my masters' retreat. One day, I saw him in the park. He was then completely unknown to me, and I was preparing to announce his visit to the château when he made me a sign to come and talk to him. I followed him, suspiciously, to an out-of-the-way spot.

"'My friend,' he said to me, "there are five louis for you if you give this letter to Madame Berenice—but to her alone, you understand, and so that no one can see you.'

"A hundred francs is always good to have and, all things considered, I wasn't doing anyone any harm in accomplishing that mission. So I held out my hand and took the letter.

"'I'll wait for you tomorrow in the same place,' the stranger went on. 'There will doubtless be a response.'

"That same evening, I gave the letter to Madame, who went as pale as marble and wrote a few lines in haste, which she charged me to take to the mysterious traveler as soon as possible."

"You didn't know what those notes contained? A wily lad like you would easily have found a means of informing himself."

The negro smiled, flattered in his self-esteem.

"The first," he said, "announced to the young woman the death of one of her children, and begged her to come into the woods at ten o'clock the following evening, to learn from the mouth of a friend the story of that death and the address of the poor abandoned child who remained, whom she would doubtless desire to see again."

"Why didn't she suspect anything, and why didn't she tell Georges what had happened?"

"I don't know. Madame seemed frightened, and was certainly too innocent to fear a trap."

"But you, wretch—you should have talked and warned your master."

Before my anger, the negro huddled in a corner, raising his arm over his head in a gesture of naïve terror. I was afraid of not learning any more, and I resumed in a softer tone:

"Go on, talk—it's the sole means of saving your skin."

"You promise to spare me, Monsieur?"

"I'm not promising you anything, rogue. Remember that I could crush you like a worm if you drive me to the end."

Porto began trembling in every limb.

"I'll tell you what I know, but I swear that I'm not guilty of the crime. If I'd been able to foresee that frightful misfortune, I'd have killed myself rather than take part in it. So, I took the letter to the stranger the following day, and he gave me the five louis he had promised me.

"That evening, Madame went out at the agreed time on the pretext of choosing a book from the library. We went through the long corridors in haste and encountered the stranger on the perron. As soon as she saw him, she shuddered and took a step backwards as if to go back into the château. I heard her moan faintly: 'My husband!'

"But the man, who was big and strong, tied a handkerchief over her mouth and carried her off at a run. I didn't see anything more, Monsieur, I swear to heaven! And what followed was so extraordinary that I'm still wondering whether I'm not the victim of a hallucination.

"After terrible crises of despair, my master seemed calmer, almost reasonable. He had the intention of traveling through France, Spain and Italy in order to try to find traces of his companion, who had lived in those three places. His preparations for departure were made, but by virtue of a sort of presentiment he kept putting off the execution of his plan. Accustomed to his eccentricities, I obeyed without saying a word, and thought that Madame Berenice would soon come back in order to return life and joy to the old dwelling.

"One morning, as I was preparing to leave my room, I heard a great cry, which seemed to come from my master's apartment. I ran, as did the old maid, and I found him unconscious with that horrible statue at the foot of his bed. How it got there, without anyone seeing anything, I'll never know. When Monsieur came round, he went into a great excitement, which frightened us so much that we wanted to break the accursed figure, but he threw himself upon us furiously and forbade us ever to go near it. Poor Clairon from that morning on began howling mortally in such a lamentable fashion that I tied him up at the back of the park, but he broke his chain and came back to whine under the windows. I thrashed him, and lost him in the country, but nothing worked. Finally, Monsieur Georges ordered me to kill him in order to have a little repose . . ."

The negro did not say any more. I had only learned one thing, which was that the murderer of Berenice was her husband. It is true that that revelation would doubtless suffice to enlighten the agents of the law, who would only have to arrest the murderer and extract the confession of his crime. I therefore denounced him immediately, and a scrupulous investigation began.

The guilty party, informed by the newspapers, surrendered himself elsewhere and recounted the facts without having to be begged.

The details of that original affair were particularly interesting, and everyone wanted to see that vengeful husband. He was a man of about forty, with a pale and ravaged face and piercing eyes. His broad shoulders and hairy hands testified to an uncommon strength.

"That woman deceived me with unparalleled impudence," he said, parading his ironic gaze over the audience. "She had fled with her lover, and for two years I searched for her without discovering the slightest indication that could put me on their track. I had promised to avenge myself, and when hazard enabled me to find the lovers, I meditated for a long time over the punishment that it was appropriate to impose on them.

"To abduct a woman, in the times we live in, and bury oneself with her in an old lugubrious and dilapidated château, it was necessary that the abductor be an unhinged, exalted, unhealthy and romantic individual, of a rare and singular species. I therefore searched for a punishment appropriate to that meritorious lover. Having resolved, to begin with, the death of Berenice, I thought that it would be unnecessary to commit a second crime and that the constant sight of the cherished cadaver would be sufficient to kill the lover. It was only a matter of giving the cadaver a decent and acceptable form.

"I therefore had recourse to the astonishing discoveries of science to attain that end. One of my friends, the savant Dr. X***, whose remarkable works you know, is especially occupied with the conservation of bodies, not by means of the ancient method of embalming or mummification, but thanks to metallization, a very simple procedure, which reproduces with the exactitude of a photograph in relief the slightest details, the projections of bones and muscles, the wrinkles, and even the abruptly petrified frisson of life.

"After having killed Berenice with the aid of the gamekeeper, whom I covered in gold—without making her suffer, she was so frail and delicate—I enclosed her in a hiding place that I had had fitted in the underside my carriage and which could only be suspected after the most attentive examination, I took her to Dr. X***. The latter, perfectly innocent, had no suspicion of a murder, having not found any evidence of violence on the body that I delivered to him."

I shall reproduce, by way of a curiosity, the deposition of the celebrated physician who, when called to the witness box, obligingly spoke at length about the marvels of his discovery and engaged those present to take advantage of it. With him: "No more slow decompositions in the horror of the coffin, in spite of embalming, which does not prevent the tissues falling into deliquescence, the flesh from drying out and the skin from blackening. No more despair before the scarcely cold body, which will soon be only an object of disgust. Metallization has changed all that; thanks to electricity, that universal benefactor, mummies can be metallized as one galvanizes a spoon, a plant or an insect."

At this point Dr. X*** put out his hands as if he were arranging flowers, and, with a smile on his lips, he said: "I immerse the subject in a chemical bath formed of a soluble salt of nickel, copper, silver or gold—according to taste or munificence—through which I pass an electric current. Under the influence of electrolysis, the salt decomposes, and the metal is deposited in a layer of variable thickness over the surface of the cadaver, the forms of which it reproduces faithfully, and which it eventually encloses from top to bottom in a metal envelope of the most seductive effect.[1]

"In practice, the thing is complicated, it's true, by a few difficulties, and the anthropoplasty demands a whole preliminary cuisine, the description of which might appear cruel to the profane, which I shall pass over in silence. I affirm that my method is unalterable, and if, in the present case, the silver envelope that enveloped the body of the unfortunate woman broke, it is because my client, who was strangely hurried, did not leave me enough time to perfect my work.

---

1 In1897, four years after the first appearance of the present story, a feuilleton serial, *L'Homme en nickel* (tr. as "The Man in Nickel" as the title-story of a Black Coat Press anthology) by "Georges Bethuys" (Georges-Frédéric Espitallier) appeared in *La Science Française*, running in weekly episodes between February and May, which features an identical hypothetical discovery, described in strikingly similar terms: a very curious coincidence, if it was, in fact, a coincidence.

"In fact, in order to obtain a complete result, it is necessary to regulate minutely the delivery of the fluid and the metallic deposit, its adhesion, its solidity and its thickness. It is necessary to safeguard the elasticity and imputrescibility of the skin, the suppleness of the limbs and the stability of attitudes. It is necessary to prevent the distension or tightening of pores, deformations, cracks and explosive effervescence: delicate and complicated problems that cannot be resolved in twenty-four hours. It is even necessary sometimes, in order to avoid a return of posthumous fermentation, to have the cadaver baked, and to perforate it in order to allow free issue to the expansion of vapors and greases, and, finally, to plunge it back into a furnace heated to a hundred degrees.

"My client, I repeat, did not give me the time to obtain a complete desiccation and sterilization; the body, under the steel envelope, was not sufficiently incorruptible. A few globules of air remaining between the flesh and the incompletely adherent metal permitted the decomposition that, swelling the tissues, led to the rupture of the apparatus. But that is a pure accident that cannot be repeated.

"What a joy for a husband—and I believed that to be the case of the accused—to see leaning over his couch, in a preferred pose, a young woman as beautiful and as gracious as in the flower of his honeymoon! What a consolation for a mother to rediscover the cherished features of her child fixed in an expression of eternal joy! What a satisfaction for a son-in-law . . ."

At this point the audience protested, and Dr. X*** withdrew with dignity.

The murderer, interrogated again, wanted to give a few final details.

"When the operation was concluded," he said, "we fixed the corpse on a pedestal with the aid of a powerful armature and, as such, I took it back to the inconsolable lover, convinced that the unexpected sight of his galvanized mistress would be more fatal than any other expiation. He would suffer for a long time, amour and terror would unite in his soul, and, little by little, the horrible nightmare, the frightful vision that he would not dare to banish and against which he would be too feeble to struggle, would lead him to death or madness.

"Now Messieurs, judge me. I have been cruel, and premeditation can certainly not be set aside in my case; but I also led a very miserable existence for two years. I loved that woman in my fashion, and it was only on finding her in the possession of another that the love in question turned to hatred. Hatred is blind, even when it premeditates its vengeances."

The defender of the accused was eloquent, and vividly impressed the elite audience that the bizarre case had attracted. Men declared the vengeful husband very intelligent and women shivered delightfully in contemplating his broad shoulders and his hairy hands.

In order to obey the law, the advocate general demanded in moderate terms a condemnation that he scarcely expected, and no one on either side mentioned the divorce that would have cut through the question so easily and so logically—but the French imagination never loses its rights.

After a long deliberation, the jury brought in a verdict of acquittal, which only a few murmurs at the back of the hall underlined.

As for me, I accomplished Georges d'Ambroise's wish; he reposes next to his tender Berenice.

THE DOUBLE STAR

And heavy cataracts
Like crystal curtains
Were suspended, dazzling
From metallic walls

There were unknown gems
And magical waves,
Immense mirrors dazed
By all they reflected.
(Baudelaire, *Les Fleurs du Mal*)[1]

I WAS not yet born, or, rather, I was already dead. It seemed to me that I had been sleeping for a very long time, a dreamless sleep, peaceful and reparative. I felt a singular lightness, and when I raised myself on my elbow in order to examine the things that surrounded me I perceived that I had wings. Oh, unusual wings, such as I had never imagined, which projected around them the blue light of electricity. As delicate and transparent as the wings of a dragonfly, they were nevertheless as hard and resistant as metal wings.

There was darkness all around me: a warm night mysteriously filled with strange music.

My curiosity excited to the highest degree, I tried at least to examine the nearest objects, by means of the light that I was emitting. I had no sooner formulated the desire to see, however, than my forehead became a luminous light-source, and everything was illuminated to a considerable distance.

---

1 The lines are taken from the poem "Rêve parisien."

I could not retain a cry of admiration, so much did what I saw surpass my wildest visions: no trees, plants or earth, but masses of stone affecting a thousand different forms, mountains of iridescent crystal, violet and red waves seeming to fall from the sky to flow into abysms, to scale fantastic obstacles, and to rear up in vertiginous crests, without making any more noise than the undersides of reptiles slithering through the grass. The soil appeared to be composed of a thick coral dust dotted here and there with stones of onyx, sardonyx, chrysolite, girasol and turquoise. Huge, bizarrely indented walls, completely transparent, rose to implausible heights; some were of amethyst, others sapphire or topaz, without a stain or a flaw, all of a piece. As for the celestial vault, it seemed to me to be as black as ink, immobile and as frightful as the vault of a sepulcher.

Soon, the masses of stone that surrounded me agitated slowly, and long wings similar to mine were deployed, illuminating everything. Then I saw strange animals moving in all directions, mingling their dazzling scales, twisting their fiery coils, walking, crawling, flying and responding to one another with profound and sonorous voices like the notes of an organ. There were sphinxes shaking their bandelets and chimeras with green phosphorescent eyes spitting fire through their nostrils and striking their foreheads with long dragon's tails. There were griffins, half lion and half vulture, clenching their red paws and stretching out their blue necks, and basilisks with violet bodies undulating in the sand. There were a thousand strange, scarcely suspected, beasts: tragelaphs, half stag and half ox,[1] alligators with the feet of roe deer, goats with the hindquarters of donkeys, owls with serpents' tails, gigantic chameleons, and terrifying monsters sometimes as tall as mountains and sometimes as slender as reeds. There were immense metal flowers on the legs of women, and dragonflies

---

1 The mythical tragelaph or hirocervus is more usually imagined as half-goat and half-stag. It is cited as an exemplar of imaginary hybridization by Plato in the *Republic*, and was subsequently employed by Aristotle as an exemplar of something that can be known without actually existing.

whose deployed wings resembled the sails of ships and whose bodies shone like steel yardarms.

Gripped by a mysterious dread, I stood up in order to flee, but when I was upright, I found myself so strong and agile that all my fear vanished. I could scarcely believe my senses. In fact, my senses were no longer the same; I was no longer seeing and hearing in the same fashion; my organism was endowed with several new faculties, notably a magnetic power by means of which it was easy for me to put myself in communication with the beings that surrounded me without the aid of speech. My muscles enjoyed a marvelous flexibility, I felt a sweetness of honey in my veins; I would have liked to sing, to love, to spread my goodwill like a river of oil over all the strange creatures that surged forth at my sides. I took a few of them in my arms; they were icy and as hard as bronze. In spite of their terrible appearance, however, they did not do me any harm, and abandoned themselves with confidence.

Then I heard their language, which was not formed by words but by different intonations. A harmonious chord was sufficient to explain the most complicated sentiments; a musical phrase substituted for a long speech. The intelligences were remarkably intuitive, vast and nimble. There was no need to enter into laborious explanations in order to be understood, no need to disguise one's thoughts to make oneself more becoming; an immediate comprehension, an absolute lucidity and a touching benevolence united us all.

I learned that my existence would last several centuries if I succeeded in forgetting the perverse world from which I came; that I would remain young and healthy without taking the slightest nourishment, the air I breathed being sufficient to maintain my new organism; and finally, that I would remain luminous— which is to say that a phosphorescent emanation would irradiate from me, as from all the beings that surrounded me, and that my impressions would also be translated by a scale of colors, bright or discreet, according to their intensity.[1]

The Chimera that I had hugged to my bosom first of all enveloped me with her red hair, and I could no longer see anything but her strangely shining green eyes. Profound and troubling sounds escaped from her throat, and this is what I understood:

"You see, son of Earth, here I dwell. I am not the fickle enchantress who flees after the kiss in a moonbeam. I do not reveal to your soul the paradise of felicities in order to abandon it half-way. My mission is nobler, my heart more generous. Look! Everything that was once only an unrealizable dream for you, a dementia, is becoming reality."

"Where am I?"

"Very far from your tottering globe, which you will never see again, very far from your sad sun, which is dying slowly in the bosom of its cold planets. Your worlds have fallen into the gaping depths of the immensity, and you would search in vain for Mercury, Venus, Mars, Jupiter, Saturn and Uranus. All those children of darkness have returned to eternal oblivion."

"Where am I? I don't understand. The sky is like a sepulcher filled with shadow and horror."

"That is because your own glare prevents you from seeing its marvels. The Milky Way is collapsing around us like a cataract of suns, the stars streaming like rivers of light, and our own magnificence would be unsustainable for the human gaze. Would you like to judge for yourself? Come, follow me."

The Chimera who had said these things to me in a single melodious and vibrant note suddenly rose up a few meters above my head. Her deployed wings formed a sort of veil of fire over the black sky, and the stones of the ground, the transparent walls and the silent waves had such a scintillation that my eyes closed almost dolorously.

---

1 Many of these ideas of alien existence, including that of nourishment by means of inhalation, echo and elaborate suggestions offered in Camille Flammarion's classic accounts of interplanetary reincarnation, *Lumen* (1865; revised 1887; tr. as *Lumen*) and the best-selling *Uranie* (1891).

"We inhabit a star," my companion continued. "Suspended in space, she is supported by a twin sister without ever touching her, for their progress in the azure is regulated by a superior principle that always maintains them at an equal distance from one another. They gravitate in cadence in the constellated fields, and whereas the sun that once illuminated you shone cold and solitary, they spread around them the ardent warmth of their affection."

"Are we far from the old sun?"

"Millions of trillions of leagues, and if you could hear from here the bellowing of your ocean, the clamors of your thunder and the rumbling of your volcanoes, all those sounds, in order to reach you, would employ the duration of more than twenty million human lives. Everywhere around you, unknown worlds shine, but our own glare prevents us from perceiving them."

As she spoke, I saw her wings sparkle with a blue radiance; then everything around me turned blue, and the colossal sister star of our own appeared over the horizon. Nothing could give an idea of her marvelous splendor.

It seemed to me that phosphorescences were crawling at my feet, that my senses were ablaze and that my entire being was quivering with an indescribable joy.

"You see," my companion continued, "that which troubles and perverts humans does not exist here: war, pillage and murder are unnecessary, for everyone finds satisfaction in themselves and their surroundings. Amour, jealousy, hatred, pride and envy cannot even brush our vast intelligences; we know that our destinies are sublime and that we are progressing incessantly toward perfection and supreme happiness. Soon you will understand that which still seems surrounded by mist. God has not wanted the initiation to be immediate, in order better to prove his elect, but our presence alone is already a promise of immortality. The angel of the resurrection sought you in the tomb, where terrestrial death had placed you, and has given your astral form a glorious envelope. While your flesh and your bones have become the prey of worms, your divine essence has traveled through space and has alighted on this star, where it has taken form in order to await the ultimate beatification. Do not forget, however, that in spite of your radiant body you ought only to be a pure spirit, and any human reminiscence might be fatal to you.

"Here, beings do not reproduce; they must neither admire one another, nor love one another, nor desire one another. Amour is a creator, and in creating, we insult the Master who, alone, can dispose of our destiny. The time that we spend on this star is a proof, a transitory epoch; submit to it courageously. Your intelligence, finally freed from its mists, will rise progressively, and, after having been subject to all incarnations, will become a star itself, first a satellite, then a planet and a sun, for all the worlds traveling in space are the servants of the supreme spirit. Only the hearts of the elite achieve that glory, and I believe that, thus far, no inhabitant of the Earth has even suspected it."

"What!" I said. "Not to love! Can one live thus?"

"Love? Yes, certainly, it is necessary to love, but to love above oneself and not the miserable beings that, like us, are awaiting their final transformation. Love the galaxies that are streaming like rivers of honey, each droplet of which is a radiant world; love the rapid comets that wander like birds of flame in the celestial tempests; love the billions of suns grouped like archipelagoes in the frightening immensity; and above all, love the mysterious power that presides over everything and inflates these globes as children blow soap-bubbles. Here, everything is silent, because we need to pray and meditate, but what upheavals there are around us! What imprecations! What shocks and sobs! You can hear me, but you cannot imagine the extreme grandeur of that chaos. A voyage through the heavens would be a fulguration; incessant electric commotions would make us palpitate like moths intoxicated by light, and the imagination would quail, dazzled, bewildered and agonizing.

"Creation is composed of an infinite number of universes, separated from one another by abysms of nothingness, and the world is only a portal by means of which errant souls are precipitated into glory and become stars in their turn. Eternity is endless and the number of universes is similarly unlimited. To the right and left, on high and down below, everything vibrates, everything palpitates, everything exists, and always progressing, because you cannot only take a single step forward. You are beginning to understand, because you are above matter; once, my thought would not have had any meaning for you. You understand the future of glory that waits you and the eternity of happiness in a colossal royalty, compared with which your temporary monarchs have not even been able to reign. You understand, and gradually, your mind will clear and perceive what was nothing for you once but enigma, mist and fear.

"Do not forget your grandeur, for if ever human being reappears in you, you will fall back into dust and everything will be swallowed by the darkness of the tomb."

"O Chimera, dear Chimera," I said, contemplating my companion's phosphorescent eyes, "how can you think me insane enough to lose so many benefits? No, the old human is dead in me, I only exist by the will of a clement God, like everything that surrounds me, and the splendor of this star is such that my imagination would never have dared to conceive the faintest reflection of it. Vile body that has compressed my soul for too long, remain in the sepulcher! Let your bones and muscles be the prey of liberating larvae. Let the gaze of passers-by turn away from you in horror! O terrestrial life, infamous and injurious life, I hate you, insult you and despise you. And you, my former brethren, who have also drunk the blood and eaten the flesh of animals scarcely less intelligent than you, who have killed for a handful of gold, and spread lies and misery everywhere, I cannot find terms vehement enough to curse you. Abject race, which crawls everywhere, poisoning the valleys and woods more surely than the worst plagues, you will perish by your own hand, you will consume one another, no longer having anything else to destroy, and your cadavers devoid of sepulchers will infect the agonizing earth . . ."

But the Chimera half-closed her glaucous eyes.

"My son," she said, "all worlds have their parasites; when you are a sun in your turn, you will sense infinitely petty beings swarming round your flank, which will torment and enfeeble you. You see specimens of all species here; they will pass, like you, through multiple transformations, and those which have been able to conserve the divine spark deposited within them will similarly attain the supreme power, in a more or less distant time, in accordance with their merits."

"O Chimera, come with me. Let us fly from light to light in this marvelous sky, let us scale these walls of gems, traverse these abysms with golden walls and these rivers with crimson waves. I want to see everything, to know everything, and to admire everything, in infinite gratitude."

"Be careful! Temptation is nigh and your heart is not yet far enough from the Earth to comprehend the Heavens fully."

"What could I have to fear with you? Are you not my guide and my safeguard?"

"I am the Chimera with rapid wings, floating hair and a fiery gaze, I gallop through the labyrinth of the heavens, I soar over the worlds, I weep in the depths of solitudes, I cling to clouds and raise oceans with my trailing tail. I reveal unexpected perspectives to all, I am the fay of eternal dementias and the vestal of eternal desires. Have you not always found me in your path?"

"Yes, always, but I am confident, since you have brought me to this place of delights."

"I have guided many others here, and I keep all the hearts of which they have made me a present."

The Chimera agitated her wings and I saw that her scales were made of a multitude of hearts stuck together. At times, droplets of blood escaped therefrom and were metamorphosed into rubies before falling to the ground.

"Would you like my heart too, O my ardent Chimera? I shall have no more need of it when I am similar to the glorious dust of the Milky Way."

"Take care, child of men! You are only at the turning in the road."

My companion had gradually risen into the air, and I followed her, effortlessly, with a smooth and gentle movement.

The mountains were increasingly ablaze, the seething waves formed strange edifices in clear gums of topaz and iridescent waxes of opals. Everywhere, a brazier crackled with cerulean glints of beryl, peridot and aquamarine, sweating tears of chrysoprase and almandine, darting tongues of ruby and emerald. Then there were towers of amethyst, Babels of onyx, plains and forests of turquoise: a thousand dazzling phantasmagorias, as soon destroyed as edified. The great walls of sapphire and jade barred the way; but we rose so high that they no longer seemed to us to be anything but bizarre crests of an incomparable splendor.

And in that prodigious world I saw not one tree, not one flower, not one blade of grass, nothing that reminded me of the Earth, even vaguely.

We flew millions of leagues; we traversed seas of flame whose infernal waves swelled, sank, hollowed out and rose up capriciously without apparent cause. Those flames were as blue as those of punch, and did not emit any warmth. From time to time monsters pursued one another over the crests of the waves, opening terrible mouths and rolling enormous eyes. Then, suddenly, in enormous depths suddenly revealed, bones appeared: strange white and nacreous bones, which did not seem to have belonged to any known being, and which collided incessantly at the bottom of an abyss of fire.

"What you see," said the Chimera, "are the skeletons of those who were unable to support the proof of this divine world so superior to those they had inhabited."

"Are there human skeletons there?"

"No. Humans are still on the first rungs of science, and the Master, until now, has not judged them worthy of entering this cenacle. Humans, who nourish themselves on flesh, fight one another and destroy one another, are only considered as inferior beings, scarcely different from the brutes they sacrifice to their needs."

"Why has God created them thus?"

"It is an effect of chance. In the times of the primary period of the terrestrial genesis, the trees, the plants and the mollusks devoid of heads, deaf, mute and devoid of sex, only nourished themselves by respiration. It is generally believed that a drop of water denser than the ambient environment traversed the body of one of those mollusks, and was the origin of the digestive tube that was to exercise such a deadly action on animality entire. The Lord turned away from your globe then, as one turns away from a spoiled work, and abandoned it to hazard.

"Here, no one eats; no one has ever eaten. Organisms conserve their molecules by means of a simple respiration, as your vegetables still do. But your sad race cannot go a single day without killing. Your law of life is a law of death. You march in blood and nourish yourselves on cadavers like hyenas and crows. Constant war is the stupid pleasure of the unfortunate and the best mode of domination of the powerful. You will never emerge from your mire!

"Here, our bodies are impregnated with the stellar electricity that sets the entire universe in vibration. We do not know combat, nor murder, nor theft, nor politics. Our intelligences, freed from any material need, rise incessantly in the knowledge of the truth. Our nervous system has attained such a degree of sensibility that our impressions surpass a hundredfold all those of your five poor terrestrial senses."

"Why have I been chosen among all for his future of glory?"

"Because, more than the others, you aspired to the knowledge of the truth, and your soul always suffered from its exile. In any case, space does not exist, and the spirit can fly immediately to the most remote celestial regions, if it is judged worthy of it. Justice reigns in the moral system of the world as equilibrium does in the physical system. The destiny of souls is only the result of their aptitudes and their aspirations.

"While simple suns like yours shine in isolation, fixed and tranquil in the deserts of space, double and multiple suns seem to animate the silent regions of the immensity by their movement, their coloration and their life. That universe is composed of several billions of suns, separated from one another by trillions of leagues, but nevertheless sustained in the luminiferous ether by the mutual attraction of all and the movement of each. While you are traveling toward the constellation of Hercules, our beautiful star is traveling toward the Pleiades; Sirius is hastening toward Columba, and Pollux launching itself toward the Milky Way. All these colossal existences are running through the eternal void, and when you are a star, you will do likewise."

We flew thus for a very long time. My eyes were burned by the glare of everything they had seen, my lips were dry, and my wings torn. Unable to do any more, I let myself fall on to a high ardent yellow mountain, which appeared to me to be made of topaz.

The Chimera continued her flight through the heavens, and soon I could no longer make her out. I was hungry and I was thirsty, but I knew that I must not eat or drink. In any case, nothing in that bizarre world would have been able to satisfy me. Everything had the appearance and the hardness of precious stones and metal.

A great despair drowned my heart and, furling my wings, I tried at least to go to sleep. Fortunately, I recalled that it was forbidden for me to sleep. Everything that was closely or instantly reminiscent of human action had to be sacrificed, pitilessly.

I stood up and looked at the surrounding objects: everywhere, gold and silver, emeralds and rubies, the same fulgurant waves and the same transparent diamantine walls.

The star sibling to ours had disappeared, and the sky had become an infernal night.

"O Chimera!" I cried, "I'm suffering, I'm afraid! I'll never be able to spend two centuries in this accursed place!"

A vague, slow and melodious sound became audible close by. "Aaaah . . ."

I looked, and at first saw nothing, so dazzled was I by the reflection of precious stones.

"Aaaah . . ."

It was nothing but a prolonged note, but how sweet it was to my heart! I had recognized the voice of my desire, the voice of faith and hope, the voice that I had awaited since my mysterious awakening.

"Aaaah? Aaaah . . ."

I bent down and I perceived, stuck to the shining wall of the mountain, a being similar to myself, whose wings were hanging down miserably. I detached her with a thousand precautions and placed her on my knees.

Her long hair trailed on the ground, her languorous eyes were half closed, and her lips were quivering. O joy! There were two of us to undertake the celestial stage; another creature of election had been snatched from the larvae of the tomb in order to make the divine stars pale. For the time being, she was as weak as me, and her flesh of a barely carnal white seemed to me to be made of ice.

"My brother . . . or rather, my sister, be welcome and recognize in me the most devoted, the most reliable and the most affectionate of souls."

"Aaaah . . ."

Oh, the lovely note! And how many bright and vibrant things it expressed, without detours as without effort. "I love you!" it said, "I am a woman, I am alone, I am weeping and I am languid. Like you I am thirsty and I cannot sleep . . ."

"It is necessary to submit to these proofs in order to conquer eternity."

"What does eternity matter if it is at this price? Does it not seem to you that the forgetfulness of the Earth is preferable?"

"I don't know. But I would be happy and proud to become a sun and spread wellbeing and amour around me in a kiss of fire. It is a beautiful destiny, for which one cannot pay too dear."

"Perhaps the stars suffer, like us; I believe that God is the torturer of the heavens."

"It's necessary, however, that there is happiness somewhere! An eternity of pain is inadmissible, for everything must collaborate in perfection. We are only hungry and thirsty because we know that we could satisfy the desires of our body, and the Lord has placed the remedy beside the evil. Our soul cannot be eternally hungry and thirsty, therefore, and the nourishment that it has been unable to find on the Earth must be given to it in the heavens."

"Poor friend! Have you not seen humans martyrizing unfortunate animals for the discoveries of science? Have they supposed for a moment that those creatures, barely inferior to them, might one day hold them to account for that obscure martyrdom? I believe that we are also the martyrs of a supernatural power and that our suffering, doubtless necessary to the experiments or pleasure of a master, is of scant importance to him."

"Let us adore that master without seeking to understand him, since he disposes of our destiny. Perhaps our spirit will be able, one day, to penetrate these terrifying abysms; let us try to persevere in virtue, and reject the miserable fears that come to us from the shameful matter that we have been unable to forget completely."

"But in order to persevere in virtue, it is necessary to live, and I sense that death in brushing me for a second time."

"Must we not remain here for two centuries? Has not the Chimera advised me to resist temptations?"

"The Chimera is the daughter of men; she lied, like everything that comes from their miry globe!"

The gentle creature that I was hugging to my heart seemed to fall unconscious; I dreaded seeing her die, so very pale and weak was she. Her extended and torn wings no longer emitted anything but an agonizing glimmer.

"Aaaah . . . Aaaah . . ."

And the note, once vibrant, was no longer anything but a sigh.

"I'm hungry and thirsty," she said. "My entrails are twisting, my blood is congealing."

I darted a desperate glance around me: there was nothing, nothing but the horrible flamboyance of that mountain of topaz, those distances of gold and bronze.

Then, seized by rage and despair, I bit my arm and applied the profound wound that I had just inflicted to my companion's lips. She drank avidly, and—a singular thing—as my blood reddened her mouth and trickled into her breathless throat, I felt stronger and more vibrant. That flesh on my flesh was an exquisite caress; that bosom, which swelled against mine, set my veins ablaze; I would have liked to remain like that forever.

But she stood up, smiling; I was astonished by her beauty.

"Thank you," she said. "I have to go on my way now."

"Go on your way? Abandon me! Remember that you cannot do without me, that my blood is necessary to your existence. Stay here. What would you seek elsewhere? I've made a tour of this world; it's the same everywhere; you cannot slake your thirst nor satisfy your hunger. Stay, flower of the desert, sweet reincarnation of what I have cherished. I sense that you will be for me a homeland, a hearth, hope and tenderness. You will give me life in taking mine, and if I can offer you one final joy by offering you my last drop of blood, I will search for it in the very bottom of my heart in order to moisten your mouth with it."

"Take care! In your turn, remember the divine threat. In spite of your dazzling body, you ought to be nothing but a pure spirit; any terrestrial reminiscence might be fatal for you. Here, beings do not reproduce; they must not admire one another, love one another or desire one another. Amour is a creator, and in creating, we insult the Master who, alone, can dispose of our destiny. The time that we spend on this star is a proof, a transitory epoch. Submit to it courageously; your intelligence, finally freed from the mist, will rise progressively and, after having been subject to all transformations, will become a star in its turn and shine in the heavens."

"Is it not the Chimera who spoke thus? You told me yourself that the Chimera, a daughter of men, was deceptive and perverse. Ought we to sacrifice a certain happiness for a problematic future?"

The white creature that I was retaining by the extremity of her wing slipped out of my hands and rose up slowly with a smooth and graceful movement.

At the idea of losing her I felt myself fainting; a mortal frisson ran through my bones; I uttered a terrible scream that made the mountain tremble.

Momentarily, my pretty fay paused, indecisively; I hurtled toward her with so much ardor that I broke her wings and we tumbled together into the depths of the abyss. But that fall was soft, as gentle as a voluptuous glide, and although we fell on blocks of gemstones cut into sharp teeth, we did not come to any harm.

Violet basilisks with trilobate crests and nisnas with only one eye and half a body,[1] reared up before us, while toads and chameleons swarmed at our feet, with blue spiders, slugs and green vipers, white larvae and others as transparent as crystal, beasts as round as balloons and others as flat as blades, toothed like saws.

And all those bodies were flamboyant, opening emerald maws and showing ruby tongues. The luminous bellies were bulbous, the claws were elongated, the coils writhed silently, and my companion wept in my arms.

"Aaaah . . . Aaaah . . ."

But the circle of monsters opened, the blue star appeared between two chrysoprase peaks. Immediately, a thousand strange insects swirled in its radiance like diamond snow.

---

1 A nisnas is a kind of monkey; I cannot locate any other reference to the fanciful being described here.

"Look," I said, "Those beings are seeking one another and loving one another. Let us love one another under the eye of the radiant star that, following the example of all lovers, cannot live alone. Can't you see that she is following the star that bears us in order to contemplate her and caress her incessantly? You are my star, and since you can live on me, I want to live on you."

As I spoke, I tightened my grip, and soon, forgetting the Earth, the universe, the stars and God, I took the sweetest and most complete of kisses from my lover's lips . . .

But my ecstasy was of short duration; sensing a horrible pain in my breast and opening my eyes, I recognized in my arms the bloody Chimera, who was digging her fingernails into my flesh and gripping my heart.

"It was me," she said, fascinating me with her glaucous eyes; "like your brethren, you have succumbed to my temptation. Die then, cowardly soul, body of mud! Oh, the pretty heart! What a pretty little heart this amorous heart is . . . !"

Anguish and suffering had woken me up. I made an effort and . . . I chased away Tigrette, my domestic cat, who had installed herself on my bosom and was laboring me amicably with her sharp claws . . .

REINCARNATION

ACCORDING to Claude Saint-Martin,[1] a man is a spirit fallen from the divine order into the natural order, who tends to return to his original state.

A man senses within him a host of aspirations toward an unknown goal, a thirst for joys that the earth cannot provide. His habitual condition is a kind of anxiety that is almost dolorous, and which increases in direct proportion to his superiority.

Only the occult sciences, without according him complete satisfaction, bring him closer to the luminous ideal that he glimpses when the veil of his habitual darkness is torn by the effort of his thought.

In these times of progress, a few elevated spirits have undertaken to initiate us into the mysteries of theosophy, the supreme science. They have consecrated their lives to the quest for wisdom and the discovery of the secrets of hyperphysical and invisible nature.

Humanity seems to be shaking off a long torpor and marching to the conquest of a veritable conscious state. What demonstrates that with all the clarity of evidence is the great religious movement commenced by spiritualism, under the flag of theosophy and the aegis of esoteric science. It is the studies of Éliphas Lévi, the Marquis de Saint-Yves, Stanislas de Guaita and Papus.

For the facts it is sufficient to consult Richet, Philips and Mesmer; for hypotheses of the ensemble Comte, Stuart, Spencer, Taine and Ribot; for the philosophy Hartmann, Schopenhauer

---

1 The ideas of the mystical philosopher Louis-Claude Saint-Martin (1743-1803) played an important role in the French Occult Revival, especially in the context of the Martinism re-established and promoted by "Papus" (Gérard Encausse) and Stanislas de Guaita in the 1880s.

and, going much further back, Spinoza, Leibnitz, Plato, Aristotle, the neo-Platonists and the Pythagoreans. All of them have sensed a state other than the one in which we are living, a kind of human doubling to the advantage of the divine element, an evolution, a spiritualization of human substance.

The most skeptical people are forced to admit certain manifestations that all their science cannot explain. Do we not see in India, "the ancestor of heavy secrets," prodigies accomplished by fakirs that we cannot admit humanly?

"Here," says Dr. Paul Gibier,[1] "a naked, motionless individual, the body in a semicircle, the legs folded, extends his fingers, and suddenly, to general amazement, a small piece of wood placed out of his reach on a thin layer of sand stands up, marches, trots and runs of its own accord, and traces the sentence thought by a member of the audience."

There, another fakir influences the vegetation in a direct manner and causes seeds taken at random from plants to germinate instantaneously.

Another folds his tongue into his throat, has his ears and nostrils blocked, enters into lethargy and is put into a coffin in that state. A hole is dug out to receive it, sealed beneath a stone slab subsequently covered by seeded soil, and two sentinels keep watch night and day to prevent any fraud. One, two or three months go by; the seeds have germinated and produced plants and flowers. The man is disinterred, almost mummified; he is warmed up and massaged; his heart resumes beating and the blood circulating in his arteries.

Another throws a rope into the air and, without anything seeming to hold him, suspends himself from the end, and then disappears from the sight of the bewildered spectators.

---

1 The physician Paul Gibier (1851-1900) had a strong interest in spiritualism and formed a circle of study in Paris similar to Camille Flammarion's. La Vaudère might have known him, and certainly used his book *Le Spiritisme (fakirisme occidentale)* (1887), from which this quotation is taken, as a crucial source for *Les Mystères de Kama*.

Several voyagers worthy of faith have witnessed these scenes and others; do they not prove that anything is possible, when the spirit of a subject is borne by an invincible force and an unshakable will is brought to support it? Unfortunately, we are always drawn outside ourselves by unexpected events, and intelligences powerful enough to resist doubt or folly are rare. Remember the possessed of Loudun and the convulsives of Saint-Médard.[1]

It has, however, been given to me to see the striking triumph of the will over matter. Amour, it is true, facilitated the victory, but is not amour the very essence of our soul, and in whatever manner we experience it, whether for a chimera, for a god or for a woman, does it not give us the power to brave anything and to vanquish everything?

The heart has a thirst for the ideal; materialism has clipped its wings for too long. That is why this story has perhaps come in its time, and however strange it might appear, I do not hesitate to transcribe it.

At the time when I knew him, Ghislain d'Entrames was thirty years old. He was tall, remarkably proportioned, and nature had endowed him with an inflexible will. Over his ascetic forehead, the shadow of a forest of thoughts descended. His elongated visage was mortally pale; he seemed diaphanous, it was as if the fire of the soul illuminated him from within. In the middle shone two cavernous eyes, as dazzling as two flashes of lightning in two clouds.

He told me that he had always realized what he had wanted, because his desire was able to impose itself in its omnipotence, in the way that whatever is great and strong imposes itself.

1 The story of the alleged sorcerer Urban Grandier and the possessed nuns of Loudun was frequently repeated in nineteenth-century texts. The curious story of the eighteenth-century "tumult of Saint Medard" was less well-known, but is told in *Histoire de miraculés et des convulsionnaires de Saint-Médard* (1864) by P.-F. Mathieu.

People had been docile instruments in his hands; he would have been able to conquer a magnificent situation in the land if his ambitions had not had higher aims.

It is necessary, for the explanation of what follows, to go back a number of years and to recount that which was his happiness, his goal and his reason for living. While very young he had been engaged to a girl whom his parents had seen born, and which a large fortune, a great name and former family relations recommended particularly to their choice.

Bérengère had an imperious spirit, and an ardent and passionate nature; having grown up with Ghislain, she was habituated to consider him as her fiancé, the natural companion of her entire life. The young man did not oppose any resistance to those plans, still indecisive in regard to his own sentiments; for the character of a man develops much more slowly than that of a woman, and a man who will one day disturb the world sometimes offers in his childhood a hesitant will submissive to an intelligence surrounded by mists.

Bérengère being the only person who was mingled with his intimacy, he experienced some pleasure in seeing her, even though a secret antagonism had already put him on his guard. There was no similitude of character between them except the same need for domination, visible in the young woman but as yet unavowed in her fiancé. But while the former was in full possession of her seductive forces, the latter was seeking to disentangle the frightful chaos of his thoughts. Immobile, as if electrified, he tried in vain to coordinate them. He was subject to a sequence of unformulated expressions that were like the imagined representation of his sensations.

Vaguely, he attempted to escape the power of Bérengère, who, using all the weapons that nature had given her, thwarted his resolutions and pursued him with her futile tenderness. Gradually, however, he shook off the yoke; his ideas became broader, his character firmer.

Everything that was simple and vulgar seemed despicable to him. When his brilliant studies were concluded, he launched himself into the complications of theosophy, seeking with a few profound minds to penetrate the mysteries of that science, which had recently become fashionable. With that elite, he devoted himself to the triumph of wisdom and the discovery of the hyperphysical and invisible nature. He seemed to be emerging from a long slumber; wonderstruck by the enjoyments of that study, he soon progressed to the conquest of his veritable conscious state. His highly assimilatory intelligence smoothed out the first reefs of initiation, and, while being remarked for a few peerless studies, he soon found himself at the head of the new school.

Until then, his work had been sufficient to his existence. Bérengère, whom he continued to consider as his companion, followed him with difficulty in his incessant discoveries, and, desirous of pleasing him, strove to find an interest therein equal to his own. Ghislain, however, was only attached to her by habitude, neither his heart nor his senses attracted him toward that woman of a different temperament, with whom he was unconsciously at odds and in conflict, awakening within him the involuntary sentiment of anger and hatred that we sometimes feel in regard to people who cannot understand us. Soon, the dull irritation that he experienced became intolerable; without any avowed motive, he broke abruptly with the young woman and departed for a long voyage across the world.

Bérengère felt a sharp dolor, in which there was more anger than real chagrin. She had fought, and had built a thousand clever plans, to conquer that bizarre nature, and, just at the moment of definitive triumph, her prey had escaped her, without her being able to penetrate the causes of that abrupt reversal.

When her former fiancé returned she tried to retie the broken bonds of their intimacy, but he evaded all advances. The reason for that was simple, and a young woman more expert in matters of amour than Bérengère would have divined it easily. Ghislain had escaped her domination because his heart had awakened and was beating for another. Suddenly, he had glimpsed the ardent joys of inspired and experienced tenderness; he had been invincibly attracted, by an unknown force, toward a being created for him, and who, it seemed to him, united all physical seductions and all moral perfections.

That marvel, however, was not one in the eyes of the profane, who only recognized in her a great beauty combined with a sovereign charm. Perhaps the young man would not have noticed her if he had not found her there just at the moment when his heart opened, avid for new joys and troubling sensations. A magnetic current was established between them, and they loved one another without ever having spoken to one another.

Djalfa belonged to one of the nomad troops that travel through France singing, dancing, and telling fortunes by means of cards. Barefoot in the sand, her hips tightened by a brightly colored skirt, she went forth leading by the bridle the meager nag attached to a caravan in which clever monkeys, fatal birds and ragged gypsies were piled up pell-mell.

The others did not have for her the affection that ordinarily unites all the members of the great Bohemian family. Another blood ran in her veins, and her distant memories of childhood traced for her an existence of affection in a regal dwelling, in which she wandered among flowers and silky furniture; but that was so long ago that she was not very sure that she had not had a sweet dream during halts in odorous meadows.

Djalha was an admirable creature. She had the nacreous complexion of a delicate seashell; her forehead was high, her nose slender and her nostrils mobile, and her pale silken hair made her a kind of bonnet of brocade woven with gold. That head would have been angelic if two large, profound brown eyes, scintillating between their double rows of black lashes, had not been animated by an almost supernatural flame. A mysterious smile wandered over her lips, and one divined, beneath the slightly frail elegance of her stature, nerves of a singular strength and an exquisite sensibility. Her slender body undulated rather than walking toward you, with a smooth serpentine glide.

70

Ghislaine had met her by the side of a road, and he had wondered whether he had before him a human being, a fay or an angel. She had started to dance, to turn and to whirl on an old Persian carpet thrown negligently under her feet, and every time her radiant face passed before him, a double flash sprang from her eyes.

"Oh, dance, dance again!" he cried, as she made as if to repose. And she resumed twirling, to the hum of a Basque tambourine that her pure arms raised above her head. Her flight became lighter, she launched forth, as frail and lively as a wasp, with her golden corsage, his diaphanous skirt and the blonde gauze of her hair spread over her shoulders.

He gave her money, but she threw it on the road with a large bunch of vervain that she took from her belt. Ghislain had departed, clutching the fresh souvenir of the gypsy woman, and whatever he did, her image no longer left his thoughts.

Two days later, while going past a small stream in farmland, he encountered her again. The caravan had stopped in a natural meadow enameled with Lucerne, clover and sainfoin. Corncockles, bugloss and black xylocopes were intoxicating the bees,[1] and the young woman, lying on the ground, was watching them flying above her head.

Ghislain had felt an irresistible attracted toward that meadow and, obedient to the mysterious force that was guiding him, he had arrived beside Djalfa. She had risen to her feet, blushing, and then, without saying a word, had fallen into his arms, as if she had been living for a long time in the expectation of that blissful moment.

Penetrated by the new doctrines, Ghislain said to himself that he had encountered the woman especially engendered for him, the twin soul that one hardly ever finds on earth, and that it was henceforth necessary to both of them that they live together. Djalfa felt an ineffable shudder throughout her being when the

---

1 This appears to be an error, as a xylocope is a kind of black bee, familiarly known as a carpenter bee.

young man's lips had pressed against hers; also learned in the mysteries of the Kabbalah and theosophy, she knew that a stranger would come and that, as one plucks a fruit from a branch by the roadside, he would extract her from her errant misery in order to create an existence of luxury and amour for her.

Throughout their peregrinations, the Bohemians have conserved intact interesting traditions originating from Tibet, which are recognizably similar to theosophical doctrines; the young woman had, therefore, studied the same grimoires as her lover; her mind was open to the same reasoning; her soul, like his, had a thirst for the ideal. She was awaiting the beloved, and when she held him in her arms, she was fully satisfied.

In fact, they complemented one another admirably. In life, human beings, imperfect by nature, march incessantly toward a goal of which they dream, which is equality and equilibrium. In order to attain it, they seek complementary influences capable of perfecting them, of enabling them to cease perpetual wandering. Thus appears the irresistible tendency of two beings to become only one, to enlace one another, to fuse in a physical and intellectual communion.

Instinct, as much as reason, seeks what might bring about that enviable state; from that are born sympathies and attractions, and, when reciprocity does not exist, despairs and follies. The passions, in fact, all flow from amour, the fundamental law of humankind. Do not our thoughts, our decisions and our actions come to us, in their turn, from our passions? And if our passions are hateful, and sometimes take on an umbrageous and aggressive form, it is because they result from secret presentiments that perceive a hindrance to the dreamed of and powerfully desired complementarity.

The more equilibrated an individual is in nature and intelligence, the greater his influence will be on others, for everyone will find in him what they lack. Ghislain represented will, strength and power. He was subjective, active and an individual. Djalfa, frail, nervous, ardent and tender, charmed him quite naturally, in the same way that the seduction she exercised on him was immediate and complete. Without argument, without resistance, she abandoned herself entirely.

"Now take me away," she said to him, when they disengaged, unsteadily from that first embrace. "My secret voices have not lied to me; I was born for you, and everything that has happened had to happen."

Plutarch says that incarnate souls have the faculty of predicting the future in this life, but that it is more or less latent, because those souls are obscured by the body as the sun is by fog. In her long reveries during her halts under the alders and the poplars, the Bohemian woman had seen her ideal incarnate; she had loved Ghislain, and when he had come, she had gone to him, knowing that he was destined for her, and that their two dreams were fated to fuse in a plenitude of wellbeing.

He took her away, therefore, to a small property he owned in Brittany, and there commenced an existence so filled with tenderness that there was no time even for reflection. They lived in a sort of radiance, an almost unconscious state of ineffable felicity.

Behind the black walls of their retreat, Ghislain had accumulated marvels: silky carpets, fabrics set with precious stones, large Venetian mirrors with multicolored flowers, and delicately-sculpted golden perfume-burners in the half-light of a tabernacle. At the end of a long illuminated corridor, that magnificence suddenly burst forth, as unreal as something out of a tale of the Thousand-and-One Nights.

Djalfa, semi-naked, clad only in diaphanous fabrics, themselves as soft as a caress, studied with Ghislain the mysterious books that they loved; then, rising with him to unknown altitudes, she seemed to pierce the future, to float in another world, populated with enchantment, as delectably rosy as a sunrise. She was no longer the same woman. Her instruction was perfect now, and her friend often allowed himself to be guided by her through the chaotic world of metaphysical investigations with which he was ardently occupied. But a sad presentiment often caused her to go pale; her eyes were veiled by tears, and all her courage seemed to abandon her.

"I sense that I shall die soon," she said. "We're too happy." And as he put his hands together in desolation, she went on: "When I am dead, I will not quit you; death only exists for those who are unable to love. I shall force the doors of the tomb, for my unique will, my inflexible will, is to remain with you and within you forever. Promise me that you will associate your power with mine, and summon me to you with all the ardor that I shall put into breaking my chains."

"I promise you that."

"Whatever happens, we'll be together, won't we, in death as in life?"

"I swear it," said Ghislain, again, and the young woman, consoled, rested her pretty head on her lover's shoulder. And that was her favorite topic of conversation. Incessantly, like a funeral knell, but very gentle in the sunlight, that phrase recurred: *when I am dead . . . when I am dead . . .*

That idea pursued her. The presentiment of a mission to fulfill beyond the tomb haunted her nights. Sometimes, stiffening in the young man's arms, she uttered a heart-rending cry and Ghislain, livid, tremulous and desolate, implored her not to think about anything any longer, to go to sleep in the confidence of his amour.

She almost never went out; the world no longer existed for her since she had encountered the beloved and understood her very reason for being. She belonged to him as the leaf belongs to the tree. They completed one another and were sufficient for one another. The leaf falls and dies detached from its stem; Djalfa did not want to be detached from Ghislain.

What about Bérengère?

Bérengère had suffered, cursed and wept. Divining too late that she had not been able to conquer her fiancé's heart, a grim hatred had overtaken her, and, attaching herself all the more the more she was scorned, she had sworn to triumph one day.

A headstrong and spirited young woman is never embarrassed; she had obtained information, had spied on Ghislain, and had divined a part of the truth. When she found out that the lovers had retired to Brittany she persuaded her parents to rent a property near theirs, and hid in the park, incessantly lying in ambush, and watched her rival's closed dwelling. In a month, she only saw Djalfa go out twice. Her lover gave her his arm and they walked slowly, holding one another tightly.

Bérengère had to admit that the Bohemian woman was charming, with her pale complexion and the extraordinary gleam of her gaze. Until then, no woman had caused her that involuntary sentiment of admiration, and in order for her to feel it, prejudiced as she was against her rival, it was necessary that the seduction exercised by the other was, indeed, very powerful.

Sensual and willful above all, Bérengère now desired Ghislain furiously. Her brutal and egotistical amour recoiled before nothing. Skillfully, with the cunning that all women have when passion drives them, she searched for schemes and drew up plans. How could she vanquish Djalfa, the accursed and execrated creature who had taken her fiancé? How could she reconquer the place she coveted so ardently?

She wrote to the young man, begging him to return to his former projects, to abandon an intrigue unworthy of him, from which nothing good could come. She appealed to his reason, to his heart, to his rectitude, and, her soul full of distress, she awaited the response.

That response was not the one for which she had dared to hope. Without denying his wrongs, he gave for their excuse the triumphant sentiment that had attracted him toward a woman capable of loving him and understanding him. The stupid prejudices of society did not exist for him, and, in order to consecrate that amour, he was ready to offer Djalfa his name and his life.

That brutal declaration cut to the quick of Bérengère's pride; her anger no longer knew any bounds. What! That schemer, that negligible young women, was standing up impudently between them! That frail creature whom a breath of wind could knock over would be an insurmountable obstacle in her life?

Her lips quivering and her eyes on fire, the young woman looked at herself in her mirror, and saw herself as she was: wild, beautiful and powerful, like an unbroken mare. She twisted her heavy, rebellious tresses over her forehead and attached them with two golden pins, which sparkled like stars in the night of that fleece. Then she smiled, suddenly appeased.

"I shall triumph," she said, "because I have the strength, the cunning and the will!"

That evening, she went to knock on Djalfa's door. The latter's husband had just left her, and, as the domestics were slow to appear, she followed the corridor all the way to the mysterious retreat. The Bohemian, lying on a low divan, was asleep, or seemed to be asleep. Her mouth was still smiling at her amorous dream; her entire face had an expression of infinite tenderness.

Bérengère shuddered to the depths of her heart. The disorder of the cushions and the intoxicating perfumes with which the atmosphere of the room was saturated exasperated her jealousy and troubled her reason. She approached and touched the sleeper, who opened surprised eyes, not understanding how that woman, whom she did not know, had arrived as far as her.

"I'm Ghislain's sister," said Bérengère, without her voice betraying her. "Won't you receive me as a relative and a friend?"

Djalfa threw the ashy curls of her hair over her shoulders, and contemplated her enemy with a soft smile at the corners of her lips.

"Be welcome," she replied. "I didn't know that my beloved had a sister, but you resemble him, and you must be accomplished."

"Truly? I resemble him?"

"Yes, a great deal. You have the same complexion, the same black hair. How he must love you!"

Bérengère frowned, and an imperceptible tremor agitated her hands. "He loves me," she said slowly, "but he would love me much more if you wished it."

The Bohemian looked at her with an incredulous expression. "No one is as good and tender as him. I'm certain that he has given you all of his fraternal heart, as he has given me all of his lover's heart."

An ardent blush covering her cheeks, she extended her hand to Bérengère, who sat down next to her and pressed her to her heart.

Only the soft whispers of the two women were audible in the closed room. An alabaster lamp suspended from the ceiling illuminated them feebly, and the servants, distanced from the retreat, knew nothing of their conversation.

When Ghislain returned, the lamp was extinct, but a tremulous voice called to him in the darkness.

He advanced, groping, and, encountering his beloved, who was also seeking him, he returned her caresses and her kisses.

That night seemed to him the most intoxicating of all those he had spent in Djalfa's arms. She enlaced him and linked herself to him, insatiable, passionate and irresistible. When he finally went to sleep, day was beginning to break.

His slumber was dolorous; terrible dreams assailed him; an unsustainable weight oppressed him, and he suddenly opened his eyes with a cry.

What he saw seemed to him to be the continuation of a nightmare, and, abruptly, he sat up on the bed, wondering whether he was not drunk or mad.

Djalfa was lying in the middle of the room, her face completely bloodless, her pupils fixed and dilated in a frightful expression of horror and suffering, her lips twisted over the enamel of her teeth. A little blood was running over her neck and making a small pool on the carpet.

He leapt forward and lifted her in his arms; he tried to re-animate her, but she was icy, already stiffened by death. There was no trace of a wound on the body. Red droplets, however, remained in her hair, which they had stuck together in little hard locks. Ghislain parted them, and found nothing.

Suddenly, his fingers encountered an obstacle: a golden pin-head gleaming in the blonde fleece. He tried to grip it, but the blood coagulated around it had, so to speak, encrusted it in the hair. At the peak of despair, trembling in every limb, he gripped the shiny little ball and, having drawn it out with some difficulty, a long hairpin emerged from Djalfa's head, which was unfamiliar to him, but which could only belong to a woman.

Who, then, had been in his bed beside him? Who had lavished bewitching caresses upon him all night long?

His forehead inundated with cold sweat, Ghislain turned his gaze in that direction, and recoiled suddenly, as if a snake had bitten him.

Leaning on her elbow, in the disorder of the pillows, Bérengère was smiling at him. A slightly ironic expression was curling her lips.

She nodded her head, responding to the terrible question that he addressed to her mentally. "Yes, it was me," she said. "I killed her, because she had taken my place. You thought you could escape me, but my will is equal to yours. I've taken you back, and I shall keep you!"

The young man felt a frightful anger seething within him. He looked around the room for a weapon in order to administer justice; red spots were quivering before his eyes; he was impatient to avenge his beloved Djalfa. As he found nothing, he advanced his taut hands, determined to strangle the miserable creature who, smiling and motionless, was still confronting him.

His fury blinded him; kneeling on the bed, he clenched his hands around Bérengère's neck. She uttered a feeble sigh, and lost consciousness.

At that moment, it seemed to him that the dead woman had made a movement. He turned round, but he had no difficulty convincing himself that he had been the victim of a hallucination. The body was still extended, rigid, on the carpet. It seemed to him, however, that she had ordered him not to commit that crime.

He concentrated his attention on Djalfa, and begged her, with his heart hammering, to let him know her will by means of some manifestation, if the will in question was that he should spare Bérengère's life.

Suddenly, he shivered. The gaze of the dead woman slowly turned to meet his, and fixed obstinately thereon, like those of certain portraits, which always seem to follow you.

That terrible gaze, in that white face, troubled him strangely, and, stirred to the marrow of his bones, he took the young woman's hand, expecting to feel it contract in his own, to warm up, to live again; but the hand fell back inert; the heart over which he placed his ear remained devoid of a pulse. He put his lips to the blanched lips in order to blow life into them, but the teeth did not unclench; a little mirror that he put to them remained limpid. It really was a cadaver that he had before him: the cadaver of the only woman that he had loved.

His chest tightened; finally exhaling his dolor, he shed abundant tears.

Then, in a superhuman effort of will, he ordered Djalfa for the second time to reassure him, to prove to him that all their research had not been in vain, that there existed a world different from the one they knew, that everything did not stop on the threshold of the tomb, and that the apparent injustice of life ceased therewith. He begged her to dictate to him the conduct that he ought to adopt, and to assist him in his troubles. Had she not repeated to him, often, the sentence that was still singing in his memory: "Death only exists for those who are unable to love. I shall force the doors of the tomb, for my unique will, my inflexible will, is always to remain with you and within you."

He heard the vibration of a feeble echo. As his thoughts retraced those consolatory words, a voice, all of whose chords quivered delectably, repeated them within him. He savored that new sensation, that exquisite understanding of the now-wandering soul that he loved; and the voice, whose sonorous waves perceptible for him alone, troubled him so profoundly, continued:

"You promised me to associate your desire with mine, and to summon me to you with all the ardor that I shall put into breaking my chains. The moment has come."

Ghislain knelt down and, his eyelids closed, his lips extended toward mysterious kisses, all his strength directed toward a single goal, he promised to carry out the dead woman's wishes.

When he got up again, he was calm and resolute, a flame burning in his eyes.

✳

Bérengère had remained motionless. He lavished his cares upon her, and succeeded easily enough in reanimating her. He said to her then, with a mildness by which she was frightened:

"You can't stay here. Get dressed and return to your parents."

"But I'd die of shame! Keep me, protect me! Have I not doomed myself for you?"

She dragged herself at his feet, vibrant with sobs, more frightened by his forbearance than by his anger or his hatred.

He picked her up.

"Have no fear; I'll protect your honor. When Djalfa's body has received the last duties, I'll marry you, Bérengère. No one will ever know that you spent the night here."

"And my crime? Can you forget it?"

"I forgive you. Go in peace."

She fell upon his hands and kissed them with transports of gratitude, but he begged her to hurry, as the day was progressing rapidly.

When she had dressed, feverishly and had disappeared as secretly as she had come, he laid the body of the Bohemian on the bed; then, having washed away the slight traces of blood that stained the carpet, he summoned the servants.

They all believed, or pretended to believe, that it was a natural death. Djalfa having no relatives or friends, no one was troubled by her decease; the funeral took place without any obstacle.

Only a few curious individuals attended the ceremony, and when Ghislain d'Entrames left the cemetery, he was not subjected to any compliment of condolence or any delicately sympathetic handshake.

For the rest of the day he wandered at random, bare-headed, his garments in disorder. Those who encountered him took him for a madman, so incoherent were his gestures and so wild was his gaze.

At ten o'clock in the evening, he went home, and, after a light meal, he ran to shut himself away in his cherished retreat, still warm with their amour, still embalmed by adorable memories.

The bed was made. Long brocade curtains covered it completely. At the foot, a bunch of white roses marked the place where the coffin had lain. Two half-consumed candles stood on the floor, in their silver candlesticks. Ghislain relit them, lifted a drape at the back of the room and activated a wooden panel, which, as it moved aside, uncovered a secret passage. He went into it, and penetrated into a small dark room of whose existence only he and Djalfa knew, which contained a few rare books, tarot cards, and various magical objects used in their experiments.

The disposition of that redoubt had been modified recently by the young man, and in the place that the bookshelves had occupied at the back of the room there was now a vast divan of black velvet, surrounded on all sides by dark curtains.

Ghislain closed the secret door again and knelt down, trembling. He was very pale, and drops of cold sweat were pearling on his forehead. His heartbeat would have been audible.

After a few minutes of meditation, he spoke aloud.

"If everything is transformed, if the progressive phenomena that we have studied must be renewed until complete perfection, if nothing dies, and if the human initiate to occult powers can direct at will the various evolutions in his life, until the supreme bliss, may my will be accomplished! Your soul is linked to mine, Djalfa, and I can no more be deprived of it than I could be deprived of air or sunlight.

"No, nothing dies; everything simply changes and is transformed, like the chrysalid that will become a butterfly and the flower of the peach-tree a vermilion and flavorsome fruit. Can we not direct at will the transformation of the beings we have cherished? Can we not, by dint of perseverance and energy, find them and recognize them, living by our side? Will the moment of our indissoluble union not come, my beloved, in spite of society and its paltry conventions, in spite of the feeble calculations of human intelligence, which believes that it embraces everything, and only sees the handful of millet that God holds in his hand?

"We have learned that the Earth turns, that the blood that circulates in our bodies is a river that returns to its source, that there are, beyond the sea of darkness, lands covered with trees different from our own, inhabited by men who are also different; but no one has yet recognized that all the creations and all the creatures in the Universe are signs.

"There are divine signs in the sea, in the profound forests, in a grain of sand, in our muscles, our bones and our flesh. Nature speaks to us, at every hour of the day, in an immensely sonorous language, compared with which all our poor science falls into dust and disperses. Those signs demonstrate to us in a manner that does not address our reason but our instinct, our soul and our heart, that we cannot disappear, that our essence is imperishable and that a divine light guides us incessantly toward the eternal light . . ."

Ghislain parted the curtains, and on the bed, the body of Djalfa appeared to him, such as he had found it on the carpet after his criminal night. He had taken care to fill the coffin with stones, in order to sustain belief in the inhumation of those cherished remains, and secretly, while everyone was asleep, he had transported the cadaver to this retreat.

Cold and rigid, Djalfa still had open eyes, and her motionless gaze, turned toward Ghislain, had lost none of its luminous gleam.

A profound silence fell. The young man, sunk in his meditations, remained on his knees. He felt himself transported into a different world, rid of his bonds, light and happy. Lost in his intoxicating dream, projected, so to speak, outside of himself, an imponderable body, an astral form, it seemed to him that the force of his vital fluid, thus liberated, attracted Djalfa, or what remained of her, and that she dissolved divinely within him. He sensed her entire being plunging into his as if into an abyss. Her voice spoke to him ineffably, a bell of amour descended from the gods, an echo of the ecstatic prayer of the angels, it vibrated in his most secret fibers, and maddened him.

The whole night passed thus, without him being conscious of it.

The candle went out, entirely consumed; a faint gleam passed under the woodwork.

He closed the curtains that sheltered the body of the Bohemian, and left quietly. His face was fearfully pale, but he seemed calm and resolute.

During the day, he had himself announced in Bérengère's house. The young woman was surprised to see him so soon. She had reflected a great deal; the remorse of her crime weighed upon her; she was gripped by a kind of obscure dread. Without regretting her rival's death, she feared its consequences. Human justice, although slow and incomplete, could not be blind to the point of absolving her, and in any case, would not divine justice attain her?

Ghislain found her changed, thinner and tremulous, with something anxious and fugitive in the depths of her eyes. He took her by the hand and drew her to him.

"Don't you want to receive your fiancé?" he asked her, with great mildness.

"I dare not believe you. How can you look at me without shivering?"

"What happened had to happen. You were only a docile instrument in the hands of destiny, Bérengère. It has been given to me to read the future; that is why I have come to offer you my name, and I am certain that you will accept it as I offer it to you, with joy and urgency."

"And will you love me as much as . . . the other?"

"Perhaps not at the beginning, but we're young and . . . time passes over everything."

The young woman shivered. "I'm afraid," she said. "A cold breath brushed my forehead, an icy breath like the exhalation of the tomb. Someone is here that I can't see: a specter that is whispering menacing words to me. Can you not hear it, Ghislain, and is it not the soul of Djalfa, the wrathful soul of the woman I murdered in a cowardly fashion?"

"Dispel those somber ideas. Those who are dead do not return. Did you not say that to me often when I pored over obscure old books in order to extract therefrom the secret of the eternal mystery in which we evolve? Did you not mock me then for my crazy imaginations, and were you not right, therefore, to take from the earth its sunlight and its dew, like a beautiful insouciant flower?"

There was a little irony in Ghislain's words, but Bérengère, glad to see him so docile and so persuasive, paid no heed to it; she smiled at him, and the cruel flame of triumph lit up in her gaze.

84

"I belong to you," she said, in a low voice. "Can you love me as I love you, and forget in sweeter intoxications the bloody intoxications of our first night of amour?"

He returned every day, and their engagement was soon announced overtly. Their parents had consented with joy to that union, which fulfilled their wishes, and the solitude in which they lived preserved them from indiscreet commentaries.

Ghislain d'Entrames acquiesced to all of his fiancée's caprices; he was only inflexible on one point: their place of residence. The old château where he had been so happy and so proven pleased him, and all prayers that young woman addressed to him in order to persuade him to sell it remained vain. Djalfa's bedroom would remain Bérengère's bedroom, the dead woman's bed would be that of the legitimate wife, and no change would be introduced to the disposition of their dwelling.

The marriage drew a great many people, in spite of the difficulty of communications. A little curiosity regarding the groom was mingled with the eagerness that people put into responding to the numerous invitations that the young woman's parents sent out. People knew about the idyll so strangely commenced and so fatally interrupted by the death of the young Bohemian, and socialites throw themselves avidly on all the romantic adventures that the spirit of calculation and egotism have rendered so rare.

People felt slightly sorry for Bérengère, who, shivering in her white silk dress lowered her eyes hypocritically.

Entrames attracted the gazes of all the women present at the ceremony. He seemed to have grown in stature, superior to the others, with something cold and willful that was imposing.

Certainly, those preoccupations were far from the one that was leading him to the altar. A different being lived within him, a suffering and anxious being who was feverishly agitated. He wondered whether he might not be mistaken, whether he was really obeying Djalfa's injunctions in giving his name to the criminal woman who awakened in his heart nothing but hatred and scorn.

All his science seemed slender to him, now that he was trying to resolve a frightful problem. Did the books that he had read so often, while charmed, contain anything but beautiful lies, gilded and fugitive? Did the stars themselves not lie? Could poor human intelligence comprehend the mystery of the worlds scattered in space like as many turbulent atoms?

He knelt down on the velvet prie-dieu and, while the choir-boys were swinging censers and the priest was intoning the words of the ritual, he made a supreme appeal to the powerful being that watches over human destinies. Had that God not said: *let there be light*, in sowing force and clarity everywhere? Departing from that principle, Ghislain lost himself in profound reasoning.

Infinity has its ether, the star its light, the organized being its magnetic fluid: the astral body or the plastic mediator. The will acts directly upon it, and by its means, submits all of nature to the modifications of intelligence. Entrames knew that he had an incomparable magnetic power, but he had only made use of that force thus far in pure experiments; might it not abandon him at the decisive moment?[1]

He knew that one could kill by means of magnetism, as one could by electricity, and there is nothing strange about that particularity, which has many analogies in nature. The fluid is matter in rapid motion, always agitated by the variation of equilibria. There is no fluid body that cannot become harder than diamond if its constituent molecules are equilibrated. To direct magnets is thus to destroy or create forms, to produce an appearance or to annihilate a substance, to exercise omnipotence over nature.

That force, insufficiently known in its effects, like electricity itself, can become terrible, and the future belongs to those who are able to employ it usefully. It has presented itself at all times; Hermes and Pythagoras mentioned it; Synesius, who sang its praises in his hymns, had found the revelation in the Platonist

---

1 The author inserts a reference at this point to Éliphas Lévi, which is garbled in the print-on-demand reprint of *L'Anarchiste*.

memoirs of the school of Alexandria.[1] "One single source, one single root of light springs forth and expands in three branches of splendor. A breath circulates around the earth and vivifies, under innumerable forms, all the parts of animate substance." It is that primal substance that is signaled by the hieratic narrative of Genesis when the Word of Elohim makes light by ordering it to be. That light, the Hebrew name for which is *aour*, is the living gold of all Hermetic philosophy.

Our plastic mediator seems to be the magnet that attracts or repels the astral light under the pressure of the will; it is a luminous body itself, which reproduces with the greatest facility the images invoked by the imagination. But cannot that luminous body, instead of receiving its form from the carnal envelope on which it depends, communicate its own to it at length, and progressively substitute one being for another by means of the disaggregation of the constituent molecules?

While Bérengère was praying, her head curbed over her joined hands, he thought about those things. His mysterious conversation with the dead woman vibrated in his memory. She had reassured him, convinced him and pushed him into that dangerous path. Next to her, he had felt strong and courageous; everything had seemed facile to him. Now, a veil of darkness descended over him. Would the punishment that he was preparing attain the culpable individual? Might it not rather strike the man who was daring to penetrate secrets thus far inviolable?

His entire body shuddered. *Djalfa! Djalfa!* he cried, with the voice of the soul, which the ear cannot hear, but which shakes and tears every being with more force than the clamors of the ocean.

No echo responded to him, but, having turned round, he was struck by Bérengère's pallor. Her fearful eyes encountered his.

"Pity!" she murmured, very quietly.

---

1 The known works of Synesius of Cyrene, who became Bishop of Ptolemais in 410 A.D. in spite of his neo-Platonist ideas, were easily accessible in both French and English in the nineteenth century.

That evening, when they found themselves alone in the room of the murder, the young woman enveloped him in her arms and drew him toward the divan.

"What I felt this morning was strange," she said. "It seemed to me that my life was escaping me like blood flowing from a mortal wound. An icy cold descended upon my heart, my ideas were obscured; I've never felt such an anguish. Might it be the punishment already?"

Ghislain did not reply. A satisfied smile wandered over his lips; he was certain now of victory.

He lay down alongside Bérengère and his mouth had no sooner touched hers than she fell into a profound slumber. With a few rapid lateral passes, and the most intense projection of the will that he was able to obtain, he plunged her into a complete state of magnetic catalepsy.

Then, bringing the mobile panel of the woodwork into play, he went to Djalfa's body, and there, kneeling down, lost in the intoxication of his desire, it seemed to him that the dead woman called to him, encouraged him, and ordered him to continue his work.

He remained thus for a long time, unconscious, radiant and transfigured.

When he returned to Bérengère, she was lying in the same position; her pulse was imperceptible, her respiration was soft, scarcely detectable, except by the application of a mirror to the lips. Her eyes were closed, naturally, and her limbs were as rigid and cold as marble.

"Bérengère," he said, "are you asleep?"

She did not reply at first; then her lips trembled, and her face took on an expression of suffering and dread. Her eyelids rose up of their own accord, as if to unveil the white line of the eyeball, and, making an effort, she cried: "Where are you taking me? I don't want to die! You've opened my heart, oh, with a needle, and the blood is escaping from it slowly . . . Ghislain! For pity's sake, wake me up . . ."

Imposing his will upon her, he said, gravely: "We have loved one another well, tonight, Bérengère. You'll remember that, won't you? You'll tell everyone that you're perfectly happy?"

She agitated feverishly. "I'll tell them, Ghislain . . . wake me up."

He made a few rapid passes, and her respiration became stronger. She passed her hands over her face, and the iris appeared in the eyeball. Immediately, a smile spread over her features.

"How content I am!" she murmured. "She didn't merit so much happiness. How I love you, and how you love me! We'll have a great many similar nights, my adored. I knew full well that your heart would come back to me, that one day you'd be entirely mine."

She got dressed and went down into the garden. She had never been as joyful. Her parents came to see her, and were astonished by her exaltation. Her eyes had a slightly feverish gleam, and her complexion was clouded, but happiness sometimes leaves the same stigmata as pain.

The Marquis and Marquise de Sainte-Laure were not overly anxious about the condition of their daughter. Subsequently, in any case, she maintained the same charmed air, even though she had changed visibly. When anyone asked for news of her health, she said that she was very well and fully satisfied, with the result that her entourage soon ceased to worry about the alteration in her features, which might have been attributable to the commencement of a pregnancy.

Every evening, Entrames plunged her into a magnetic slumber and put her in communication with the inert body of Djalfa; then, breathless and with his soul swollen by hope, he followed the mysterious work that was occurring in her organism.

Certainly, he hated Bérengère with a grim hatred; all his aspirations, all his tenderness went to the other, the murdered woman, the only adored. He indulged in orgies of memory. His spirit was burning fully and broadly with an incessantly increasing flame. He insulted the accursed woman and desperately summoned the idolized mistress, as if he could reanimate her and enable her to live again by means of his savage energy and the devouring ardor of his passion.

Bérengère sighed and wept, but her plaints remained futile.

When he interrogated her, she accused him of pricking her heart with a long needle in order to let the blood out drop by drop—and it was a frightful torture! She writhed and struggled; her fingernails dug into her flesh and her lips twisted in impotent cries; and every morning, a more profound change was produced in her. Her features now seemed to be melting and diminishing; her complexion was paling in places; her eyes were clouded; even her hair was changing color; her robust figure flexed; one might have thought that she was shrinking.

Her humor, however, was constantly joyful; no worry seemed to affect her. She only spoke to her husband with the greatest tenderness, and reassured her family, who could not understand her metamorphosis, and were beginning to become anxious about it.

That state of affairs lasted for several months.

Ghislain acted with the most extreme prudence. The domestics, kept well away from the conjugal chamber, could not discover anything, and when she woke up, Bérengère carried out meekly the orders given to her while asleep. Her memory, moreover, remained mute. She only knew one thing, which was that her husband adored her, that he had given her the most convincing proofs of it, and that every night brought the same intoxication.

Now, every night edged her a little closer to the doors of the tomb, and as soon as the power of her administrator of justice was extended over her she fell into a horrible slumber traversed by terror, anguish and despair. And the invisible and impalpable substance of her being, which constituted her individuality, her energy and her life, was projected outside: the entity that although infinitely diluted, was nevertheless her own being—which is to say, according to the expression of Indian occultists, her astral body, which is to the body what steam is to the machine that it fills and what electricity is to the apparatus that it enables to act.

The young woman, previously the mistress of her carnal envelope, was already no longer mistress of her astral body, which the Hindus also call the Linga Sharira.

Can the astral body that receives its form from the human envelope not metamorphose in its turn, and communicate a different appearance to that envelope? Can there not be a substitution of substance? Could Ghislain, who held Bérengère's life in his hand, not employ his strength to a more complete punishment than death, which destroys and does not repair? Was he not the master of the terrible secret of life and death? Did he not have the power of the adepts who hide in the solitudes of the Himalaya? Is not everything transformed after the last sigh? He was only hastening that transformation and directing it at his whim, like the adepts who have the power to make matter pass through matter. Everything that exists is merely an aggregate of infinitesimal molecules, whose dissociation is not impossible.

Every night, he knelt down before Djalfa's remains, and, his soul filled with an immense hope, concentrating all his strength in his desire to succeed, he listened to the secret voice that led him into that mysterious labyrinth. He had vanquished incredulity and suspicion; everything seemed possible to him now.

Already, although she was inanimate and as cold as marble, Djalfa was visibly changing. In contrast to Bérengère, her features were accentuating, taking on a harshness that they had not had during life; her beautiful blonde hair was darkening and twisting into unsubmissive locks. And Ghislain went from one to the other, establishing the magnetic current in spite of the cries and supplications of Bérengère, who was convulsed by unspeakable suffering, imploring him to spare her, or to kill her immediately. The blood of her veins was always leaking away drop by drop through the imperceptible prick that she felt in her heart, and her rival, like a vampire crouched upon her, gradually penetrated her, gorging on her life.

In the morning, Entrames ordered her to forget the tortures of slumber.

"You will be cheerful, loving and communicative," he told her. Then he woke her up, and the young woman immediately threw herself into his arms, thanking him for the happiness that he had given her.

Ghislain's strength, however, was running out; he sensed the necessity of terminating his work of justice. It seemed to him that by concentrating all the energy of his will in a beam, he would triumph over the last resistances of matter. But he needed to act in solitude. He therefore informed his wife, during one of her magnetic slumbers that she had to get rid of her parents on some pretext or other.

The Marquise de Sainte-Laure suffered from chronic bronchitis; the air of Nice had been recommended to her a long time ago, and if she had deferred her departure, it was only to watch over her dear daughter, whose pallor and diminution troubled her.

Bérengère was so persuasive and so insistent that the good lady no longer hesitated. Her departure was settled for the following day, and everyone employed themselves with it so ardently that she was obliged to take the train at the agreed time.

The heart of a mother has surprising divinations; solid links always attach it to her child, and nothing in life can break them. Enclosed in her coupé, the Marquise wept recklessly and claimed that she was hiding something from her, that a misfortune was hovering over her, that she felt it, that she was certain of it—but Bérengère smiled at her and reassured her.

"What do you fear for me? Have you not always seen me fully satisfied? Did you think that I could pretend to the extent of deceiving you? No, no, Mother, depart without fear. Ghislain loves me, and no shadow of a cloud has ever risen between us."

When the old lady had gone, the spouses returned to their retreat.

"I don't know what's the matter with me," said Bérengère, as they followed the dark pathways. "My thought escapes me now for long hours. A physical metamorphosis is also taking place in me. Does it not seem to you that my hair is lighter in color, that my body is no longer the same?"

"In fact, you now resemble Djalfa."

But she uttered a loud cry. "Don't say that! Don't say that! I'm afraid. Oh, your gaze is cruel—what do you want?"

"I want the resemblance to be complete. I want the dead woman to be resuscitated in you."

The young woman fell to her knees. "Is that the punishment, then? Will you be pitiless?"

"I am as pitiless as you have been."

"But I can escape, flee, return to my parents, ask them for protection from you . . ."

"Try, then. You're feebler than a child, for your will is submissive to mine. Come."

She followed him meekly, incapable of resisting.

He traversed the long corridor, the silent chamber where he had loved and suffered so much, and then, tripping the catch in the woodwork, he penetrated into the secret redoubt.

"Lift that curtain," he said, when her gaze had become accustomed to the gloom.

But she could not obey; she went frightfully pale and collapsed on the carpet. When she came round, her eyes immediately encountered the funereal couch, and she started uttering such clamors that Ghislain put her to sleep and threw her, impotent, on to the cadaver of her rival.

"Oh, Djalfa," he said, "let your astral body, disengaged from terrestrial bonds, melt for me into this palpitating mold. Let this prodigy be accomplished by the power of our amour. Since nothing dies, you cannot be annihilated, and I sense you hovering, like a bird of light. You will live again, in all the plenitude of life, by taking possession of this body, which I have liberated for you, and which is already offering itself to give you shelter. Take its strength, its suppleness and its warmth, while its impotent thought will go to inhabit your inert cadaver."

Ghislain put the bodies of the two women in contact. After a moment, it seemed to him that a sort of vapor floated over the bed; that vapor was born on the breast of Djalfa, at the place of the heart. It rose up in a blue spiral and extended like a light cloud, uncertain of the direction to follow.

Entrames did not speak; all his power was in his brain, whose lobes were functioning with an extraordinary activity. Upright and motionless, he was thinking of nothing but the miracle that he desired, and the hope of success doubled his strength.

It that surge of his entire being toward the adored woman that he wanted to revive, he was insensible to Bérengère's suffering, and to the fact that the latter, although asleep, was agitating desperately, making vain efforts to flee. She was experiencing a kind of rip in the region of the heart; her life was flowing away through it, slowly and dolorously. Her empty brain became icy, at the same time as a sensation of breath, going from the exterior to the interior, caused her a frightful suffocation.

After a few further passes, she remained motionless. Above her extended a white form, but of a hue so faint that it as scarcely perceptible, a cloudy silhouette of the dead woman. At one moment it was accentuated, and became so clear that Ghislain, frightened, as if before a supernatural manifestation, was troubled, and ceased momentarily to project all of his force upon it. Immediately, it vanished. But a further change had taken place in Bérengère, a change so emphatic that she was almost no longer recognizable.

Woken up, she left the room automatically. She did not seem either to see or understand what was happening around her. Obedient and resigned, however, she was submissive to whatever was demanded of her, walking, sitting down, eating, and even responding incoherently to the questions that were asked of her.

Her movements had an unaccustomed stiffness, and her features remained immobile.

In the evening, however, when Ghislain wanted to take her back to Djalfa, she struggled with a desperate energy. Consciousness of her wretched situation seemed to have returned to her; her cries became convulsive and heart-rending. Finally, out of strength, she submitted; her face was flooded with tears, her breast was heaving with hectic sobs. She fell on the funereal couch, and went to sleep as usual, under the magnetic influence.

From that moment on, Ghislain felt fully reassured. He acted coldly and calmly, certain of the final success. All resistance he thought, was smoothed out, whatever it might be. He also understood that he had to carry out progressively, by almost insensible degree, that transmutation of one being into another, for fear of failure, of breaking the fragile instrument that he had in his hands.

His victim, her teeth clenched, her limbs quivering, seemed to be enduring frightful tortures; her nostrils were pinched; a little foam came to her lips. It was necessary to act with excessive prudence, for suffering has its limits, and can become mortal in attaining the limit that nature has fixed.

Bérengère was no longer cataleptic, for she would have remained insensible to Djalfa's influence, and in any case, the ordeal would have been infinitely longer. The limbs had to conserve their flexibility in order to lend themselves to the desired transformation; the blood had to circulate freely, in order to receive the new elements and assimilate them.

Although unconscious, the young woman was suffering in her flesh, gripped by an inexpressible anguish by virtue of the puncture in her heart, through which her life was leaking. The vampire that was obsessing her, gradually taking it, was melting into her, invading her, giving her its form and its thought.

She sensed that confusedly, albeit intolerably, and impotent tears ran from her eyes.

When she left the room, Ghislain was obliged to support her, she was so weak. He dressed her and covered her with thick veils, in order that no one would perceive the new change that had taken place in her.

Reason now abandoned her. When someone spoke to her, her fearful gaze fixed on them and her lips moved, but then she fell back into prostration. A frightened domestic spoke to Ghislain about the necessity of calling a physician, and that incident persuaded him to hasten the denouement, in the dread of not being able to complete his frightful proof.

The following night, he concentrated all the energy of his will like a beam in order to act upon his victim more powerfully. In the beginning, it seemed to him, for the first time, that his efforts were vain, that an insurmountable wall loomed up between him and her, and that his force buckled, as if against armor, bending like a reed.

Then he fixed his thought ardently on the goal that he was pursuing; he evoked the adored soul of Djalfa, and begged her not to abandon him on the threshold of paradise. Had he only succeeded thus far in order to taste the dolor of disappointment more intensely? Must he fall back into the world of darkness, after having nursed the ineffable hope of finding her again? Was he not worthy of that recompense? Had he not traveled his calvary with courage and patience? Had he not obeyed her as he would have obeyed God himself, in the ardor of his respectful amour?

He prostrated himself, with his face to the ground, and from all his being, plunged in desolation and tenderness, sprang a profound cry, a supreme prayer. Immediately, his courage returned, he felt reinforced and sustained. His nerves and his muscles obeyed him; no exterior impression could any longer distract him.

Under the effort of his fluid, the jet of gray vapor emerged from Djalfa's breast, rose up turbulently, folded upon itself and came to float and extend over Bérengère. The latter writhed, and sought to escape it, but an order from Ghislain maintained her motionless.

Then, the mysterious spring still flowing, the vapor took on a vague but recognizable form: the form of Djalfa.

For a moment, she remained hesitant; then she descended, enveloped Bérengère like a light veil, and gradually melted into her.

At that moment, a ray of light slid under the mobile panel, and Ghislain, fearful of being surprised, rapidly made the usual passes to awaken the sleeper. But the latter was mortally pale; her lips tightened and creased, as if in a spectral impression of death, and an extreme chill spread over the surface of the body.

Under the pressure of an inexpressible horror and terror, Entrames sensed the pulsations of his heart stop, and a cry of despair almost escaped him. Had he forced the dose, and had the exhausted organism of the patient been unable to support it?

He threw himself on to her mouth and blew air into her lungs; he dragged her into the bedroom and opened both windows wide.

Finally, a slight tremor ran through the body. However, the young woman could not recover the use of speech; she was confined to bed and remained in the same depressed state all day. Her face was white and drawn, her lips blue, her hair completely colorless. She seemed to be at the utter extremity.

Ghislain hid that condition from the domestics carefully, and, in order to deflect suspicions, talked about a violent migraine and a need of absolute solitude for the invalid.

In the evening, he dared not continue his work. Prostrate before the cadaver of the Bohemian, he remained plunged in painful meditations.

Until then the body had remained, as on the first day, smooth and white, like a beautiful marble; the features had conserved their admirable serenity. That evening, however, a slight alteration was produced, and Ghislain shivered on observing that the gaze was becoming vitreous, and that symptoms of decomposition were becoming noticeable.

There was not a moment to lose, for his proof, so skillfully conducted, might fail, and how miserable his existence would be then!

Brutally, he took hold of Bérengère, who was no longer making any movement, and dragged her to the bed.

Absorbing himself completely in his terrible desire, he concentrated all his will upon her, all the living forces of his being, with such impetuosity that he felt faint, as if the blood were flowing away from his heart in order to ooze out of him in seething waves. His hands were icy and a nervous tremor agitated him from head to toe. He clutched the two bodies in a convulsive embrace, and for the first time, he gave his execrated spouse a long, frightful kiss, which threw him back on the bed, half-dead. A soft caress brought him round.

He almost fainted a second time, under an expression of supreme delight. Bérengère, who was no longer Bérengère but the perfect reincarnation of Djalfa, was smiling at him and holding out her arms to him.

He threw himself upon her and covered her body, whose every sinuosity and all its charming coverts reminded him of his lost love, with mad kisses. Yes, those really were Djalfa's silky tresses enveloping him, like a blonde gauze; they really were her large, luminous and profound eyes, and her moist lips, made for caresses and sweet confessions.

She spoke, and her voice rose up like the echo of ancient prayers and ancient amorous sobs.

"Finally," she said, "our desire is accomplished. I have returned to you, and nothing that is not me can any longer distract us from our enchanted dream. Remember my words: *When I am dead, I shall not quit you for that; death only exists for those who are unable to love. I will force the doors of the tomb, for my unique will, my inflexible will, is to remain forever with you and within you. Promise me to associate your power with mine and to summon me with all the ardor that I shall put into breaking my chains. We have kept our promises."*

"Djalfa!"

"Yes, Djalfa, whom your tenderness has delivered from death, and who has been reincarnated, in order to recommence with you an existence of uninterrupted happiness. Come, let us flee this sinister bed!"

Ghislain cast a glance at the couch. A formless cadaver lay there; a broth of flesh in complete decomposition; a horrible mass of bones and blood.

The two lovers took one another by the hand, and, having closed the door of the frightful sepulcher again, they quit that accursed place forever.

ASTRAL AMOUR

PHYSIOLOGICAL psychology has been very fashionable for some time. The phenomena of thought, the motor functions and their different phases have been localized with precision in one part or another of the medulla or the brain. The bizarreries of hypnotic suggestion have been explained and are not a secret for anyone. Some researchers have read the German studies of Weber on sensibility, those of Fechner on the measurement of sensations; the research of Helmholtz on vision and on music; various appreciations that have been combined and condensed by the learned Wundt, professor of psychology at Leipzig. France has the endeavors of Boca and Charcot, England those of Huxley, Maudsley and Carpenter. People are occupied with heredity and transmission; Ribot was the first to transfer that question from the purely medical domain into the philosophical domain.

"The question of suggestion," says Paul Janet, "raises many others: that of the relationship of hypnotism to hysteria; the question of hypnotic phases (lethargy, catalepsy, somnambulism); the question of passages from the normal to the suggestive state and vice versa; not to mention the philosophical questions more or less engaged in the debate; and finally, and above all, the question of the doubling of the self."[1]

The truth is that we are at the stage of hypotheses, and that the mystery that is within us and around us will last as long as our miserable reign. How can we explain what we do not understand?

---

1 The writings of the philosopher Paul Janet (1823-1899) were prolific; the quotation probably comes from *De la suggestion dans l'état hypnotique* (1884).

Our imperfect nature deprives us of a host of enjoyments that beings better organized and more intelligent than us might experience. Our clairvoyance does not even embrace all the phenomena of creation; we do not have special reagents for all natural agents. Our senses permit us to appreciate sound, form, taste, heat and light, but we do not know whether the air that we breathe contains free electricity or not. At the most, we have a vague sensation of malaise on stormy days. If the atmosphere of the globe had been devoid of lightning and thunder, perhaps we would never have had any presentiment of that force, which, says Monsieur Noegell: "plays such a great role in inorganic nature, which provokes chemical affinities, which, in all the molecular movements of organized beings, probably has a more decisive influence than any other force, and of which, finally, we expect the most important enlightenments in order to explain physiological and chemical facts still in the state of enigmas."[1]

Our eyes are sensible to the colors of the spectrum, but they do not grasp the ultra-violet that is distributed around us in vegetation. Thus, there are natural phenomena around us that escape us. Our present sensations only embrace a small number of the facts necessary to our existence. However, certain more refined, more vibrant, organizations have the prescience of invisible things, and sometimes the sudden revelation of some mystery hitherto unexplained. Light is cast, and becomes bright, in a moment. The contact of two exceptionally endowed intelligences ought to cause that wellspring of unsuspected good fortune to gush forth. I also believe that if I had not encountered Viviane, everything would have remained obscure in me, and that, following the example of other men, I would have sought to satisfy my despicable instincts, ignorant and disdainful of higher felicities.

I have always seemed bizarre to banal natures; the explosiveness of my imagination, my occasional invincible silence, or the surge of my speech, which escapes in sonorous or enthusiastic

1 The reference might be to the German physician Hermann Franz Noegell, but the quotation is untraceable.

phrases, without apparent reason, all awaken mistrust around me. People have called me mad, but do we know, as yet, whether madness might be the quintessence and the sublimity of intelligence? Mad! Because we see that which will forever remain in darkness for other humans? Mad! Because the sensibility of our organism has developed to the point of exasperation, and that good as well as evil has become familiar to us? But where does good end, and where does evil commence? A common cowardice has fixed the limit of that which, in reality, has none; everything depends on the motive, circumstances and secret influences that are almost always inexplicable. Those who dream by day have knowledge of a host of things that will remain forever unknown to those who only dream by night. Visions are strewn with fulgurant lightning flashes that, at times, unveil eternity for us and permit us to retain a few scraps of the terrible mystery.

I was orphaned at a young age, and was taken in by an aunt who lived in the country with her daughter, a few years younger than me. Viviane had inherited the paternal fortune, which was immense; her education had also impelled her into the most elevated regions, which her remarkable intelligence explored without fatigue.

I associated myself with her studies, glad to be anticipated in the solution of a difficult problem, or to be able to converse with her about matters that are generally closed books for the majority of women.

In any case, Viviane was only a woman by virtue of the softness of her voice and the charm of her smile. She was extremely thin, her complexion almost diaphanous, and beneath the somber forest of her black hair, her pupils, in their blue enamel, resembled two coals that an interior fire sometimes ignited. She was tall, straightforward, and all her movements seemed harmonious. When I evoke her terrestrial image, I see her clad in loose, silky fabrics, leaning on the back of an armchair in an abandoned posture, her profound eyes half-veiled by the sweetness of a dream.

She did not awaken any desire in me. I loved her mind, her heart, her thought—in sum, what it is conventional for us to call the soul, not being able to define more clearly the second being that lives within us and commands slavish matter as a master.

Viviane was a soul, nothing more, and like a beautiful mystical flower, all dream and all perfume, I plucked that soul.

It happened on a foggy day in October; nature had the melancholy charm of fêtes that are about to end. A few yellow leaves dotted with crimson patches rolled at our feet. The sun, at times, appeared through the clouds like a feebly illuminated unpolished globe.

The spirit of things seemed to be weeping over the nullity of terrestrial splendors, and I thought that, like those leaves writhing on the damp earth, our youth would fall from the tree of life, and that cold winters would suspend their tresses of frost and snow there.

I searched around me for something a little more durable than the others, in order to support thereon my paltry hopes, which take so long to die, like all those born in the human heart. My gaze traveled through space, and, as if attracted by a powerful magnet, came to fix upon that of Viviane, who, silent and immobile, seemed to be lost in a dream. Suddenly, her eyes sparkled, a sort of electric shock was produced, the darkness that surrounded us was dissipated, and in the same way that two beams of light that encounter one another are confounded, our souls were no longer secret for one another. I felt myself warmed, comforted; I read within her, as in an open book, the infinite tenderness that she had for me. Her soul was radiant; I was dazzled by it, and such a flood of delight sprang from mine that she lowered her eyelids, delectably moved.

From that moment on, speech became unnecessary between us. I seized one by one all the vibrations of the heart that beat next to mine. My companion's ideas became palpitant and sonorous, if I might put it like that. Our two intelligences, in immediate contact, conversed with one another, understood one another, and, disdaining the efforts of conversation, so painful and so fruitless, rose to vertiginous heights.

There is nothing comparable to that divine fusion, that eternal caress, which never wearies, and which falls from the supreme limits of what a being can feel.

What did the years matter, old age and death? Our souls, forever infatuated, would dissolve in one another, would savor increasingly ardent ecstasies as they were purified and drew closer to the ineffable deliverance.

Until then, Viviane had remained the strange girl that I have described: too thin, too dark-haired, and too paltry; but even if she had been frankly ugly, I would not have been disquieted by it. Her body did not exist for me; I lived a completely intellectual life, so far outside common existences that nothing of what habitually charms men interested me.

However, the age of puberty was approaching; a change, insensible at first, occurred in my companion, and then, gradually, like a plant in spring, her young body filled with sap and developed; a livelier blood circulated beneath her delicate skin, and her gaze, her beautiful limpid gaze, became slightly troubled, like deep water at the approach of a storm. From that moment on, she ceased to belong completely to me. I made vain efforts to read within her, as I had done so easily before, and, gripped by hatred, I began to curse the expansion of the carnal envelope that was increasingly devouring the divine substance of her thinking being.

One evening, by the light of the flock of stars that hastens in the fields of infinite space, like as many lambs submissive to an invisible master who will slaughter them one day, I forced her to combine her thought with mine by an effort of will, as she had done so passionately before.

"Oh, stop tormenting me," she said. "I'm tired, horribly tired."

"What!" I cried. "It's thus that you withdraw yourself? Haven't you sworn to belong to me forever?"

She tilted her head, and tears rolled down her pale cheeks.

"Is it my fault that a strange force is drawing me away from you? It seems to me that there are sweeter things in life than those you have enabled me to know. Is it our role down here only to exist through thought, and are we not insensate to disdain what makes the happiness of the people around us?"

I contemplated her; she had metamorphosed, as if by a miracle. Her red lips were swollen voluptuously, and beneath the light fabric of her dress, her bosom rose and fell, moved by a new emotion. The lashes of her long eyelids put a soft shadow over her grace; she trembled before me, knowing full well that I was scornful of her now that she had revealed herself to be similar to other women.

"That's all right," I said, with a sigh. "You'll come back to me, Viviane, for everything that awakens your desire will wither, as you will wither yourself. I don't release you from your promise."

And, fixing my gaze on hers, I plunged into the utmost depths of her being, until a mysterious impact, followed by an infinite sweetness, had put us in perfect communication, one last time. She could not support the ardor of my will, and lost consciousness.

Some time after that, the requests for her hand in marriage commenced, for she was very rich, and dowry-hunters would espouse a girl in her cradle if they could.

Viviane seemed the same for all of them: indifferent and slightly weary, waiting for her parents to fix a choice for her. I counseled her gently, astonished to find myself so calm and resigned. Is it the case, then, that our destiny is written in advance, and that, secretly in agreement, we were acting in accord with a ready-made plan, without even discussing that strange connivance between ourselves?

I would only have had to say one word to change the course of events. In that tightly-knit family, everyone's opinion was taken into consideration, and mine would have been heeded like the others. What did it matter to me? My torment was not of the earth; it was not a wife that I wanted, it was not her physical and palpable beauty that troubled me, but her hidden being, her astral essence, which, like a perfume in a sealed bottle, was dormant beneath her pale envelope of flesh.

That treasure of amour, I had once possessed, when, through the frail wall of her diaphanous body, it had sent me its radiance and its intoxicating effluvia. Now, that inebriating flesh had reclaimed its rights; that was the enemy; I detested it and, if I had dared, I would have annihilated it like a harmful beast.

That another would take it and make it suffer was acceptable; that the martyrdom of maternity would weaken it and twist it in slow convulsion was better still; for I, who demanded nothing of the despicable joys of life, was certain of being victorious one day. No, my ambition was higher; I was thirsty for ineffable kisses that never weary, mystical intoxications of thought that float in tenderness dazedly, like an opium dream or a divine ecstasy, like monks in prayer before their virgin, invisible but present.

It was necessary that Viviane's destiny should be accomplished; then she would come back to me more confident and tender, her soul would be assimilated to mine and would, so to speak, dissolve in me, a light vapor, an astral form, visible and yet embalmed like a smoke of incense. And my eyes, my nostrils and my lips would see her, respire her and drink her.

We spoke again about that supreme felicity. She shivered, and her soul sparkled in her eyes and palpitated on her mouth, but bonds attached her to her terrestrial envelope and I had the desire to squeeze that flexible neck with my clenched fingers, or cause the life of her ardent heart to spring forth in red droplets . . . But a dread, an obscure presentiment, retained me, and I awaited events without impatience and without disturbance.

Viviane was seventeen years old. Increasingly, the splendor of her beauty seemed to extinguish the radiation of her somber eyes. The soul escaped me, and I sensed it going to sleep in the wellbeing of health. She faded away, becoming disinterested in the long reverie in which we had once confounded ourselves. The woman had all her curiosities and her desires awakened; the troubling monster surged forth, with the smile of her red lips and the impudence of her pale flesh. I then had a sentiment of grim hatred, and in the fear of not being able to contain myself, I went away, certain that I would suffer less at a distance.

Viviane seemed happy with my sudden decision. My will still dominated her, and that power, which she could not vanquish, gripped her dolorously, like an obsession.

I remained absent for nearly six months, horribly tortured, without news of my relatives and without the courage to ask for any. When I returned, the peaceful dwelling was illuminated, peasants were pressing against the railings in order to see, through the high windows, the elegant silhouettes of women in silky ball gowns. A harmonious murmur reached me, and lackeys hastened to offer me their services.

I went into a vast drawing room, which bronze chandeliers charged with candles illuminated abundantly. Viviane was standing near a table, signing her marriage contract. Her shoulders, devoid of jewelry emerged like the flesh of a camellia from their long sheath of lace, her dark hair made a helmet of jet for her radiant face. She looked at me fearfully, and then went pale, and suddenly collapsed on the parquet.

I complimented her fiancé. He was a tall blond young man with a mild and attractive physiognomy. He had a meager fortune, but a great name; Viviane was not noble, and that equilibrated the advantages of the future spouses. By the urgency that he put into helping the young woman I saw that he loved her with all the impetuosity of his heart and his senses. In fact, she was so admirably beautiful that all men must have desired her. I conceived a more intense chagrin in consequence, and the Comte de X***, her fiancé, became particularly odious to me. He, on the other hand, had immediately taken me in affection, and I was obliged to promise him to go to see him often in a villa that he possessed on the Mediterranean coast, in which he intended to reside immediately after his honeymoon voyage.

The next day, when Viviane appeared in her long dress of white moiré silk, she could scarcely sustain herself.

"Go away," she said to me. "I've been happy since your departure, but now the strange madness that you once communicated to me seems to be gripping me again. I love the Comte, I tell you, and it's to him alone that I want to belong."

"You're mistaken," I murmured in her ear. "You don't love him, and whatever you do, I shall always possess you."

She shivered. "No, no! Go away, I implore you. I'm afraid. I don't want to lend myself to your crazy imaginations any longer. You're accursed! I hate you!"

She adjusted her veil, which quivered over her shoulders and descended in light waves all the way to her feet. People were arriving from all directions, and, drawing away indifferently, I went to install myself in the chapel, near the choir, in order not to miss any of the ceremony.

Viviane knelt down on the red velvet prie-dieu, and although she did not turn round, she certainly divined my presence, for her shoulders were trembling slightly, and the missal that she was holding slipped from her hands and fell on to the paving stones.

I summoned her thought with all the force of my will, and at times I sensed it fluttering around me like a heavy moth afraid of alighting. Then, suddenly, an impression of emptiness and desolation invaded me; I found myself more abandoned than I had ever been.

The newlyweds fled as soon as the ceremony was terminated, as if their happiness would only really commence beyond the frontier. I did not enquire as to the itinerary that they had mapped out; their actions were of scant importance to me, and I knew that Viviane was too narrowly linked to me by an immutable power to escape me thus, no matter how much she might desire to do so.

After that departure, however, darkness fell upon my spirit; I lived mechanically, having no appetite for anything, bleak and despairing. In my long feverish nights I evoked the absent thought, but no secret voice responded to my sad appeals. Had Viviane yielded, then, to physical amour, so incomplete, so despicable and so disproportionate to the idea that one has of eternal ecstasy? Could she love that banal being made in the image of all, who held her in his arms as he had held many others, with the unique ambition of material pleasure? Could she desire that lover, who would go to sleep sadly over her quivering lips, already forgetful of past felicities, and who would find in the annihilation of his strength the annihilation of his amour?

How much sweeter were our old intoxications! We did not talk to one another, but we read one another like open books. Our hands scarcely touched, but our souls, all vibrant with amour, embraced one another madly. And that was the true, the only durable happiness, the one that religion has enabled us to glimpse as the supreme goal of our efforts, the one that, not being of the earth, can never end.

"Viviane! Viviane!" I cried in the night. "Come and place on my lips your divine form, white and as transparent as a cloud; let it press thereupon, dissolve therein, and give itself to me in a kiss!"

But the darkness thickened, an icy cold descended over my heart, and the ardent fusion did not take place.

Perhaps another had taken my beloved's soul!

At that idea, I shivered in anguish, and was haunted by ideas of murder. But could murder efface that which is ineffaceable? Would not killing those lovers give them to one another more surely, since it is only beyond life that the real and indissoluble union commences?

What other man could have penetrated those mysterious destinies?

Few human intelligences have that quasi-divine prescience, I said to myself, *and if it is sometimes given to them to perceive the truth, it is only a flash of lightning in their habitual darkness.*

✳

It had been a year since the young couple had quit Paris, and if I sometimes received news of them, it was only indirectly, via the family.

One day, I learned that Viviane was a mother. I conceived a profound chagrin in consequence, for it seemed to me that the little being who was scarcely breathing would take all the solicitude of the woman. Nature has determined that there should be an infinite tenderness in maternity, in order that the torture of childbirth should be braved and desired even by those faint hearts who do not understand the futility of their mission and the cruelty of their obedience. An admirable folly that consists of making with one's flesh and blood sad and paltry beings whose life will be spoiled by the thought of death, and who will toil daily without a single moment of real happiness! A proud folly that consists of building temples and palaces that the wind will sweep away, and which will have scarcely more duration than the pygmies who constructed them! But human vanity is only equaled by human weakness, and until the end of the world, they will struggle in the void, commencing and recommencing their illusory labor.

Viviane was a mother! Her affectionate parents announced the great news to me joyfully, and, in order not to offend them, I wrote a letter of congratulation. The Comte de X*** replied to me that his wife was having difficulty recovering, although she was receiving admirable care, but that the child, on the other hand, was superb: the very portrait of his father.

I wrote to Viviane a second time, begging her to tell me about her life, her hopes and the plans. I did not obtain any response, and I understood that, if I did not make a supreme effort, the mysterious link that still attached us to one another would be broken forever.

From that moment on I extended all the power of my will toward the person that I wanted to reconquer. Not for an instant did I cease to think about her, to summon her irresistibly, to order her to manifest herself, so determined to convince her that it seemed to me that I could hear her timid objections in the distance. And I wanted her, I desired her madly, I was thirsty for her mystical kisses that did not touch the lips but fell upon the heart like a current of flame.

One misty afternoon in April I was sitting next to the window in my large bedroom hung with pale golden-red Cordovan leather. The sky, not yet cleansed of the impurities of winter, remained a jaundiced gray, giving everything a desolate appearance. However, the almond trees and the cherry trees were beginning to flower; buds of a delightful pale green were bursting forth on the branches; but those promises of renewal squeezed my heart like a happy smile on a death mask.

I remained motionless, lost in my obstinate dream. Gradually, the shadows of night invaded my retreat, and my wide-open eyes could no longer distinguish things. I was indifferent to the present moment, to the world, to existence itself; a devouring fire rose in my breast, extending to my fibers, penetrating into the creases of my organism in waves of flame. And my soul agitated like a captive butterfly, ardent and feverish.

Visions of the past unfolded slowly, as diaphanous and light as the veils of the evening over which they were gliding. I saluted them with my heart and my lips, reproaching them for having fled me so quickly, and no longer being anything but phantoms of happiness. But they did not turn away from their route, for even our regrets escape us, and we cannot savor their dolorously bitter charm for long.

My childhood appeared pensive to me, so narrowly linked to Viviane's that I rediscovered her influence in the most insignificant details. In reality, she had been the complement to my thinking being, the reason and goal of my being. It was necessary that she return to me; she belonged to me as a tree belongs to the soil. She could not exist without me, and without her I remained somber and desolate.

The desire to receive the confirmation of my immutable rights returned to me more obsessively. I gazed into the darkness and I listened to the silence with so much intensity that my heartbeat accelerated and my muscles were violently contracted.

Suddenly, it seemed to me that I was no longer alone. I could not see anything yet, but a strange sensation alerted me, a sudden anguish, something like the rapid, soft and vertiginous fall that we believe we are making into the void in a dream. A pale light emerged from the depths of the room and vacillated momentarily on the wall like the projection of a lantern swathed with cloth. A slight creaking, and then a silky friction awakened my attention. I listened intently, in an anguish of superstitious terror, but the sound was not renewed. Resolutely and obstinately, I kept my eyes fixed on the mysterious light.

A few minutes went by, and then I saw a white form detach itself from the wall and follow the luminous path in my direction. I extended my arm to grasp it, but it retreated rapidly, seeming already to be extinguished by distance. I recalled it softly, and it regained confidence, swaying from right to left, still indecisive. It was nothing but a vague, almost transparent silhouette: the astral form of Viviane.

By a superhuman effort of will, I had obliged her to quit her carnal envelope and to obey me. I was in possession of a supernatural power and I took advantage of it to attempt miracles forbidden to all human beings.

I thought about those fakirs who, under the radiance of their astral fluid, summon objects that are displaced and come of their own accord to place themselves in their extended hands, of those yogis who have their eyes, nostrils and mouth blocked and who, after several months of sojourn in a tomb, emerge again alive and strong. Was I not the master of life and death?

"Viviane!" I cried. "I doubted you, but you have come to reassure and console me! Viviane, do you still love me?"

She drew nearer, and a soft and perfumed air struck my face.

I divined her response rather than hearing it.

"Come and take me back," she sighed. "I'm afraid of my weakness, and if you don't extract me from the hearth I'll be lost to you."

"I'll leave tomorrow, my beloved. Have confidence! Don't abandon me!"

I stood up impetuously and extended my arms toward her, but darkness fell, and I tried in vain to recall and to fix the fluttering soul. Suddenly, in the place she had occupied, I saw, distinctly, an open coffin, and in the funereal cavity a cadaver enveloped by its shroud. A fleshless hand dangled over the edge, and on the little finger shone a gold ring set with a ruby, which I recognized perfectly; it was the one that I had given Viviane at the moment of her marriage.

Stupefaction struggled then in my mind with the profound terror that I had felt at first. I sensed that my sight was becoming obscured, that my reason was fleeing, and it was only by means of a violent effort that I succeeded in steering myself to the mantel-piece and lighting the candles of the two large bronze candelabra that habitually illuminated my bedroom. The flame sprang forth, and the surrounding objects appeared to me in their customary order: the tapestries of fabulous individuals fell hermetically over the doors, and there was no draught from outside.

I got undressed and went to bed. One by one, the candles went out, and toward dawn, I fell into a profound and heavy slumber.

＊

When my valet de chambre, slightly anxious, woke me up, mid-day was chiming. Bright sunlight entered through the window, and things around me had an almost joyful aspect. In reality, my body alone had rested, for my mind had never ceased to evoke the strange nocturnal apparition.

"Make preparations for my departure as quickly as possible, and have the carriage ready in two hours," I said to the man who was awaiting my orders.

"Is Monsieur going to be absent for a long time?"

"Perhaps a week, perhaps a fortnight, perhaps a month. Don't forget anything that might be necessary to me."

Having dressed rapidly, I went to supervise my servants personally, who were making haste, being long habituated to my eccentricities.

The air was light, the sky a pretty turquoise hue. A large flowering pear tree sent me through the window the adorable perfume of its white corollas; I felt satisfied and resolute, as if the journey had been planned for a long time.

In the train, I closed my eyes in order to savor more fully the emotion that gripped me delightfully. An urgent but submissive appeal of my thought to a distant thought had sufficed to overturn the order of things: hearth, duty, and family would cease to exist for the soul that I had vanquished, if it pleased me to recall it to my power.

Life is nothing, I said to myself, *and it is not the comprehensible and logical causes that reign but the mysterious power that is within us, and which rises above all human plans. Like the pieces on a chessboard, we obey profound calculations of which we are unaware. We come and we go, sensate in appearance, but in reality unconscious of the mission that we are called upon to fulfill down here.*

When I rang at the Comte de X***'s villa, I had a sudden conviction that I had come to accomplish an irremediable action, the consequences of which would engage my entire existence. I had come guided by an irresistible force, and nothing would turn me away henceforth from what it demanded of me.

The gate was not locked; I pushed it, and as soon as I entered I saw my cousin at the end of a long driveway bordered by giant rose bushes and myrtles, paler and more tremulous than me. She had had a presentiment of my coming and had come to meet me.

Some distance from the gate she stopped, and her face contracted dolorously.

"You, here?" she said, in a muffled voice. "Why are you troubling my repose?"

"Have you not summoned me to you, dear Viviane?"

She put her hands together, terrified. "My God, protect me! He knows my dreams, he sends them to me! He still dominates me!"

"It was against your will, then, that you manifested yourself to me, in order to ask me to join you?"

"I want to love my hearth and my husband," she said. "I want to live as other women live, tranquil and honored. I want to do my duty as a Christian and a mother."

"You no longer belong to yourself, Viviane. Your body alone is here next to your husband and child, and whatever you do, your ardent thought will follow mine as a bee follows a perfume in order to drink at its source."

She drew closer, and her dark gaze, wide and profound, dared to fix itself on mine. Immediately, the strange and delicious commotion that we knew so well was produced within us, and the severe words that she had on her lips died away in a vague stammer. What did it matter? I had read once again in her beautiful eyes, those doors open to the soul!

The Comte de X***, alerted by his domestics, had joined us, and, smiling beside his wife, he extended his hand to me amicably.

"I'm delighted by your visit, my dear monsieur; I hope that

you will prolong your stay for as long as possible, and not disdain our beautiful land."

I accepted the hospitality that he offered me eagerly, and that evening I was installed in a lovely bedroom with a view over the Mediterranean. The exquisite perfume of spring flowers rose up to my window, and my eyes went from the blue of the sea to the blue of the sky, dazzled by those two sublime and terrible immensities.

✳

What remains for me to relate is so strange that few minds will understand me well enough to absolve me.

For long years I savored my triumph, and my happiness was complete.

Today, I doubt, I weep and I suffer.

May this sincere confession of my life bring a little calm back to my heart!

I installed myself, therefore, in the Villa des Roses, and from the very start, I understood that a struggle had been engaged between Viviane's material nature and the divine, exquisite, passionate individual that hid within it like a dragonfly in the heart of a lily. I neglected nothing that might increase my domination.

The presence of her child might have disarmed me, but I loved too intellectually to be influenced by human considerations, and the little being who loomed up between us inspired nothing in me but aversion.

My cousin avoided me, scarcely looked at me, and strove to fix her attention on the vulgar things of life. Oddly enough, I only really rediscovered her when I could not see her; for although she remained mistress of her wakefulness, she was not of her dreams. Every night, her astral form quit the inert envelope that hid it from the profane and came to find me in the darkness of the closed room. A milky radiance struck my gaze, and the warm and perfumed apparition glided all the way to my lips, swaying like a flower of light. Her golden voice resonated within me; I was inundated by celestial joy, and until morning, I heard her sing her canticle of amour.

It was thus that, dissolved in one another, ecstatic and unsated, we compensated ourselves for terrestrial lies.

I was only living for those exquisite hours, disdainful of all the rest.

I was pale and feverish; Viviane also seemed to be wasting away. I rediscovered her now as I had known her previously: emaciated and indolent, with excessively bright eyes beneath the forest of dark hair that seemed to be consuming her thin face.

At times, she begged me to go away, to have pity on her and her child. But the unforgettable ecstatic memory of each night was too present in my mind to allow me to yield to her pleas.

A bizarre phenomenon occurred: I began to detest the woman that I saw during the day, who incessantly avoided me or begged me to leave, in order to redirect all my affective forces on the adorable individual who only lived for me and was only manifest in darkness. But that was too little, I would have liked to discover her incessantly, to possess her at every moment, to intoxicate myself with her mystical kisses, as a morphine addict savors his dangerous ecstasies at will by injecting a little of the poison into his veins. Those forced cessations exasperated me, and I confided my pain to Viviane's soul.

"Alas," she sighed, "like you, I detest that insensible body, which cannot quit the earth and enchains me to its obscure labor. I hate it with all the force of my love for you!"

"And will it always be thus?"

"Listen," she continued—and her voice vibrated in every fiber of my being—"Listen; I can, if you wish, belong to you without partition, dissolve in you for eternity. But it will be necessary to deploy great courage, and I fear that you might weaken at the decisive moment."

"Speak! What must I do in order not to quit you any longer? Tell me, I implore you."

She hesitated; then, gradually, I sensed that she disengaged herself, retaking possession of herself, and I saw her draw away, a light shadow, an impalpable and yet tangible form, like a snow-cloud.

In the very place that she had quit, the hideous coffin that I had contemplated before loomed up, with its funereal burden. I could not perceive the cadaver that it contained, the shroud covering it entirely, but the same livid hand dangled out of the bier.

Suddenly I saw it move, clench upon the shroud and tug it violently. I sat up in bed, shivering, my throat tightened by an inexpressible anguish, my soul desperately engulfed by a whirlwind of emotions, of which perhaps the least terrible, the least devouring, was a supreme terror. In the effort that it made, the hand dropped the ring that it bore on its little finger, and I thought I saw drops of blood falling with it along the bier.

Viviane's face now appeared to me, whiter than the sheets that surrounded her, and a breath as cold and damp as the exhalation of a tomb reached me. At the culmination of horror, I launched myself toward the frightful vision, but everything vanished.

Prey to an indescribable emotion, I dreaded understanding. Would it be necessary for me to become criminal to possess the dearly beloved fully? Did our strange amour require a human sacrifice in order to bloom in the sunlight? Certainly, I felt that I was strong enough to kill, and two victims were designated by my hatred: her husband and her child.

The next day, Viviane was suffering and did not show herself.

"She's been very troubled for some time," the Comte de X*** told me; "an intense fever grips her during the night, and incoherent words escape her lips. I would have summoned a physician already if she had not begged me not to do so. What do you think, my friend?"

I dissipated his fears, giving him a host of good reasons.

"Your wife has never been very strong; she is greatly occupied with her child, and that is doubtless the cause of her fatigue."

He did not insist, but remained anxious.

I waited for nightfall with impatience in order to discuss the matter with my beloved.

She came at the usual hour, and as soon as I sensed her within me I begged her to deliver me from the horrible suspicion that had come to me.

"What are you demanding of me, then, Viviane?"

"A crime!" she replied. "My body is an obstacle to our complete union; that is what you must annihilate."

"Kill you! But I would never have the willpower or the courage."

"It isn't me that you'd be killing but the other, the obscure and suffering obstacle; it's the inert chrysalis that is keeping the butterfly of amour imprisoned."

"Kill you! But how? People will know, and imprison me; I'd be an object of scorn and horror for people!"

"No, it's my husband who will be accused. He alone has an interest in my death; he's poor and I'm rich; I've left him my entire fortune in my will."

"That's horrible!"

"No, it's human. Do you want to have me entirely and forever?"

I did not reply, bewildered by fear, and I sensed that the adored soul was disengaging from me. Then I made a supreme effort to retain her.

"I give in, Viviane, I give in! I'll be a wretch, a liar and a criminal, provided that you absolve me from baseness, deceit and crime. How can I kill you without betraying myself? How can I reach you?"

"Nothing is easier. You'll go along the balcony and you'll enter through the French windows of our bedroom. As the weather is very warm, I'll leave them open."

"But what about your husband?"

"You'll pour him a narcotic this evening, at supper. He won't wake up, and the next day, on finding him bewildered beside me, covered in blood, there'll be no hesitation in accusing him."

"So be it. I'll do as you order me to."

"You swear it?"

"I swear it."

"Until tomorrow, my love, and forever."

She glided away like a shooting star and was lost in the night.

I was still motionless, entirely intoxicated by the memory, when a sound of footsteps resonated on the parquet. The Comte had just come in, a candle-tray in his hand. He begged me to help him and to help Viviane, who was writhing in a crisis of nerves. I followed him, and approached the young woman, but as soon as she perceived me she hid her face in her hands.

"My child! My child!" she moaned. "Don't take me away from him. Have pity on him!"

I understood that a terrible battle was taking place within her, and I felt myself weakening in my resolution.

Throughout the following day, she held her son tightly in her arms; her lips trembled; she cursed me and begged me by turns.

I did not have the courage to resist her, and I went to bed early in order to hide my distress.

Toward midnight, her spirit arrived, as usual. The milky radiance departed from the depths of the room and the diaphanous form undulated toward me. But she did not press herself upon my lips or dissolve into my being like a delicious fruit. I begged and wept in vain.

"You've never loved me," she said. "Otherwise you wouldn't have hesitated to liberate me from the burden of life."

"Did you not implore me today to make me abandon my resolution?"

"It's the human creature who moaned, trembled and suffered! My soul remained impassive and scornful; it's her alone that you ought to consult."

"But I too am human, and everything human touches me!"

"Human life is nothing, it's the beyond that I envisage. What does it matter to us whether I disappear in a day, a month or a year? Time is of no account in eternity. And besides, are you not sparing me struggles, chagrins and malady? It's the sole means of proving to me the immensity of your tenderness. Leave the miserable body that is only able to tremble and complain to moan; our ecstatic dream is not of the earth; our souls, overflowing with desires, are thirsty or eternal possession. Afterwards, no more doubts, no more weaknesses: a sea of happiness, as blue as the sky, and likewise limitless; an abyss of sensuality in which our feeble bodies will be annihilated."

"Tomorrow! Tomorrow!" I cried, drunk on hope and covetousness.

The soul shivered.

"After having struck, you'll lean over the lips of the expiring woman," she said, "and you'll respire me, you'll drink me, in a supreme kiss."

From that nocturnal moment on, I was no longer my own master. I felt that I was driven by a mysterious, irresistible force and I was only living any longer for the accomplishment of my crime.

The first light of dawn caressed the surrounding objects; cockerels responded to one another, and soon a volley of roulades departed from every branch and a cloud of butterflies from every thicket.

I got up and went down into the garden to refresh my forehead in the morning breeze. The French windows of the conjugal bedroom were ajar. I saw that it would be very easy for me to penetrate therein via the balcony. A curtain was floating over the gap; everything therein was silent and calm.

I did not go in again until it was time for the morning meal. Viviane was waiting for me, standing by the table. She was frightfully pale; her convulsive hands came together at times, and her eyes were staring at me with an expression of terror and prayer.

Her husband noticed the alteration in her features, and spoke several times about going to fetch a physician, but I dissuaded him with a calmness that still surprises me today.

During the day we went to sit down in the shade of a plane tree of which we were fond. The child, lying in his perambulator, was looking around with his bright blue eyes at the leaves that a warm breeze was agitating softly, and Viviane, leaning on the Comte's shoulder, was weeping quietly.

She was so frail now that the light fabric of her dress creased around her shoulders and her wrists moved easily within their golden bracelets. A branch had caught in her hair, and in order to free it she had taken out the long tortoiseshell pins that secured it, with the result that the regal black fleece, darker than the night, undulated all the way to her feet. She was adorable and touching. No pity came to me, however. I considered her anxiously, and told myself that it would not be necessary to use a great deal of force to kill her.

Her husband left us alone for a few minutes in order to go and lift his fishing nets. When he had disappeared through the gate she threw herself at my feet and begged me to have pity on her, with heart-rending sobs. I picked her up without responding. Then she leaned over her son and contemplated him ardently, while two streams of tears ran over her cheeks and fell on to the infant's blond head.

I took her hands and forced her, by a supreme effort of will, to fix her thought on mine.

Her soul immediately sparkled in her eyes.

"Do you still want it, Viviane?" I asked her. "You can release me from my oath."

But she was transfigured.

"I want it! I want it! Take me and keep me entirely. This struggle between spirit and matter is horrible. I'd like to dominate myself, but I can't. Don't abandon me, my beloved!"

"If you put up the slightest resistance tonight, I'll be lost, for the Comte might wake up and accuse me of the crime."

"I no longer desire anything but death, I tell you, in order to belong to you, no longer to be anything but one with you, like your muscles and your blood. You will drink me in the only kiss that you will have ever have given my perishable body."

Slowly, I turned my gaze away from hers, and, reconquered by matter, she knelt down beside her child and surrendered once again to her despair.

The day was exceptionally hot. At dusk, a storm was unleashed with extraordinary force. For several hours, the rolls of thunder and flashes of lightning succeeded one another without interruption. I was in a circle of iron, and my will to act, doubtless exasperated by the ambient electricity, attained such an intensity that I saw red, and had great difficulty containing myself.

Viviane retired to her bedroom early, asking that she should be allowed to repose. The Comte was, therefore, alone with me at the evening meal, and I deployed all the resources of my eloquence to distract him from his preoccupations. He was listening to me with interest, He drank mechanically, and I never left his glass empty. Hunting and fishing were his favorite pleasures, and I talked about them at length, inventing anecdotes, citing facts, and describing distant countries that I had never seen. My listener was under my spell; his dilated pupils were fixed on mine avidly.

At dessert, without him noticing, I poured a few drops of a powerful narcotic into his wine, and then I drank to the health of all the disciples of Saint Hubert.

He drained his glass in a single draught and replaced it on the table. By a skillful transition I then turned the conversation to Viviane's malady, and, suddenly recalling that she had been more afflicted than on the preceding days, he got up with alacrity in order to go and join her.

I remarked that he was very red in the face, and staggering slightly.

"I don't know what's wrong with me," he said. "I'm falling asleep."

I went up to my room in my turn. I could hear the domestics coming and going on the ground floor; then the noises faded away gradually, and everything fell into silence.

I had opened my window. The cooler air of the night refreshed my forehead, and over the narrow rectangle of the sky I saw innumerable stars scintillating, as if in a tabernacle. The tempest was still growling in the distance, however, and at times the trees writhed, and high waves jostled one another convulsively, like unsated lionesses.

The occult power that had dominated me since the morning still held me in its power. External facts had no purchase upon me. I was continuing my dream, speaking, walking and acting like a sleepwalker. And the obsession triumphed, lacerating, almost terrible in its intensity. If the evil spirit that was haunting me had ordered me to gouge out my eyes, tear out my tongue and slash my wrists, I would have obeyed without hesitation. Its empire was all the more redoubtable because it was excited within me by the most noble of sentiments, amour. I loved as no man had ever loved. I loved a pure spirit, and the idea of her eternal possession gripped me so ardently that I sensed myself fainting in an ineffable spasm.

Soon, she would be mine! A reckless ecstasy made me totter like a drunken man. Burning drops of light fell into my heart, and beyond the glimpsed felicity, nothing existed any longer; human conception was arrested, impotent.

I waited for another hour, a stranger to all reasoning, all dread. The thought of the crime was as intense as a burn. Finally, I sensed that the moment had come, and I slid on to the balcony, barefoot, in order not to make any sound.

The spouses' French windows were ajar, as they had been the previous night, and only had to be pushed gently; I slipped into the room, illuminated by the tremulous glow of an alabaster lamp suspended from the ceiling.

Viviane looked at me with eyes dilated by fear. Her entire body was quivering, and her teeth were chattering convulsively.

The Comte, lying next to her, seemed to be plunged in a deep slumber.

On the wall of the room, draped in pale velvet, there was a panoply of Oriental weapons: helmets and bucklers of steel damascened with gold, sabers and daggers with ivory or jade hilts, sharp stilettos and krises with teeth like saws. I hesitated momentarily, and then chose a slender dagger whose blue-tinted blade cast a gleam in the shadow. I took the weapon down with a thousand precautions and, having tested it delicately on my arm, I approached the bed.

Viviane had sat up, as pale as a corpse, her face so distressed that I almost hesitated to recognize it. A feeble plaint escaped her discolored lips; in her immense eyes, the dilated pupils had devoured the iris. She tried to cry out, but her contracted throat would not allow any sound to pass. I tore the lace of her chemise, in spite of her convulsive efforts to push me away, and, with a vigor of which I would not have believed myself capable, I nailed her to the pillow with one hand while, with the other, I plunged the sharp weapon to the hilt in her breast.

She uttered a frightful, heart-rending, superhuman plaint, but I leaned toward her mouth and, applying mine to it, sucked in her soul, her ardent soul, frenetically, in an ineffable kiss. When I sensed it within me, it was like a liqueur that rises and fills a vase; my heart swelled with intoxication, and there was the anguish of a spasm in which I felt myself dying . . .

I was getting up with a triumphant cry in order to flee with my prey when a hand fell on my shoulder, and the Comte, almost as pale as the cadaver that lay beside him, sat up in the alcove.

Blood had spurted everywhere; we were both covered in it, and the curtains, the carpet and the wall-hangings seemed to be streaming with a sanguine flood. Then there was a dazzle, and as the domestics arrived from all directions, I allowed myself to be tied up without any resistance.

✳

For twelve years I have been in an insane asylum. For eleven years, Viviane's soul remained faithful to me, and we savored indescribable ecstasies. Oh, I did not regret my liberty! For what greater happiness could I have been ambitious? Always alone with my dream, I found between the four narrow walls of my cell an entire paradise of intoxication!

If only I had died in my divine error! For, today, I doubt. My body and my mind have weakened, and as they weakened, I felt Viviane's soul withdrawing from me. The dreams that charmed me have vanished into a nebulous distance. I find myself once again in the midst of the miseries of life. My sky is veiled by livid clouds; I feel desperately alone.

The director of the asylum says that I am cured, and tomorrow, the doors will be opened for me.

Yes, but tomorrow, I will have ceased to live, for my divine madness raised me above other men; with reality, I am nothing more than a vulgar murderer.

YVAINE

I
Père Lazare

EVERY DAY I saw him go out. He seemed humble and un-happy. His deformed hat fell over his eyes, his trousers and jacket were tattered and sordid rags.

Intrigued, I sought information from the concierge, and I learned that the old man had been living in the house for ten years. Rich at first, he had lost his fortune in insensate alms, given without choice and without discernment, by virtue of caprice, a love of squandering. Originally a tenant of the first floor, he had successively moved through all the stories; now he lived under the eaves, by charity, in a garret deprived of air and light.

Our building was a former town house in the grand style, once built almost outside the city, but which presently found itself in an enclave surrounded by new buildings, regular and banal. The few fine trees in the garden remained there as if in the depths of a well, extending their pale branches like long arms toward the sky. Moss was eating away the stones, a green-tinted damp oozed beneath the ivy that had invaded everything. One might have thought it a corner of a forest put in prison, a corner of nature agonizing in mute despair. And in that obscure peace, which made one shiver, Père Lazare came to sit down, his face hidden in his hands, his long bony carcass shaken by unappeasable sobs.

I observed him for hours with a complex sentiment of mistrust and compassion. I do not know whether the other tenants saw him, as I did, through the small window-panes of their apartments, but no one talked to him, no one seemed to take any interest in his misfortune. Sometimes, he raised his head, and I shuddered before the fixity of his gaze and the dolorous crease of his thin lips.

One rainy morning he slipped on the edge of the sidewalk, after having distributed his alms, as was his custom; he could not get up again, and a passing cart crushed his leg above the knee. He was taken to the hospital, covered in blood, and for several months no further mention was heard of him. Then, suddenly, he reappeared, went up to his attic, and continued his former existence as in the past. With his crutches beside him—for he had been obliged to suffer the amputation of his leg—he still remained for long hours on the mossy bench in the garden.

Several times, I tried to start a conversation, but he did not seem to see me, and for six months I could not get a word out of him.

He lived in the midst of people without even knowing those to whom he gave alms, indifferent to everything and everyone.

Winter came again, the sky's smiles were effaced; the mildness of golden and topaz sunsets was succeeded by the desolation of ashen firmaments empty of stars and wing-beats.

Père Lazare resumed his taciturn walks; the bench in the little garden no longer offered him sufficient shelter.

However, his resources were diminishing incessantly, and a moment arrived when he no longer had anything left, absolutely nothing. His pockets were empty beneath the clenching of his feverish fingers and so were the hands of the paupers, which were held out to him in mute prayer.

That day, a cold wind ran along the walls and whistled in the bare branches of the plane trees, and somber clouds galloped through the sky, almost brushing the summits of buildings. The old man went along painfully, moving his crutches one after the other with a great effort that lifted his shoulders and stiffened his arms. The twisted leg that remained to him vacillated from right to left and his chest heaved convulsively. He was paler than usual and I had no difficulty perceiving that he was hungry.

128

Having arrived in an isolated spot, he leaned against a boundary marker, and then suddenly collapsed like a limp rag.

Aided by a few passers-by, I carried him into a pharmacy, where he regained his senses after a long half-hour of futile cares. His first gaze was for me: a bright gaze that chilled me to the bones, and which I could not sustain. Until then, in any case, I had never observed his eyes very closely, which a formless felt hat usually covered. When I saw them, I recoiled instinctively, in surprise. They were round and pale, with a strange and cruel fixity.

For a minute, they stared at me, full of an expression of grim anger and frightful irony; then the iris rose again into the yellow cornea and he seemed to lose consciousness for a second time. But it was nothing of the sort; only his thought had fled into the dream, while his body, a sad human rag, remained palpitating before us. Several times his lips trembled, twisting silently, like two leaves of parchment bitten by a flame, and then he uttered these incomprehensible words:

"Two! There are two, now!"

"Who do you mean, Monsieur?" I asked, softly, in the hope of obtaining a few explanations.

He was not listening to me, but he raised his arm as if to defend himself against invisible enemies.

"Two! Two! Two! There are two! How do you expect me to resist them?"

"There are two of them tormenting you?"

"Since I tell you that I no longer have anything! Do you want my skin? But no, you'd prefer to claw at me relentlessly, to dig your murderous hands all the way to my heart!"

"Pull yourself together . . ."

"I no longer have anything . . . I no longer have anything . . . all these beggars are going to devour my entrails like wolves!"

I put a louis in his hand. "Come on, my friend, go home. I'll help you, because we're neighbors . . ."

He was planted on his crutches, and by means of superhuman efforts, he succeeded in standing up, but when he was offered something to eat, he said: "It's the share of the poor. I'm rich and have no need of anything."

Arrived home and laid in his bed, Père Lazare went to sleep immediately. I had some provisions brought for him and returned to my apartment, very intrigued by the mysterious existence of the man.

Against all expectation, he recovered rapidly, and as money seemed to have fallen upon him from the sky during his illness, he recommenced his futile charity.

He went out in the morning and dragged himself along until nightfall, barely dressed, under the rain and the snow. All the vagabonds of the quarter knew him and welcomed him. Pale rogues turned out his pockets and robbed him of anything that might have any value. One night he came back completely naked, under a green sheet of canvas taken from a peasant's cart while the peasant was asleep on his seat.

"What a state have you've been left in, Père Lazare?" I cried, when I encountered him on the stairs. "Have you encountered malefactors on your route?"

Without speaking, he pointed at his chest, covered in long black wounds.

"It's necessary to complain to the police," I went on. "You're in a frightful state!"

He shook his head. "I burned myself this morning with red-hot pincers."

"Burned! Great God, why?"

"The two wretches had ordered me to."

"What wretches?"

"You can't know and I can't talk."

"From what I understand, you have enemies who are harassing you, and whom you don't want to denounce?"

"If I denounced them, human justice could not attain them."

"Are they too highly placed, then?"

"Perhaps."

I could not get any more out of him that evening.

After having helped him back to his mansard—for he was so weak that he would certainly have collapsed before getting there—I sat down beside him, clawed by an avid curiosity. Soon, the phenomenon that I had observed before was renewed; the irises of his eyes rose into the gray sclerotic, seeming to convulse as they disappeared under the eyelids.

He's a hypnotic, I thought, a hypnotic who enjoys the rare faculty of hypnotizing himself. His brain becomes congested, supercharged with astral light; instead of seeing externally he sees internally; everything that surrounds him becomes foreign to him, his mind sends itself into the fantastic world of a dream. He must perceive, in images, the reflection of his impressions, and his impressions must be terrible, for I have never seen a human face metamorphose to that degree.

While I reflected, the old man's limbs began to tremble, and his hands, which I was holding in mine, became ice-cold.

I was painfully impressed myself, because the fluid, being the common milieu of all nervous organisms and the vehicle of all sensitive vibrations, establishes between impressionable individuals a veritably physical solidarity, and transmits from one to another the impressions of imagination and thought. Sometimes, in fact, something inert is set in motion under the action of the universal fluid, and its movement obeys the dominant impression, to reproduce, in its revelations, sometimes all the lucidity of the most marvelous dreams, and sometimes all the bizarrerie and all the deception of terrifying nightmares.

Raps struck on furniture, the agitation of objects and the vibrations of musical instruments are, I believe, illusions brought about by the same causes.

Exaggerations, on the one hand, produced by the fascination that is the special intoxication occasioned by the congestion of astral light, and, on the other hand, real oscillations or movements imprinted on inert matter by the universal and subtle agent of the movement of life; that, I said to myself, *is at the bottom of all these disquieting things.*

But those movements of my accelerated heart, and the chill of the hand that I was holding, penetrated me with horror. It seemed to me, then, that the wood panels were creaking as if they were about to split, that the newspapers scattered on the floor were agitating, that the green-tinted and leprously stained walls were oscillating and liquefying. Now, I observed all those phenomena curiously, which would have been no less marvelous if my imagination alone were responsible for them, so much reality was there in their appearances.

"Are you asleep?" I asked Père Lazare, whose lips were agitating convulsively. "I beg you, make an effort to come round!"

He shivered from head to toe, but did not respond.

"Père Lazare, say something to me . . . are you in pain?"

A few minutes went by; then he seemed to summon up all his energy, and murmured, almost unintelligibly: "Save me!"

At hazard, I attempted the magnetic passes that cause the hallucinations of slumber to cease. For some time that had no result; then the irises of the eyes returned slowly, and the pale and cruel gaze fell upon me angrily.

"What are you doing here?" he cried. "Who gave you permission to enter, to spy on me?"

I did not take offense; the man's insanity interested me to the highest degree, and, while beating a retreat, I promised myself to keep watch on him as closely as I possibly could.

For him, evidently, error triumphed over real life and his reason was now perpetually asleep. The state of hallucination that I had observed very often, even in people seemingly devoid of any anomaly, exists in all degrees. The passions, in sum, are intoxications and transports of relative and graduated follies. But the old man must have been endowed with a great tenacity; his rectangular forehead and his sturdy jaws revealed obstinacy and materiality; his broad shoulders and his powerful muscles, atrophied now by poverty, testified to an exceptional former vigor.

By what combination of circumstances and what slow disintegration of his energy had he arrived at trembling like an infant before the evocation of an imaginary danger?

Those enigmas posed to my searching mind became thereafter the occupation of my leisure. Unfortunately, I could not study my subject as often as I wished. He shut himself away in his room, and if the concierge had not taken up a little bread and meat every morning on my part he would certainly have died of starvation. The destiny of that sick man, abandoned by everyone, seemed to me to be sinisterly mysterious, and I interested myself in him in spite of his pale and terrible gaze.

It has been said of a certain German book: *Es lasst sich nicht lesen!*[1] The character of that man was similar to that discouraging book. One could turn its pages, but no light sprang therefrom for the intelligence. There are secrets stronger than time and death! Terrible secrets that, undoubtedly, could only be written in blood, and which living beings would refuse to reveal! Individuals writhe in unspeakable convulsions, breasts are torn under the force of sobs, without being able to cast off the burden that is oppressing consciousness and gradually stifling it.

My imagination wandered at random, forming a thousand suppositions that it subsequently abandoned with disdain. I reasoned paradoxically regarding the sentiments of circumspection, composure, malevolence, distress and horror that I believed that I had read in the livid face of the old maniac. Who could he be? Where did he come from? And what somber drama had left its ineffaceable and illegible imprint on his features?

---

1 The quotation is from Edgar Poe's "The Man of the Crowd," in which the narrator does not name the book about which he is supposedly talking, but translates the phrase as "it does not permit itself to be read." Poe's text, which might well have inspired the present story, continues: "Men die nightly in their beds, wringing the hands of ghostly confessors, and looking them piteously in the eyes . . . Now and then alas, the conscience of man takes up a burden so heavy in horror that it can be thrown down only into the grave."

II
Losange

Weary of contemplating the muddy street through the small windows of my room, into which the daylight filtered every morning so pale and crepuscular, I resolved that year to flee on the first fine day to some spa town or beach resort. It was necessary to react, to deflect the incoherence of my somber ideas.

Père Lazare had not brought any new document to my observation. He rubbed along, frail and sinister, impelled by habit or dread of the mysterious beyond. I recommended him to the charity of my concierge and I quit Paris at the beginning of July in the glory of a regal and generous sunlight.

The train that carried me away rocked me gently; my gaze wandered over the countryside seething with waves of golden buds, bubbles of poppies and a foam of daisies extending all the way to the horizon. Then there were files of squat apple trees and peach trees distributed along a wall; a village church whose ocher profile disappeared under the amorous mesh of a giant ivy, with low yellow buildings all around it, grouped there like chicks under the wing of an attentive hen. Sometimes there was an overflow of verdure, an ascension of trees jostling one another dementedly in the brightness, and, behind that curtain, tearing it as if to drink the light, an old château flanked by towers.

The building, curbed by age, undermined by cold winds, showed its façade strewn with windows sculpted in ogives and triple crosses, fitted with glass the color of dirty water, its roof of blackened tiles patched with green. Then there was the small house of some modest bourgeois with its pond surrounded by symmetrical rocks like the cardboard décor of nativity cribs, its glass ball and its bushes carved into almond shapes, with borders of box.

When I arrived at Losange-sur-Mer it was dark. The train had gradually emptied, and there were only four passengers left. A few omnibuses were parked outside the station. I took the first one, which conveyed me to a hotel of modest appearance in the main street of the town.

Intoxicated by all the verdure and all the daylight, I was falling asleep. So, after a summary meal, I asked to be taken to my room. The bed did not appear to me to be too inhospitable, and I fell into a heavy slumber, devoid of anxiety and dreamless.

I did not know Losange; its broad leafy pathways pleased me by virtue of the contrast they formed with the immense sandy beach, as even and as gentle on the feet as a thick woolen carpet. On the one hand, there was a sensation of twilight and melancholy, which descended from dense vaults that only filtered a violet light, and an odor of damp that rose from the earth felted with fallen leaves at the foot of rusty grilles corroded by ivy, where placards swayed; on the other, there was life, warmth, eternal movement under the dazzle of a naked sky as vast as the sea itself. Here one could love and dream, there one could live and believe.

After a few days, my hotel horrified me, with the reek of cooking and the banal faces of its guests. I rented a chalet hidden in a nest in a clematis wood and I had my luggage taken there. The house was frail, trembling in the slightest wind, and draughty, but I was at home there in the warm perfume of the vegetation, the buzzing of bees and the caress of my dreams, which no banal awakenings came to disturb.

It is true that an unspeakable sadness gripped my heart again, as in my Parisian lodgings. That isolation, those somber paths, that light, decanted with a violet tint, acted upon my still-too-vibrant nerves.

It seemed to me that I had not escaped the influence of Père Lazare, that the fears that tortured him were going to invade me here as in Paris. I had not left of my own accord but in order to obey a mysterious order, an occult power that governed my destiny. The first dazzle, under the deluge of sunlight that had calmed the stormy anguish of my mind, had ended.

That lost little house, the well of moisture beneath the trees, was reminiscent of the muffled and unhealthy melancholy of the little garden strangled between the four walls of my courtyard. A kind of macabre sensuality was driving me, it seemed, to choose analogous places in which to live my constant ennui. I analyzed myself and found that I was in a dislocated state of mind, submissive involuntarily to violent impressions, tormented by dolorously tensed nerves, vibrating without cause and against my reason. That struggle overwhelmed me here, as it had back there. I went out at daybreak, along the gray, level roads, along rare patches of grass eaten by dust, where I lay down in the warm sand, allowing the sea to bathe me gradually, caressing me with its white foam.

Losange was deserted; the large hotel only had a dozen guests in spite of the persistence of the good weather. Posters stuck to the walls announced imminent distractions: bicycle races, operettas, new comedies and balls with great orchestras. I read the names there of stars who were absolutely unknown but nevertheless emerged, it seemed, from the Vaudeville or the Gymnase, and who proposed to perform, by turns, comedy, opera and tragedy.

I visited the casino, ornamented by numerous gaming rooms, where the green baize, still virgin, displayed its soft seduction. The mirrors reflected my doleful face, framed with thin hair that was already turning gray, and as I contemplated myself sadly, a perfect lucidity suddenly illuminated the vagueness of my anxieties. I understood that, for a year, I had doubted myself and others, that a tortuous suspicion had prevented me from loving and being loved. My life lacked that essential and consoling thing: tenderness. The women that I saw seemed to me to be too heavily plastered with make-up in body and soul; their eyes concealed lies, I avoided the kisses of their excessively red lips. The courage of amorous escapades had ebbed away with youth; my fatigued brain no longer let itself go to the hauntings of the imagination, the generous nurse of nightmares and fear! In me, commencements of thought were aborted, a rubble of ideas that blazed fervently and suddenly collapsed, burned to a crisp.

I let myself fall on to a divan, and, my head tilted back, a cigarette between my lips, I became torpid in a semi-dream. A few visitors came into the gaming room, made a tour of the tables and went out silently, disappointed. The hours passed. I had even dozed off, I believe, when a slight sound attracted my attention. I turned round. A young woman was standing behind me, motionless, beside a man of about forty whose ravaged face and evasive gaze were immediately antipathetic to me. I returned my gaze to the young woman, who smiled at me, while talking in a low and rapid voice to her companion. She was petite, scarcely developed, almost boyish, but nevertheless plump.

Her bright eyes had an indefinable, almost cruel expression, and appeared even brighter by virtue of the proximity of artificially bleached hair coiffed in a soft velvet bonnet and gathered at the nape in a superb mane. A tight dress outlined her torso, molded her hips and, beneath the light lace that descended from the shoulders, her arms allowed a glimpse of a little light skin above the gloves that covered them. She was bizarre and charming, with irregular features and an almost unhealthily pale complexion.

"We've come too early," the man said. "There's no one here yet."

"Bah! We'll go to bed. After our recent late nights, it won't do us any harm."

The couple went out, and I remained in ecstasy, already forgetful of my vain sadness.

III
Baccarat

"Place your bets, Messieurs . . . no more bets!"

There are lots of people in Losange now; the rooms of the casino are overflowing with dancers and gamblers. August is in full swing, the hotels have no more vacant rooms, and there are insufficient places in the dining rooms.

I have stayed, in spite of my hatred of crowds, in order to see my unknown woman again, and I see her every evening at the baccarat table. She is more charming than ever, and her gaze now remains fixed on mine for long minutes.

The circle at the Losange casino has nothing in common with the Jockey Club, the Ganaches or the Pommes de Terre. Anyone can come in; it is a former cook who guards the door and his new functions have not augmented his pride. I have asked him for information regarding the young woman and he has told me that her name is Yvaine d'Argens and that she is accompanying Baron de Ziler, the individual with the pale complexion and the squint who had displeased me so much at first sight. They arrive when the game begins and only leave when the candles are extinguished, when there is no longer anyone to compete with them. I understand: Yvaine and her friend are there to attract players, to "light them up," to get the game going, and perhaps also to change the run of luck.

Of all gambling games, baccarat is the one that lends itself most to "systems," and a host of strangers, decked with sonorous names, bring new ones every season that they try out in the casinos of seaside resorts and thermal spas. I had learned, at my expense, that it is necessary not to play quinze, poker, écarté, and, above all, baccarat.

Ziler never ceased dealing, going from one table to another for hours on end. I observed him with the greatest attention, doing my best to dissimulate it. I thought that I remarked that he dealt the cards by making them describe a broad trajectory, which is known as "rainbow dealing." I also saw him dispose three cards in a fan, and thought that he held them like that in order to allow a colleague to see that he was "telegraphing" them and "palming" them.

I had frequented a number of tolerated gambling clubs and elegant dens in Paris; I had left a good deal of my plumage there, and almost all the tricks were known to me. I had had to suffer, particularly, "Marseillaise" palming, the alteration of the sequence of the cards. A few elegant players, of whom I had been told that they possessed the greatest wealth, often forgot to place a "shirt" under the last card in order to make their point, on seeing the "shepherdess." Some pinched the fabric of their coat, previously steeped in water, delicately, with the thumb, the index finger and the middle. Others wore a ring with a resplendent bezel, which permitted them to see the cards.

The tricks of those messieurs were innumerable, and often ingeniously original. Do people not cite, among the most remarkable inventions, that of a gambling house in Pensa, near Moscow? Russians who had lost enormous sums in that den alerted the police. The banker was arrested, along with the scoundrels planted in the place, and an investigation was carried out. The walls and the ceiling were decorated with painted paper representing stars, and in the ceiling, holes were pierced in the middle of those stars in such a way that a man lying on the parquet of the floor above could see all the players' cards. By means of signals whose wires ran along the walls, he indicated by means of slight taps plied to the soles of the banker, the cards held by his opponents. The accomplices were exiled to Siberia.

In France, four cheats exploited a gambling den fitted out in an even more curious fashion. The system of signals also consisted of wires, but they did not come from the ceiling and did not lead to the banker's boot. They departed from a section of the parquet forming a pedal and came to set in motion, by means of electricity, a spring placed under the padding of the banker's chair. One of the accomplices stood with his foot on the pedal and transmitted hands at the pontoon by leaning lightly on the pedal. The spring, moving up and down, struck the banker's thigh through the fabric of the chair.

The method had the advantage over the one employed in Pensa of not producing any sound. It was, however, discovered in singular circumstances. The man responsible for communicating the pontoon hands had almost to stand on one foot and only to lean very lightly on the pedal. The latter could be consolidated by means of a simple pressure on a button hidden behind a curtain, but during the operation, it was scarcely sustained, a void having been created beneath the electric apparatus. One evening the operator was distracted, and placed all his weight on the section of parquet, which gave way, and the mechanism sank down while the banker uttered a terrible scream. The spring in the chair, receiving too forceful a shock, had just traversed the fabric and penetrated the thigh of the unfortunate cheat, while the other, his leg partly plunged into the parquet, could not get it out again. The causes of the disturbance were investigated and everything was discovered. The surprise was great, for the banker was a highly placed "philosopher"—so highly-placed, in fact, that the affair was hushed up for fear of the frightful scandal that would have been produced.[1]

If cheating is easy in the gambling clubs of Paris, where it is presumed that all the players are known, it is almost the rule in casinos to which anyone is admitted. Every year the Sûreté générale sends special instructions to police commissaires relating to the casinos within their jurisdiction, but surveillance is impossible with individuals who change their names, and even their faces, according to circumstances. Then, articles appear in the *Courrier des Plages* or the *Echo des Vallées* of this sort: "Would the Sûreté générale care to tell us by what circular or regulation it authorizes the entry into the gaming houses and casinos of *** of young women who are only women by virtue of their sex? These creatures cheat, flirt, spread scandal, lie and serve marvelously the actions of the men of every sort who escort them."

The editors of these virtuous newspapers are often less grim than their prose, and allow themselves to be led astray by the "creatures" of which they speak with so much scorn. However,

---

1 Author's reference: "*Le Monde où l'on triche*, 1 vol., by Hogier-Grison." The book in question, thus signed in some editions, is credited to Georges Grison in the two-volume 1886 edition; it is an exposé of methods of cheating at cards, which La Vaudère had presumably read avidly while working on the present story.

one cannot give too much credit to the lamentations of fathers of families whom the marriageable "demoiselles" turn sour, like overripe fruit, while awaiting the sage monsieur who will talk to them about beef stew and flannel waistcoats between a gallop and a polka. Every year one sees them returning to Losange after the conjugal rat race, ardent for the boston, in their harness of virginal ribbons and saddle-cloths of holy muslin. They twirl and twirl, to the sound of a resigned orchestra, but the *tirage à cinq* has reckoned with their overripe graces and their convulsive smiles.[1]

Yvaine d'Argens was enthroned in the midst of the old guard that composed the ordinary feminine clientele of the green baize. With her naturally pale complexion, the keen gaze of her large eyes and her disdainful mouth, she seemed to belong to a different race, more vibrant and more refined. While her companions decked themselves out in pearls and diamonds, her exposed neck remained devoid of jewelry, without a single stone. From her shoulders to her knees, her tight dress, of a pale pink hortensia shade, espoused the exquisite forms of her young nudity precisely, and would have seemed indecent without the light foam of English needlepoint that covered it.

A penetrating odor floated around her, surrounding her, so to speak, with an aura. I felt gradually invaded by her strange charm, and, in spite of the repugnance inspired in me by her lover and the players that surrounded them, I scarcely quit the baccarat room any longer.

One evening, she came up to me and, without any preamble, asked me why I never played.

"My God, Madame," I said, "I played a great deal once and lost a great deal. I mistrust gambling dens in general, and casinos in particular."

She smiled in a singular fashion. "Really? You'd be lucky with me. Would you like me to advise you?"

---

1 *Tirage à cinq* is a method of drawing and laying out Tarot cards in order to tell fortunes.

"Would I win?"

"Certainly. With me one always wins."

"Be careful—I'm a police agent."

She recoiled sharply. "Oh! You're spying on us?"

"What does it matter? Have you something to fear?"

"Nothing," she replied, dryly, looking me up and down, "but I don't like snitches."

I started laughing. "You thought I was serious?"

"Well . . ."

"Well, don't be deceived. I'm just a friend . . . a friend who can give you some good advice, if you wish."

"What good advice can you give me?"

"This, for example: don't play any longer."

"Oh, it's not for my pleasure that I'm playing, it's a matter of obedience."

"Revolt!"

"Later, perhaps. At the moment, I'm cowardly, any effort of will would be painful for me."

She sat down beside me and put her little hand on mine.

"All women have their story, don't they?"

"Certainly, but there are vulgar stories that don't interest anyone."

"You'd be able to reveal many secrets?"

"No, for everyone here knows what matters about the past of his neighbor."

"Do you know the Prince de X***? That little brown fellow with a yellow carnation in his buttonhole."

"I knew him when he was a notary's clerk named Poirot. Look, there's the Comte de B***, who was convicted of forgery, fraud, embezzlement and other pleasantries; Baron de Z***, who has tried all métiers and only succeeded at baccarat; Monsieur C***, whose amiability with women has saved him from poverty; the banker **** who made off with the receipts and came back one day completely cleaned out; the Comte de W***, whose name was Auguste when he was only a groom; the Prince de C***, whose gallant and tragic adventure generated some talk. His mistress is beside him, and still seems seductive in this light. There's little Vicomte de R***, who is made up like a woman and never quits his friend, the opulent Arthur D***. There would be an enormous amount of other things to say about all the stars and the nonentities of this gaming room, but my evening wouldn't be sufficient. In any case, these types have already been put in the light be talented novelists. You'll find several thick books entirely filled with that flavorsome subject."

"However," she said, "there are a good many honest players here."

"They're the majority, unfortunately. Without them, gambling would no longer be possible."

"You haven't mentioned my friend Baron de Ziler. What do you think of him?"

"I don't think anything. Your friend is completely unknown to me. Is it the first time you've come here?"

"No, we've done all the casinos, but we come back to Losange for preference, especially during the races."

"That existence doesn't weigh upon you?"

"Yes, sometimes . . . I don't have the right, alas, to be difficult."

She scrutinized my eyes with her steely gaze, seeming to offer herself.

Baron de Ziler had turned round and summoned her in a curt tone. Then, as if regretfully, she got up and left me, after a final smile.

IV
Yvaine

That conversation was followed by many others. I now saw Yvaine at any time of the day. She even accompanied me sometimes on my morning walks while her lover lingered in bed, fatigued by late nights.

She didn't tell me about her life and I didn't ask. What did it matter to me? She was doubtless no better and no worse than many mistresses I had had, and what she would have told me would only have been a story invented to please, to magnify her in my eyes. Did she think I was rich? I don't know. However, I am inclined to think that what entered into the choice she had deigned to make of me was a little curiosity and a good deal of the love of change that drives certain women to compromise their situation stupidly for an improbable new sensation.

The Baron de Ziler was not unduly worried by our long conversations. Perhaps he was only seeking a pretext to break with her, judging that such a mistress was somewhat dangerous for a man like him.

Yvaine often bore long blue marks on her shoulders and arms, bruises that she sought in vain to dissimulate. I interrogated her, and she ended up saying that she now existed in a continual state of fear, her lover coming back drunk almost every morning and beating her.

"Is it out of jealousy?"

"Him, jealous!" she made a scornful gesture. "He doesn't care about me, but he's afraid that I might talk, reveal who he is and what he's worth."

"Is he very culpable then?"

"I won't betray him, because I've sworn."

Yvaine was very pale; I closed her mouth with a kiss, and put my arm around her waist.

For some time, I had succeeded in drawing her further into the country. While chatting, we set off exploring along pathways that were already yellowing slightly. Until lunchtime we wandered among the trees, she a trifle nonchalant, close beside me, her large straw hat pulled down over her face.

At the end of the path a watercourse snaked between willows; we liked its banks, which were always delightfully isolated and cool. Alongside us, green shimmers made a tremulous network of light in the stream, whose sunlit mesh enclosed the broad leaves of nympheas. We went upstream for an hour, along the sand amassed at water level, trampling reeds, and discovering little sections of sky in the midst of aquatic plants, fallen there like mysterious blue flowers.

Yvaine laughed. "It's funny to come to the seaside to contemplate a stream lost in the depths of a wood."

"At this moment, the seaside is a depressing banality; all the bourgeois go there like ducks to a pond. Here we can dream together with no one looking at us. Aren't you comfortable with me?"

"Yes, since I stay. I wouldn't have thought that a year ago. One might think that you'd cast a spell on me."

We turned round. In the distance, at the end of the path, a curtain of trees bathed in vapor closed the horizon; then, to either side of the stream, smaller trees advanced in a bouquet, penetrated with light on the edges. A sheet of water undulated away from us, profoundly green, in which silvery scales quivered, thousands of fireflies borne by the current. The breeze was singing in the hedges of wild rose-bushes, florid with coral grains, and surprised birds threw the bridge of their rapid flight from one bank to the other.

Yvaine sat down in the grass, pressed against me; we remained silent, lost in contemplation of a water spider skating in the midst of the ripples that widened around it; we followed the fall of leaves frosted with gold or rust, which were going to join the heap of previous years, forgotten there like the dead memory of former springs.

A wave of melancholy drowned my soul and I lifted up the tilted head of my companion, imagining that her fibers were vibrating in unison with mine.

"Would you like to be mine, Yvaine? We could both run away and forget the past."

She frowned. "No," she said. "That man would avenge himself. I'm bound to him. You don't know what there is against us."

Suddenly chilled by her refusal, I drew away from her, and we did not exchange another word all the way back to the hotel where she was staying with her lover.

V
The Theft

One day, as I opened the blinds of my house, I saw her running toward me, very emotional.

"Save me!" she said, as soon as she perceived me. "He's tried to kill me. Look . . ."

She showed me her gashed breast, from which blood was flowing abundantly. Fortunately, the wound was not deep, and I dressed it as best I could.

When the young woman was lying in my bed, smiling and calm, I asked her for a few explanations.

"Everything is finished between that man and me! I no longer have anyone but you in the world, my friend—don't abandon me!"

"But again, what has happened?"

"You know how violent he is? After a frightful scene, I threatened to leave him, and in a moment of fury he stabbed me."

"Didn't he know that we love one another?"

"That doesn't matter to him. It wasn't my love he wanted but my obedience, my absolute submission."

"By what right?"

She leaned over, and in a lower voice, said: "It will be necessary, one day or another, for me to confess the truth to you; know right away, then, that I'm linked to that wretch by a secret . . ."

"If it's painful for you to reveal it to me, don't say anything; I forgive you your past errors, my poor Yvaine."

"You wouldn't be able to forgive a crime!"

"A crime?"

"Yes. I'll tell you everything; afterwards, perhaps you'll chase me away, but you'll know that I loved you enough to make you the sacrifice of my life."

"Speak."

146

"I was scarcely fifteen years old. I was alone in the world, clad in rags and in the most profound poverty."

"Your mother?"

"My mother abandoned me, I don't know her. I lived as I could in the home of a worthy woman who had a little fruiterer's shop. I went to the market, I ran errands, I served the customers. When my protectress died I was thrown out, and I tried to sell flowers at street corners. That didn't go well, I was truly about to die of hunger when Ziler, who had been watching me for some time, offered to take me home with him. You can imagine how glad I was. The Baron wasn't difficult, for I was only skin and bone, with a bad cough that might have carried me off between dusk and dawn. He cleaned me up, cared for me, and even had me given lessons in reading and writing, so well that I became a woman like others with the gift of the gab, white flesh and vice. Then the fellow showed the tip of his ear. If he had raised me tenderly it wasn't for his personal pleasure but for the accomplishment of a plan he'd been ripening in his brain for some time. He only needed one thing, a blind instrument, a woman who was sufficiently attached to him by gratitude not to betray him. With a thousand reticences he explained what he expected of me."

Yvaine's face was contracted; her eyes were flashing. I tried again to impose silence on her, but she continued.

"I won't give you all the details, because the whole story has remained mysterious; this is only what the Baron found himself forced to tell me. Sixteen or seventeen years before, it appears, he had been deprived of an inheritance that he had coveted for a long time, and which ought to have come to him after the death of a relative. That inheritance, which was very considerable, had been deflected by a foreigner; it was a matter of reconquering it, because we were in an excessive financial embarrassment that it was not even possible to dissimulate."

"I can't see the role that was destined for you in all that."

"Oh, that was quite simple. I had to seduce the heir, who lived alone in an isolated apartment at the back of a garden, draw him to my home, intoxicate him with amour, take possession of his keys and . . ."

"This is a novel that you're relating to me. What a singular means for a gentleman!"

"We didn't have a choice."

"No choice? It seems to me that if your lover had been defrauded of an inheritance, he could attack the testament . . ."

"He'd done that, but fruitlessly. He had even been accused, at that time, of complicity in the murder of the Baron de Falcaz, the testator."

"Damn! What a complication!"

"I'm repeating to you, of course, what he told me; myself, I don't know."

"The story doesn't matter. You were, then, to seduce Baron de Falcaz' heir?"

"Yes, a man named Gauthier, a vile man who led a joyous life and received lots of women at his home."

"The seduction was easy, then?"

"Not at all. When Gauthier saw me at a public dance-hall to which I'd followed him, he turned his back on me. I came back to sit beside him and tried to engage him in conversation, but he got up abruptly and left the hall."

"That's at least strange."

"Would you believe that I followed him everywhere for a month—to the café, to the theater, in the street? A sort of rage possessed me, I hated him and desired him at the same time, having to reckon with his repugnance. I was profoundly humiliated by Ziler's sarcasms . . ."

"This Gauthier interests me . . ."

"If only he'd remained the same!"

"He gave in, then?"

"All men give in. One evening, he took me home with him and talked to me for two hours about a host of bizarre things to which I listened curiously. I thought he was delirious. Then, after those ramblings, he sent me away brutally, putting some banknotes in my hand. I'd examined everything around him and I knew where he locked up his valuables."

"With the consequence that you've robbed that man?" I drew away from Yvaine, my soul filled with disgust.

"I didn't know," she begged, in a whining tone. "I was so young! Now, certainly, I'd rather die . . ."

"But in sum, you stole!"

"Things didn't happen absolutely as you suppose, and the difficulty of my enterprise might render me less odious. Gauthier continued, in spite of that first conversation, to testify a singular aversion to me. In my presence his eyes sparkled and his lips trembled. I was almost afraid of him. However, I feigned passion so well that I ended up attracting him to my home. His keys never quit him; it was a matter of taking them and giving them to Ziler, who was waiting in an adjacent room. Drunk with caresses and wine, toward midnight, he let himself fall on to the back of his armchair. I hastened to search his pockets, but he hadn't lost the notion of reality sufficiently because, as I handed the keys to my lover, he got up abruptly and uttered a cry. Ziler then fell upon him and tried to strangle him. Both robust, they rolled on the floor, fighting, and then Ziler got up. I was frightened mute, not daring to intervene . . ."

Yvaine, very pale, supported herself on the pillows, looking at me with an imploring gaze.

Indignant at so much criminal lack of conscience, I contemplated her with horror.

"Not only have you stolen, but you've murdered a man!" I murmured, in a quavering voice.

"No, no, he didn't die. Ziler, who had left him inanimate, was trembling in all his limbs, and clung to me in the fear of his action . . . we were already wondering what we were going to do with the body when Gauthier came round. He stared at us for a few moments, and then a scornful smile creased his lips. 'It's futile to kill me,' he said. 'You won't find anything in my house. My valuables are in a safe place. Let me go and I swear that I won't denounce you.'

"But Ziler didn't trust him. 'What reason do you have for sparing us?' he asked.

"'Oh, the best of all. I'm as guilty as you are, we're as bad as one another.'

"'Aha!' said the Baron 'I've always suspected it. You won't denounce me; that's as well, but it's only natural that you compensate me for my complaisance. Sign me a note for a hundred thousand francs and you're free. That's very little compared with what you've stolen from me.'

"Gauthier straightened up. 'I haven't stolen anything from you. Monsieur de Falcaz, your relative, nominated me as his universal heir. If I give you these hundred thousand francs, it's not because I'm afraid of you, but because I'm rich enough not to care about such a paltry sum.'

"Ziler thought that he hadn't asked for enough; however, he didn't manifest any regret, and he permitted Gauthier to leave. Such is my crime, my friend."

Yvaine was no longer interrogating my eyes. "I was so young," she said, then. "I didn't know what I was doing. Can you forgive me?"

I had a chill I my heart in thinking that the young woman I had collected, and almost loved, had fallen so low. I no longer experienced anything but aversion for her. However, in making me that confession she had certainly not rendered account of her indignity.

"You're infamous, Yvaine! It will require some time for me to forget!"

She started sobbing, and the dressing covering her breast came apart, tearing the wound, which bled abundantly. As she did not cease to agitate I held her in my arms, and put my lips to her eyes as a sign of forgiveness.

VI
A Cheat

The wound closed rapidly. After a fortnight, there was almost no more trace of it; only a small round vermilion mark remained on her breast. As I was anxious, Yvaine smiled.

"You're looking at that mark? I've always had it, it's a birthmark. The spilled blood prevented you from seeing it. One might think that a rose petal had fallen there, mightn't one?"

"Yes, it's singular, a rose petal! But would you like the entire rose to bloom under my kisses?"

I had already forgotten Yvaine's criminal past, in order only to remember that of the lover, who revealed herself exquisite and new.

Sometimes, fear made her face pale.

"What I told you will remain between us?" she asked, in a quavering voice. "You won't denounce me?"

"Why would I denounce you, since the past no longer exists?"

Ziler had disappeared, at the same time as a domestic from the club whom the players had almost caught playing the "brush trick." The trick in question consisted of the Baron dropping the ash from his cigar in front of him and calling his accomplice, who was waiting for the signal. The latter arrived with his brush, lifted up the cards in order to brush more effectively and then withdrew. In the hand that lifted the cards he had placed a two-shot "rigollot."[1] Ziler employed the trick when he suspected that someone was about to go banco, the cards not having been stacked at the beginning of the deal.

"Oh, they haven't seen anything," Yvaine told me when I told her about the Baron's latest exploit. "I know many other tricks more extraordinary."

---

1 The literal meaning of *rigollot* refers to a cataplasm, but in this instance it is presumably an alternative spelling of *rigolo*, a slang term for a small firearm.

"You cheated with your lover?"

"Well, you'll understand that the hundred thousand francs didn't last long."

"The rogue initiated you into all his secrets?"

"Yes, all of those in which I could serve in his calculations. Once I was his accomplice I was no longer to be feared. In any case, he couldn't work alone."

"He's never played honestly, then?"

"It was rare. When it appeared that he was being watched, he moved on."

"What were the tricks he employed most frequently?"

"I don't know; it depended on inspiration. He had the angling trick, the sticky trick, the consumptive trick, the sower's push, the silent punt, the piano player, the muffler, the mute cram and many others that I forget."

"It's to replace you that Ziler has taken on the domestic from the club?"

"He needed someone, but the man wasn't a novice; he was hovering around us from the first day. Like me, he must often have positioned himself opposite the Baron and made him imperceptible signals to tell him whether the hand in front of him had baccarat, two, three, four or five."

The Baron dealt with elegance and brio, without emotion, like a good player, whereas he was in reality a vulgar card sharp, and very dangerous. In Paris there are thirty men of the world who lend their "collaboration" from time to time to certain administrators and hosts of games. They are loud, quarrelsome and insolent, and seem to want to save themselves by the excess of their audacity. Those high-ranking thieves know one another, protect one another and share the loot. Ziler, in wanting to act alone, had attracted hostility; perhaps he had also lacked prudence . . .

We were able to remain in Losange for another fortnight in the sweetest intimacy. Yvaine was no longer Yvaine, but a creature of tenderness and sensuality of whom I was proud and jealous.

A muted joy slid within me, the great and intimate satisfaction that a man feels after the creation of a masterpiece. Had I not saved a soul? I thought myself better and stronger, a profound serenity spread within my being, like a fête of my consciousness, a renewal of hope and faith. The days that I spent in the little villa bathed in mystery were certainly the happiest of my life.

Unfortunately, the rain began to fall persistently, and it was no longer possible to go out. The air was impregnated with the odor of damp leaves and the sea, whose threatening breakers could be seen from a skylight in the grain-loft, grim beneath a grim sky. In the house the silence was only broken by the sound of the downpour or the friction of bending branches. Clouds fled overhead, somber and ragged, which swelled and pursued one another, seeming to catch on to the trees. Instantaneously, everything became sad and cold.

In the villa, summarily constructed, the wind came in through the broken windows of the attics and shook the doors, whose battens rattled. The tarnished mirror wept silver tears; the wallpaper, holed by tears and scratches, began to peel along the woodwork, and a dank odor rose from the saturated ground. We looked at our discolored faces in the mirrors, marbled by the patchy silvering, and my pale Yvaine looked like a victim of drowning. It was necessary to leave, the rain having penetrated our bedroom through the ruined ceiling.

Our preparations were quickly made. As we were loading our luggage on to the omnibus, however, the sun reappeared. Then, as if by magic, the villa, reanimated by the warmth of the air, was stripped of its wretched appearance. It was rejuvenated, adorned for our departure. Something like a fond farewell was exhaled by the grass and the plants.

I felt my heart constrict as I crossed the threshold of that modest dwelling, passing under the starry arbors of the clematis. Then, I don't know why, the specter of Père Lazare suddenly loomed up in my path and ordered me to speak.

"You don't know," I told my companion, trying to smile, "that there's an old man in my house who is very strange. We'll go to see him together."

"Why?" she asked, astonished. "The old man is indifferent to me."

"When you've seen him, he'll interest you, as he does me."

Yvaine enveloped me with a singular gaze, a bright and hard gaze that I did not know. After a moment of hesitation, she murmured: "Don't talk to me about that man!"

"But you don't know him!"

She pressed herself against me, shivering. "I'm afraid! I don't want any stranger between us. Let's be everything to one another. Believe me, don't let anyone into the confidence of our amour! You've made another woman of me, keep me in the warmth of the nest, beside you, always."

VII
Fatality

When Yvaine awoke after her journey and a night of fatigue, she rubbed her eyes and, in the first confused palpitation of her thought, believed that she was still in Losange. Her silky bedroom, however, bore no resemblance to the bare white bedroom of the villa. I had had my bachelor apartment hastily adapted so that it would be in rapport with my new sentiments. A friend had been charged with carrying out my desires faithfully.

All the colors of the fabrics in the old dwelling were now mild and melting. The eye went from pastel China blue to sulfur yellow and the softest pinks. The tinted windows with narrow panes enclosed, in a pale golden light, the entire gamut of the colors that came there to die. On the ceiling, the suns of Chinese standards radiated, ocellated like peacocks' tails with little glass eyes with golden eyelids. Everywhere, there were low divans, cushions, and amusing trinkets. I had wanted, above all, to sow cheerfulness around our slightly fearful tenderness.

Yvaine looked at the butterflies and the flowers of the wall-hangings, which, following the play of the sunlight, seemed to be sinking into the shadow or blooming in a magical radiance. She also gazed at a dressing-table decked in lace and ribbons, on which a thousand little things in blonde tortoiseshell or silver were placed.

Nothing resembles happiness like amour, and nothing equals amour, since happiness is only an ungraspable mirage.

Our first week continued the dream of Losange, and was a week of enchantment. In order to describe such felicities it would be necessary to strew the paper with words like flowers. We went to sleep in long idleness after exquisite sensualities, only existing for the present, strangers to anything that was not our adorable twofold egotism. Every morning, all our kisses of the previous day sang in our memory, and we quickly made a new harvest for the following day's awakening.

Finally, on the eighth day, Yvaine stood at the window and forgot herself in a vague reverie. The garden seemed to be a hole of shadow from which the trees launched toward the sky, to breathe in a little pure air, like captives through the window of their prison.

"Wouldn't one think it was a corner of our garden in Losange? I've certainly seen that garden and his house before," murmured the young woman.

"In a dream, then? You've never been here."

"Yes, yes . . . wait . . . there, that door, that perron . . ."

She uttered a scream, and fell back, utterly pale, into my arms.

Père Lazare, sitting on the stone bench, was gazing at us, and his vulturine eye had an expression of cold cruelty. I turned my head away involuntarily, invaded by an inexplicable terror.

Yvaine came round almost immediately, and leaned avidly toward the window, but the old man had disappeared.

"That man . . . ? That man . . . ?" she demanded.

"Well, that's Père Lazare . . ."

"Yes, yes, Lazare Gauthier! That's the man we wanted to rob, to murder!"

"Get away! He has no money."

"It's really him, I tell you. I recognize the house now. He lived on the ground floor, behind that cemetery garden!"

"But he's almost a beggar . . ."

"He hasn't always been. In any case, he recognized me . . . didn't you see his eyes, then?"

I was devastated. Was the woman's accursed past going to loom up between us, then? What singular hazard had brought her into proximity with her living remorse?

"We can't stay here," I said, sadly. "I'll go today to start looking for another apartment."

"Oh yes, go, that Gauthier only has to talk! For you as for me, it's better to leave . . ."

"Don't leave your room. Don't open the door to anyone . . ."

"Don't worry, I'll ask . . ."

I went out, and after making a few enquiries, I settled on a beautiful new house with large cheerful windows overlooking an avenue. Everything was arranged with the concierge, who also took charge of our housekeeping, for I had no domestic.

Almost joyful, I hastened to return home in order to announce the good news to my mistress.

On penetrating into the antechamber, the door of which was open, I heard the sound of voices. Frightened, I listened, and soon distinguished a few words. Yvaine was weeping and begging, while a man was proffering threats. I showed myself abruptly, and recognized Père Lazarus, upright on his crutches, his face livid, with foam on his lips.

"It's that woman who caused all the harm!" he cried, as soon as he perceived me. "Finally, I've found her again!"

"This woman is my friend! I love her, and I forbid you to insult her."

"You don't know her! Do you even know where she comes from? I tell you that she's mine. It's heaven or hell that gave her to me! It's the two of us, my little Yvaine!"

My fist was about to fall on the wretch's shoulder, but I considered his weakness and contented myself with pushing him toward the door.

He clung on to the frame.

"Before having encountered you, slut!" he howled, "I was living tranquilly, if not happily; my fortune didn't weigh upon me! It's since the horrible evening when you offered yourself to me in order to rob me more easily that my life has become an eternal torture. Look at her, with her cruel eyes and her face of death! Is she not an envoy of Satan?"

Yvaine and Lazare seemed to be challenging one another. I shivered in finding them similar to one another in expression and gesture: their thin lips were twisted, and in the ignoble visage of the old man shone the same strange eyes as in the blank face of my mistress.

"Père Lazare," I said, "we're leaving tomorrow; you will never see us again."

"I don't want you to go! I've suffered too much because of that creature. It's necessary for me to avenge myself!"

"Since you've forgiven once, the past no longer exists."

"I forgave because I thought I was strong enough to conserve my reason. But *they* come back every night! It's her who sends them to me!"

The young woman shrugged her shoulders. "This man is mad. Throw him out."

I dragged the old man away; he clung on to all the furniture, growling and groaning by turns. On the landing he made one last gesture of menace, and, his face contracted by a hideous fury, he howled:

"I will avenge myself!"

VIII
The Confession, the Crime, the Death

All of the next day was employed in preparations, Yvaine agitating furiously or remaining motionless, her lips pursed, mute. Then I hugged her in my arms, and tried to console her, like a child. But her body remained cold; she did not respond to my caresses.

"We're leaving—what more do you want?"

She looked at me, her mysterious eyes, the pupils spacious and distant, her breast heaving and her hands trembling. Her mental distress seemed immense.

"I belonged to that man," she said, finally. "I horrify myself. Whatever you say, you can never love me."

I hugged her again, but I was embracing a dead woman. She wept on my shoulder, inert, in an infinite desolation.

Exhausted by emotion and fatigue, we went to bed early. By virtue of having turned in every direction, my mind had arrived at a dead point, and remained insensible. I found myself in a complete torpor, which extinguished my reason before I went to sleep. Yvaine, next to me, had her eyes closed and seemed to be asleep. I contemplated her, with more curiosity than tenderness, already wearied by the difficulties of that amour, to which I had been subjected rather than having sought.

For a long time I had rested like a plant in the sun, or a hare in its form, happy in my liberty, and this belated adventure was beginning to encumber my life.

How long I remained plunged in that semi-sleep I don't know. Suddenly, someone rang violently at the door of the apartment, and, after having put on some clothes in haste, I went to open it.

It was Madame Duflos, my concierge.

"Come quickly, Monsieur," she said, in a confused voice.

"Why? What's happened?"

"It's a frightful thing! Without the help of Providence, we'd all have died!"

"Explain yourself!"

"Père Lazare has set fire to the house!"

"Fire? Fire! Quickly, wake Yvaine!"

"Don't worry, Monsieur, the danger is past; but the old mad-man's still there. He's asking for you now."

At hazard, I followed the concierge up to the mansard that the unfortunate fellow occupied.

The door was open, and what I saw surpassed all the horror that I could have imagined. The old man was lying on the bed to which he had set fire, which was still smoking. The flesh of his legs stood out, forming profound black holes, which one might have thought hollowed out in mud. His corroded face no longer had anything alive but the eyes, which seemed paler than usual.

We tried to dress his wounds, but he struggled so desperately that, in the fear of aggravating the damage, we let him be. A physician, summoned in all haste, declared, in any case, that any remedy would be futile, and that the invalid would not last the night.

I asked to stay with him, which won me the most sincere praise, and there was certainly some merit in remaining in that frightful place. The destroyed lips of the dying man left his teeth visible; the cartilage of the nose, half eaten away, was bleeding; the skin of the cheeks was cracked and shriveled, resembling two wood shavings twisted on a stove; his fingers were digging into his breast like claws; and from those miry remains an insupport-able odor escaped that turned the stomach.

"It curdled my blood!" declared the concierge. "Fortunately, his neighbor arrived in time to put the fire out. Without him, we'd all be dead! Since you're willing to stay with the old man, Monsieur, I'll go back to my lodge. I believe I'm going to have an indigestion."

I was soon alone beside the horrible bed, which no longer seemed to be bearing anything but a cadaver.

After a few minutes, however, Lazare's gaze fell upon mine, and I read such an expression of distress therein that I resolved to put him to sleep in order at least to spare him the final suffering.

I also hoped to know the mystery that enveloped his past, over which all my efforts had not yet been able to triumph.

Without further delay I commenced the passes that I had recognized, in my numerous experiments, to be the most efficacious. He was certainly influenced by the first projection of my will, but, although I deployed all my energy, no other sensible effect was manifested for a quarter of an hour. I gazed at him intently, concentrating all my nervous force in the fire of my pupils, changing my lateral passes into longitudinal passes. His eyes, already a trifle vitreous, did not vacillate, and after further attempts, I recognized that my energy was breaking against his, which imminent death had not been able to defeat.

At length, his pulse became imperceptible and his obstructed respiration became increasingly wheezy. Then a heart-rending sigh emerged from his bosom, and the noisy breath ceased. I contented myself with observing, despairing of putting him to sleep, as I had initially attempted to do. Then, suddenly, as if he were obedient to an occult power, I perceived unequivocal symptoms of the magnetic influence. The vitreous fixity of the eyes had changed into the strange expression of inward gaze that one only sees in cases of somnambulism, and which I had noticed several times before in the patient.

The eyelids palpitated, and then closed; the arms fell back alongside the body. I recognized that he was in a complete state of catalepsy. The most absolute calm had been established within him, his limbs were cold and rigid. After a sufficiently long time, his entire being was agitated by a slight tremor, his eyelids lifted of their own accord, revealing the white line of the eyeball, a hoarse sound passed between his clenched teeth, and I leaned forward anxiously to try to seize the words that he was doubtless about to pronounce.

In fact, after a minute, he articulated clearly, albeit in a bitter and ragged tone that seemed to be rising a long way from the depths of some abyss: "Yes, yes, I'll talk, since *they* wish it. It will be my supreme punishment."

"What do you have to say, then, Père Lazare?"

But he did not hear me, and seemed to be obeying imperious orders that only his mind received and heard. I therefore ceased my questions and remained still, my ear attentive.

"Yes, yes," he continued, as if addressing invisible beings, "You're strong! You're avenging yourselves, and I'm dying! Oh, if I'd at least been able to set fire to the infamous woman!"

"Are you talking about Yvaine?"

That name seemed to strike him like a slap in the face; his fingers clenched in a gesture of fury.

"I'm nailed here, and those executioners are torturing me!"

The old man's appearance was so hideous, at that moment, that I made a movement toward the door.

"Stay," he ordered. "It's necessary that I tell you everything. I can't die before then—*they* wish it!"

I came back meekly, while avoiding Père Lazare's gaze, which only inspired an invincible repulsion in me.

"You see," he went on, "all the crimes for which ancient sorcerers were once punished by death are real, and are the greatest of all crimes. Even forgotten by human justice, sorcerers are condemned to perish violently, to become the prey of vultures whose beaks empty their eyelids and gnaw their entrails eternally. Have they not stolen the fire of heaven, like Prometheus? Have they not ridden winged dragons and flying serpents, like Medea? Have they not profaned holy things and even made the body of the Lord serve for their accursed work? In sum, have they not plundered the astral light for the satisfaction of their shameful passions?

"Magnetism, suggestion and entrancement serve for their spell-casting. By those means they arrive at the omnipotence of the will. Their brain is a book printed inside and outside, but if the attention vacillates slightly, the characters melt and the initiate touches madness. Fiction triumphs over reality in an incurable slumber. It is necessary to advance with extreme prudence in order not to fall into the profanations of black magic. They are aerial cadavers that one evokes by those dangerous practices; they are larvae, dead and impure substances, with which one puts oneself in rapport.

"They seem to be inert, but they communicate thoughts and dreams to us. Since my damnation I have always been in an exceptional state that contains something of sleep and death. I enjoyed the power of magnetizing myself, and I arrived at a sort of waking and conscious somnambulism. When I have ceased to be, doubtless in a few hours, my culpable and accursed astral spirit will remain on earth. Its vices will appear to it and will pursue it in monstrous forms; in order to avenge itself, it will torment the spirits of the living in its turn. Perhaps my victims might forgive me via your mouth. Listen to my confession and judge me!"

I interrupted Père Lazare. "I don't need to know your past. I only have to pass judgment on your last crime. You wanted us all to perish, then, in the flames?"

"Yes. I hate my fellows; I hate you, you who helped me, and, above all, I hate that woman, who made me the wretch that I am."

"Yvaine?"

"Yesterday, I went into her abode to kill her, but you protected her. She has cast a spell on you, as she did on me."

"That is dementia!"

"Oh, I'm not mad. Let me speak, and you'll be convinced. It's necessary for me to make haste, listen . . .

"My childhood was sad and laborious. Raised by charity, I worked with all my strength to enable me to earn my living without the assistance of others. My true character was only revealed later; then, I only had determination, audacity and ambition. I'll pass over rapidly the banal years of which, in any case, I only retain a vague memory. I had the opportunity in my twentieth year, to encounter a great lady who was looking for a tutor for her son, an impressionable and delicate child whom she desired to keep close to her. I pleased her by virtue of the vigor of my constitution and the mildness of my manners, which I was already able to bend hypocritically to the greater benefit of my interests.

"The Château de Falcaz had a fine appearance. Situated on top of a hill, it outlined its imposing mass against the sky; an avenue planted with several-times-centenarian oaks led to the main door. But when one risked oneself under the vault of the inextricably entangled branches, that door appeared in a mysteriously distant verdure, and seemed to give access to some fabulous dwelling in a land of dreams.

"Everywhere that the gaze extended there were thick woods, in a debauchery of overflowing sap, and in the distance, embracing the giant forest, a broad watercourse scintillated. The château, flanked by four stout towers decorated with turrets with pointed roofs, pinnacles and florid gambles, conserved a feudal and majestic appearance.

"I stayed in that peaceful milieu, supervising and educating my young pupil, who, in spite of our cares, remained melancholy and paltry. It was said around me that the mother would not see him grow up, and as she was a just and generous woman, people felt sincere compassion for her. I had acquired a singular influence over her and her son. They listened to me with respect, obeyed my slightest advice, and I gloried in that little empire, so easily conquered. An entire leaven of evil sentiments was fermenting within me; beneath my apparent gratitude, I hated those people who, in order to be happy and heaped with all the benefits of existence, had only had to take the trouble to be born.

"Without parents, devoid of fortune, brought up by charity, my energy had never been sustained by the sweetness of a kiss or a caress. Now, the generosity of my benefactors humiliated me once again. Although I felt superior in terms of intelligence and determination, it was necessary for me to show a hypocritical humility. The constraint that I imposed on myself became a veritable torture, in spite of the affection that surrounded me.

"Against all expectation, and although the son was condemned by the physicians, it was the mother who departed first. The testament was opened; there was nothing in it for me, but I was recommended to the Baron de Falcaz, and I knew his amity too well to fear that he would ever leave me lacking anything. I had been at the château for eight years, and my pupil was approaching his majority. I hoped that, once in possession of his wealth, he would leave its direction to me and that it would be easy for me to dispose of it as I wished.

"He did nothing of the sort. Jean de Falcaz, although generous and weak, nevertheless had the innate prudence that enables drunkards to walk with impunity on the edge of an abyss without ever falling in. I obtained from him all the money that was necessary to me, but when I showed myself more demanding, he shook his head with a little mocking laugh, and I was made to feel the shame of my futile request. However, I had intense passions: pleasures, gambling and women attracted me irresistibly, and I was perpetually borne away beyond my resources.

"In that epoch I encountered a singular creature, beautiful and utterly vicious, who took possession of my mind from the first moment. She had no money, and was traveling in quest of adventure. Her past of expedients and shame mattered little to me, however; she happened to be in my path and I took her, because she realized the type of charm and perversity that I loved most of all. Perhaps she had been lying in wait for me for a long time, having divined that I would be a docile instrument in her hands. She was quickly able to impose herself on my heart and my imagination, in order to withdraw whatever still remained there of honor and virtuous sentiment.

"Maubel had taken up residence a few leagues from Falcaz in an elegant villa, where she received joyful company. Her appetite for luxury was excessive and I plagued my master with requests for money, which he almost always refused, thinking that the pension that he gave me was more than sufficient, and not imagining what need for expenditure I had in that remote region.

"A vague rancor germinated within me and increased every time that it was necessary for me to humiliate myself before him.

Finally, the violence of my desires inspired the Machiavellian idea of using the mysterious empire that I had always had over Jean's mind to oblige him to give me, against his will, what he refused me of his own accord.

"In order to arrive at that goal, I studied books of occult science, practical instructions regarding animal magnetism, and treatises on the physiology, medicine and metaphysics of hypnotism. In his book on magic, does Monsieur du Potet not affirm that one can, by means of a powerful emission of magnetic fluid, kill a living being?[1] I was not thinking then about such a terrible usage of the power that I seemed to have over the Baron's unhealthy imagination, but I thought that it might be possible for me to suggest to him the idea of confiding his fortune to me. As my studies advanced, I was no longer in any doubt that, with the knowledge of the mysterious laws that subjugate the empire of good to the powers of evil, the result might be easily obtained.

"Any superior will produces a magnetic current, the action of which is to draw and sometimes to excite beyond measure, impressionable and nervous natures, temperaments disposed to hysteria or to hallucinations. A thousand strange forms exist around us that our vulgar senses can only perceive by means of progressive training. It is necessary to put oneself in an exceptional state that has something in common with sleep and death, to arrive by means of magnetism at a sort of lucid somnambulism. The evocations of magic can produce veritable visions.

"In the great magical agent, which is the astral light, all the imprints of things are conserved, all the images formed by radiations or reflections. It is that light which intoxicates the alienated and draws their dormant judgment in pursuit of phantoms. I was the evil genius of Jean de Falcaz, as Maubel was mine. That strange woman dictated her will to me by means of a simple

---

1 Author's reference: "Du Potet. *La Magie dévoilée ou principes de science occulte*, 1852, 1 vol." The author cited, Jules Denis, Baron du Potet (1796-1881) was one of the leading French practitioners of mesmerism and his ideas had a considerable influence on both Éliphas Lévi and Madame Blavatsky.

gaze; before her I became as weak as a child. Without her advice I would doubtless have abandoned my culpable projects, but under her diabolical influence I was no longer the master of my actions.

"Thanks to her, I became skillful in the art of magic and evocations; I exercised it for a long time in secret; then, I disposed a small room in Jean's château in which I conversed overtly with demons. There were four concave mirrors there, a sort of altar whose upper surface of white marble was surrounded by a chain of magnetic iron. On the marble, the sign of the pentagram was represented, and the skin of a white lamb was extended at my feet. In the center of the table were two copper stoves with charcoal of alder and laurel wood.

"I only penetrated into that redoubt in a white robe with countless pleats, my forehead circled by a crown of vervain held in a golden chain. In one hand I held the ritual, and in the other a naked sword. I lit the two fires with the requisite substances and I commenced the invocations.

"Jean assisted in my experiments with a domestic raised in the house, a boy who was entirely devoted to him and whose discretion was certain. He would not have been able to remain alone with me, the ternary or the unity being rigorously required for the magical rites.

"My voice swelled by degrees, the smoke rose in dense spirals, and then the flame sprang forth and caused the objects around us to vacillate fantastically. After a more or less long time, we seemed to sense the shock of an earthquake, our ears rang and we felt faint. I put branches and perfumes on the stoves, and sometimes, in the inundating light, a vague figure appeared, unnaturally large and terrifying in appearance.

"When I had the courage to do so, I recommenced the evocations, placing myself in a circle that I had traced and calling upon the spirit that I desired to see in a loud voice. After a delay of a few minutes, the depths of the mirror in front of me were brightened by a white form that was gradually designed there; a new weakness gripped me and I fell into a profound trance.

166

"The effect of those experiments was inexplicable. We were certainly no longer the same; something of the other world had passed into us. The result of the preparations, the perfumes and the cerebral effort that I made was a veritable intoxication that was bound to act powerfully on a person already impressionable and unhealthy. But those attempts were a continual danger for me, and my reason would undoubtedly have stopped there if I had not precipitated the denouement.

"Every day, Maubel became more pressing; a fortune was required for the child that was about to be born of our amour, and I must not recoil before any crime in order to satisfy her. Jean was not declining swiftly enough for our liking, so I tried to cast a spell on him, the science of evil pushing me to the ultimate limits.

"We can act by means of imagination on the imagination of others, by means of our sidereal bodies on theirs, by means of our organs on theirs, with the result that, by means of obsession, we can possess one another and we can identify with those on whom we wish to act. Bewitchment can be compared to a veritable poisoning of the astral light. It excites the will to the point of rendering it toxic, even at a distance; but it exposes the person who uses it to being killed first by his execrable massacres . . ."

"And how can the spell be cast?" I asked, interrogating Père Lazare.

"In several ways. By touching some animal with the hair or the clothing of the person one has chosen; by killing that animal with a single thrust of the magical knife, extracting the heart in order to envelop it, still palpitating, in the magical objects; and finally, by plunging into the heart, for several days, red-hot nails and pins.

"One can also nail to the ground, in the form of a cross, the footprint of the person that one wants to torment. There is bewitchment by means of a toad, by means of wax images, and by the gaze, or *jettatura*. I employed all those means, but Jean, having nothing for which to reproach himself, evaded all my maledictions, bewitchment acting in the fashion of contagious diseases that first strike those who are afraid.

"The goal of the procedures of black magic is to trouble the reason and to produce all the feverish exaltations that procure the courage for great crimes. Sacrilege, murder and theft are indicated or implied as means of realization in the works of sorcerers."

I interrupted Père Lazare again. "Yes," I said, "I've read that the sorcerers of the Middle Ages profaned tombs, composing philters and unguents with the fat and blood of cadavers. They mixed them with aconite, belladonna and poisonous mushrooms; then they cooked and simmered those frightful mixtures over fires composed of human bones and crucifixes stolen from churches, they mingled therein the powder of desiccated toads and the ash of consecrated hosts. When the infernal unguent was ready they rubbed it on their temples, hands and breast, traced the diabolical pentacle, and evoked the dead beneath their gibbets or in abandoned cemeteries. Their howls were heard from afar, and belated travelers saw legions of phantoms emerging from the earth."

"That was the magnetism of hallucination and the contagion of madness."

"But what was your goal in imitating those sad examples?"

"My goal was simple: I wanted to weaken Jean's intelligence, to madden him, to knead him to my whim, to bring him to consider me as a supernatural being, as a god! It would then have been easy for me to acquire the direction of his wealth and to dispose of it as I wished.

"Unfortunately, I was only an instrument myself. Maubel, who held me in her power, drove me to evil with all the force of her will. Every evening I ran to join her in her pretty dwelling and there we rehearsed, as in the theater. Half-naked, only veiled in diaphanous fabrics as soft as a caress, she studied with me the operation of the scenes of the terrible drama that I was playing next to Jean de Falcaz. There was no similarity of character, however, between that woman and me, except the same irresistible need for domination.

"While she held me by all the magic of her tenderness, I sought in vain to disentangle the frightful chaos of my thoughts. She used all the weapons that nature had given her skillfully, and defeated my good intentions whenever I chanced to take a step back and refused to obey her. Her eyes became languid then, and, making a bond for me by knotting her arms around my neck, she said: 'It's for our child; don't you want him to be rich and happy?' So, if I desired to cast a spell on my best friend, I was certainly bewitched by that accursed creature!

"Passionate sympathy necessarily submits the most ardent desire to the stronger will. Moral maladies are more contagious than physical maladies, and there are such unexpected infatuations that they can be compared to leprosy or cholera. One can die of a bad influence as from an unsanitary contact, and the moral corruptions that result every day from an equivocal sympathy are terrifying.

"The sorcerer who practices bewitchment poisons for the sake of poisoning, like certain heroes of fiction who, in order to avenge themselves on a rival, infect themselves with an incurable disease and transmit it to his mistress. I damned myself in order to torture more effectively, I aspired to Hell, I wounded myself mortally in order to kill more effectively.

"Under Maubel's kisses I had the sad courage, without suspecting that the mixture of my cupidity and my amorous passion had weakened my power. A desire, being an attraction, counterbalances and annuls the power of projection. Spells cast in those conditions fall back on the person who casts them, and are more salutary than harmful to the person who is their object, for they disengage him from a hateful action that destroys itself in being exalted excessively.

"Falcaz, whom I had condemned in my sacrilegious practices, seemed, by a singular irony, to acquire a firmer grip on existence. The two hectic circular stains that had marked his days until then gradually weakened; his shoulders, once so narrow, became more developed. He thanked me for having led him to study the marvels of magic. With my bad conscience, I thought he was accusing me, or that he suspected me, when his affection was manifest in everything he said.

"He listened to me, admired me, would have liked to open with me all the tombs of the ancient world, to make the dead speak, to see the monuments of the past again in all their splendor, to understand the enigmas of all sphinxes and penetrate into all sanctuaries. He would have liked to possess the true Tarot and, like the Rosicrucians and the Martinists, to use a supernatural power. 'Faith,' he said, 'is only a superstition or a folly if it does not have reason for a basis, and one can only suppose that which one does not know by analogy with what one knows. To define what one does not know is a presumptuous ignorance; to affirm positively what one does not know is a lie. Oh, how I would love to know!'

"He raised himself to summits that I could not attain; he soared in the light while I was crawling miserably in the mud of my criminal desires. His physical organization was better disposed than mine for the great revelations of the occult world. His sensitive nature found the realization of its dreams in the astral light, for certain maladies modify the nervous system and make it, without the assistance of the will, a perfect apparatus for divination.

"For me, given to follies and abominable practices, magic was nothing but a long nightmare, the monstrosities of which seemed real to me, and I was astonished not to have any purchase on the soul of Jean de Falcaz.

"I tried, in order to subjugate him to my power, the gradual employment of narcotics; I made use, by night, of a series of luminous disks that I agitated abruptly before his dazzled eyes; I simulated frightful apparitions menacing him with the worst tortures. The wind plunged into the long corridors, causing the woodwork to creak and the doors to oscillate; mysterious gleams passed through the stained windows while nocturnal birds launched their sinister plaint into the air. In that domain of terror everything served my designs; I did not have to do much to awaken the nightmares of madness.

"Black magic is really only a combination of sacrileges and murders graduated to pervert human will forever and to realize in an individual the hideous phantom of the demon. It is the religion of the Devil, the worship of darkness, the hatred of good brought to its paroxysm. It is the incarnation of death and the permanent creation of Hell.

"Jean had a relapse; with a tremulous hand I had poured him a few drops of a liquor that Maubel had prepared and which must have contained poison, for the effect it had was terrible. In two days the Baron became unrecognizable: his eyes bulging and luminous, his lips thin and blanched, and his nostrils pinched, he remained immobile for hours, without pronouncing a word. In spite of the objurgations of my mistress, I did not make any further use of the liquor and returned it to her.

"In any case, Jean now gave me all the money I wanted, without counting it, without even asking me what I wanted to do with it. I would have been content with that enviable situation, but Maubel was obstinate in her crime; it was no longer an occasional handful of gold that was required, it was the complete heritage of the Baron de Falcaz. I had, therefore, to oblige him, by all possible means, to make a testament in my favor. Alas, if his reason seemed to vacillate in every other regard, he did not abandon it in regard to the employment of his large fortune and rendering a detailed account of it.

"As in the past, he heaped me with evidence of affection, seeming to suffer when I left his room. His entire body then seemed to have a singular trepidation, an excessive nervous agitation. His hands were moist, his forehead hot.

"The physicians summoned to care for him conferred regarding his malady and could never find themselves in accord. Some claimed that he was fatigued by mental over-exertion and the excessively frequent use of energetic stimulants, and that the violent action of the nerves had vitiated the entire organism;

others only wanted to see in his condition a chronic infection of the stomach. Neurosis, intestinal irritation and pulmonary or cerebral anemia were the pretext for the most contradictory remedies.

"To the amazement of everyone, life and warmth returned to that wretched body. Mentally and physically, Jean de Falcaz emerged once again from apathy, immobility, insouciance and death. However, I required his fortune; I desired it with an insane ardor, with an inexpressible passion. I had to have it, whatever the cost.

"Any desire that is not manifest in action, Maubel told me, is a vain desire. It is action that makes force, it is action that proves human will. She was scornful of me for having hesitated for so long, and I searched for a means that would make it possible for me to attain my goal. The only one that seemed possible to me was to oblige my friend to make a testament in my favor, and then to hasten his demise by the evocation of certain cruel mysteries of magic.

"With an infinite skill, I talked to him about the fatality that sometimes scythes down the most healthy, and engaged him to make his final dispositions, thinking about the profound affection that I had always testified for him and the poverty in which he would leave me if misfortune determined that . . .

"He did not let me finish. 'I'm cured, my good Lazare,' he said to me, 'what's the point of thinking about these macabre things? You know very well that while I'm with you, you won't lack anything . . . and I have no desire to go away!'

"I didn't persist, but a muffled anger clouded my eyes; I had to make a great effort to master myself, and only succeeded in doing so with great difficulty.

"When I interrogate that tenebrous past, I have some difficulty comprehending the constant cruelty of which I gave proof. Maubel must have maddened me and blinded me to the extent of robbing me of all human sentiment.

"Alas, she still dominates me with that horrible power, for your Yvaine is the perfect incarnation of Maubel and my tomb will not find mercy before her!"

Père Lazare stopped, exhausted. I thought I perceived that he was struggling against an invisible force and that, having arrived at that painful part of his story, he was trying to escape it. Although he had been talking for an hour, his voice was as clear as it had been at the first moment—which seemed inexplicable to me, in the state that he was in.

The darkness of doubt still envelops the positive theory of magnetism completely, but its extraordinary effects are almost universally admitted. It is proven that a man, purely by the exercise of his will, can impress his fellow sufficiently to throw him into an abnormal condition, the phenomena of which are unlimited.

The influenced individual can accomplish actions completely opposed to his nature, and even create another nature, once awakened, in order to obey the orders that have been given to him during the magnetic sleep.

If, however, he only employs effortfully—and, in consequence, with little aptitude—the exterior sense organs, he nevertheless perceives, with a subtle perspicacity, and by way of a mysterious channel, the objects situated beyond the range of the physical organs. His intellectual faculties are excited in a prodigious manner, his susceptibility to hypnotic impressions increases in proportion to their frequency, at the same time as the obtained phenomena extend and are accentuated.

It was evident that Père Lazare, although apparently immobile, was struggling with a desperate energy against the astral influence of one or several beings invisible to me. An occult power was forcing him to speak: a superior intelligence free of terrestrial shackles was floating above his and terrorizing it.

What he could see was surely terrible, for his visage, at which I was only gazing now with an extreme reluctance, was literally decomposed under the empire of fear.

My nerves were vibrating and contracting; the situation was becoming painful to such a degree that, in spite of my desire to know the strange history of the man, I thought again about abandoning him to his sad end, any charitable intervention being, in any case, futile.

Having divined my thought, however, he began to weep.

"Don't go! *They* want me to confess to you . . . don't abandon me. I'll tell you everything . . . everything, although it costs me . . . Jean, Jean de Falcaz, is dead, killed by me! It's necessary that I tell you how, in the smallest detail . . .

"He continued to vegetate, with periods of decline and amelioration. After several months of incredible resistance, his face had become the color of lead, his eyes were almost entirely extinct and his thinness so remarkable that the skin was adhering completely to the bones of the face. His voice was low and indistinct, his pulse imperceptible. He conserved all his faculties, however, in a singular fashion, and a certain quantity of physical strength.

"My efforts to hypnotize him and suggest the idea of the testament in my favor were as futile as on the first day, and, while talking to me continually about magic, cabalistic mirrors, fascinations, charms, bewitchments and spells, he never lost sight of safeguarding his interests.

"There were two of us caring for him, and I would gladly have strangled the mute witness attentive to my culpable maneuvers. That was a fellow named Maxime Gérard, brought up in the house and a very faithful servant. Maxime was tall and vigorous, but, by a singular contrast, my magnetic power had always been exercised upon him with complete success. While Jean, delicate, nervous and ill, remained refractory to my fluid, the superb and solid Maxime, built like a Hercules, fell into weakness before me at the slightest projection of my magnetic will.

"For us, the magical equilibrium, the triangle of pentacles, the conjuration of the four, the flamboyant pentagram and the septenary of talismans had no more secrets. We occupied ourselves with necromancy and transmutation; we read the book of Hermes, the writing of the stars . . . I took part in the witches' sabbat and the black mass of the damned, in spite of the horror that my pupil felt for that kind of practice. However, he did not get any worse; I seemed, against my expectation, to be prolonging his existence; and what the physicians had not been able to do with their drugs, I accomplished with the science of evil and death!

"Poor Maxime served for our experiments; we put him to sleep, by turns, in spite of his pleas and his rebellions. Although he was only a domestic, we considered him as our equal; all three of us seemed united by the narrowest bonds of affection.

"I plunged completely into Manicheism and into its aberrations, reading and re-reading the books of the likes of Sprenger, De Lancre, Del Rio and Bodin, as well as all the grimoires of the ancient sorcerers. In spite of Jean's disgust, I assured him that it was necessary, in order to evoke Satan, to make bloody sacrifices. I only took one meal per day, devoid of salt, after sunset: a meal composed of black bread and blood, seasoned with broad beans and narcotic herbs. I carried out evocations in cemeteries, illuminated by candles of human fat. I perfumed myself with aloes, storax, ambergris and camphor, and I burned those various ingredients mixed with the blood of moles and bats. My folly was boundless!

"Maxime Gérard lent himself to everything, without seeking to understand, as soon as his submission was demanded by the master he adored.

"Jean and Maxime were the victims that I was soon to immolate to my cupidity and hatred, for Maubel, the vampire, was within me.

"The poison of my maleficia extended over everything; I no longer knew what spells to invent, so prodigal had my imagination been thus far. Having cast my gaze on the Baron's favorite dog, I cut his throat in secret, and extracted his heart, still palpitating, in order to make use of it in my experiments.

"Jean wept for his faithful companion, but forgave me once again.

"Meanwhile, when everyone was asleep in the château in silence and dread, I led a joyful life with Maubel. Her bedroom, hung with silky fabrics, was bright and warm; dishes of all kinds and choice wines awaited my pleasure. As I had fasted all day, I threw myself on those provisions avidly, while my mistress talked to me about her plans. The term of her pregnancy was approaching, and we were in haste to quit the region. We needed money, and I no longer had the courage to play my futile comedy.

"One evening, Maubel, looking at me intently, asked: 'Doesn't he always carry his keys on his person?'

"'Yes.'

"'Well, it's necessary to take them. You know the secret of the strong-box. Go, and hurry; we'll leave tomorrow.'"

Père Lazare interrupted himself.

"Don't you find it strange," he asked, after a few minutes of reflection, "that this Yvaine, that detestable creature that you've brought, also tried to take my keys? The more I think about it, the more it seems to me that Maubel and Yvaine are one and the same conception of the demon. Do they not have the same features and the same voice? One led me to the crime; the other brought me the punishment!"

"Come on, Père Lazare, calm down. Yvaine is a poor girl who was drawn into evil. Her heart has remained good, I'm certain of it. All is not lost for her."

"Be careful!" cried the madman, trying to sit up. "That woman is accursed. Throw her out like a rabid bitch! You don't know her!"

"Yes, she was with Baron de Ziler . . ."

"Before then, where did she come from? What did she do?"

"I don't know. There are so many unfortunate women without resources in the world. If, by chance, one takes an interest in them, it's necessary never to ask them their past. It isn't them who made it, but fatality."

Père Lazare uttered a sigh.

"Go fetch her for me."

"No, no, she's suffering. You can see her tomorrow."

"Tomorrow I'll be dead."

The old man remained silent for a moment, and then his lips trembled.

"It's necessary that I finish. *They* want it. Listen to me, I'll be finished soon.

"It wasn't an easy matter to take Jean de Falcaz's keys. In any case, Maxime scarcely quit him, and I searched for some time before finding a realizable plan. This is how I put it into execution . . .

"It was nine o'clock in the evening—a mild and balmy September evening. The voices of crickets were chirping on the lawns and the stars were gazing at us with their golden eyes through the wide-open windows.

"I had drawn Jean into a library a long way from his bedroom and I was talking to him about a few rare volumes that I thought I had seen there the day before. Maxime turned his back on us, actively searching the shelves, overloaded with books, for those I indicated to him.

"I had made the Baron take a powerful narcotic and I knew that it wouldn't take long to act. In fact, after a few minutes, his eyelids fluttered, he beat the air with his arms, and then let himself fall into an armchair, uttering a sigh.

"The astonished valet turned round, but before he had understood, charging my gaze with magnetic fluid, projecting my will outside myself with an irresistible force, I ordered him to go to sleep, to obey me faithfully and, if necessary, to assist me in what I was about to do. In a matter of moments I had mastered him absolutely. He stood immobile by my side, devoid of a gaze and a voice.

"Immediately, I took from Jean's pocket the key that never left him and ran into his bedroom in order to take his valuables therefrom.

"Hesitating over the word that it was necessary to form in order to open the door of the safe, I searched for a long time, cursing myself, almost crying out with impotent rage. I tried to force the lock, and employed everything that came to hand: a spade, tongs, a saber and a dagger detached from a panoply. The strong-box still resisted, and I redoubled my efforts, fearing that the Baron might wake up.

"Finally, after an hour of work, I was able to find the secret of the lock, and I lowered my hand over the gold that I saw shining there, overturning the papers, scattering at random everything that seemed to me to be useless.

"In the middle of that operation it seemed to me that I heard a slight sound behind me, and I saw Jean's haggard face appear in a mirror that was facing me.

"I turned round, paler than him, and for a moment we looked at one another without exchanging a word. He was trembling from head to toe; I felt a mad anger grip me gradually: a blind, homicidal anger.

"Finally, he took a step forward and, lifting his arm as if to strike me, he cried: 'Wretch!'

"He had no sooner uttered that cry than I leapt at his throat and tipped him over on the parquet. 'Coward! Coward! Thief! Murderer!' he howled, as he struggled.

"Then I saw red, and, seizing the weapon that I had used in order to open the strong-box, which was glinting at my feet. I set about sawing his neck with such fury that the head was almost detached from the trunk.

"A warm flood gushed into my face, and ran over the parquet, forming a red pool that was incessantly enlarged, elongated and thickened, flowing in great surges into the corners of the room.

"At that moment, all the horror of my crime suddenly appeared to me; I extinguished the candles in order no longer to see anything, and remained lost in my fears, trying, however, to reflect on what it was possible to do to save myself.

"My situation was terrible, the crime evident, impossible to deny or to hide, even until the next day. There was certainly flight, but where could I flee? Would not the law end up finding me?

"I don't know how long those horrible reflections lasted. I had lost an exact notion of time; a mysterious force retained me there, my feet in the blood and my hands and feet also red.

"At length, my eyes became accustomed to the obscurity. I could see Jean's body distinctly now, in front of me in its bloody mire. Soon, the walls were crimson too; everything was flamboyant in a fiery light; it seemed to me that the parquet was giving way beneath me and that I could hear the shrill laughter of lamias, stryges and empusas fighting over the cadaver."

Père Lazare stopped again, and I sensed the frisson of the little death running along my vertebrae.

Nothing was more fantastically terrible than that supreme confession falling from that lipless mouth, emerging from that torn throat, all of whose vessels were laid bare. And while he was speaking, no movement agitated his body, black droplets oozed from his wounds, lugubriously illuminated by the smoky flame of a candle.

I had nausea and vertigo; it seemed to me that I was falling into an abyss in a dream. I closed my eyes, my eyelids sticking as if in a spasm. And yet, I was in haste to know all the infamy of that man; he fascinated me, holding me fast by the horrible eloquence of his crimes.

His involuntary confession, hastened by the throes of death, in that hovel filled with a pestilential smoke, had something irresistibly poignant about it. I thought for a moment, in the disarray of my reason, that death had seized both of us, that I was traveling the domain of specters, a specter myself, a wandering and terrified soul.

I was, in fact, the victim of a hallucination, for I now saw two indistinct forms, transparent and slightly luminous, leaning over Père Lazare. They were standing to either side of his bed, oscillating slightly from right to left, like vapors agitated by the wind.

I tried to persuade myself that it was the smoke that was becoming more compact, but the head of the moribund, which had remained motionless until them, turned toward them and his teeth chattered.

"Yes, yes," he murmured, "I'll finish . . . Jean . . . Maxime . . . Oh, I remember: I had killed my companion of childhood, my friend, my benefactor; I had committed the most execrable crime, and yet I didn't repent! My sole preoccupation was to get out of trouble, to escape the punishment of murderers.

"As I was still meditating, a light glided over the wall, and Maxime came into the room quietly, doubtless thinking that his master was asleep.

"Immediately, my decision was made. I felt relieved of a great weight. The thief and murderer would be Maxime! Maxime, the faithful servant who would have given his life to save his master!

"That thought inundated me with such joy that I uttered a sonorous burst of laughter. 'Maxime, my good Maxime, come here,' I said. 'I want you to see something that you've certainly never seen.'

"The unfortunate fellow took a step forward, and, perceiving Jean's decapitated body, uttered a howl that had nothing human about it; then, before the scattered papers and the open safe, suddenly understanding the drama that had unfolded, he bounded toward me. But I lowered his fist as easily as one lowers the wrist of a little child, and, in spite of his tears and supplications, I plunged him into magnetic sleep.

"I was saved! That scene had scarcely lasted five minutes. 'Maxime, my dear Maxime,' I continued, 'you know very well that I'm innocent of your master's murder. I loved him too much to wish him the slightest harm, so my grief is boundless. Oh, wretch, what have you done?'

"The valet fell to his knees and put his hands together. 'Yes, wretched thief, murderer!' I cried. 'How could you forget all the benefits that Jean never ceased to heap upon you? How was the folly of gold able to make you fall into such an abyss of infamy?'

"Maxime was writhing at my feet. 'Mercy! Mercy!' he groaned. 'My good master, my gentle master, my adored master! Oh, kill me, crush me! I've merited the worst tortures, I've cursed God and man!'

"'Perhaps God will pardon you, but it's necessary that human justice take its course. Your head belongs to the executioner; you can't escape him.'

"Maxime had thrown himself on Jean's cadaver and was pressing it recklessly to his heart. 'Will you swear to obey me?' I asked him, in a terrible voice.

"'Command, I'm in your power.'

"In the fear that the emotion might be too strong and that he might wake up, I hastened to suggest his conduct. 'Well, I'm going to denounce you; you'll be arrested, you'll confess your crime, and you'll give all the details. You needed money, you hear, it was necessary for your pleasures and your vices, for your mistress and for gambling. Jean didn't give you enough, so you resolved to put him to sleep by means of a narcotic, take his keys, open his strong-box and steal everything it contained. Unfortunately, you searched for a long time for the secret of the lock, and when you finally discovered it more than an hour had passed in fruitless attempts. Your master, woken by the noise, appeared on the threshold and you suddenly saw him in the mirror that was facing you; then you turned round, panic-stricken, and, seizing the weapon you had used to spring the lock, you pounced upon him and cut his throat, persisting in that butchery until the head, almost entirely detached, fell on to the shoulder. You've understood me fully, my dear Maxime? Repeat what I've just told you . . .'

"Maxime repeated, word for word, that account of my own crime, and I woke him from his magnetic sleep, having convinced him that he wouldn't forget a single sentence of his lesson.

"What I had anticipated happened; the poor fellow, under the power of suggestion, recounted the crime as it had happened, without omitting a single detail, and accusing himself energetically. He was tried, convicted and guillotined.

"Not for a moment did suspicion fall upon me, for in that same strong-box that I had opened so unnecessarily, a testament was found written by Jean de Falcaz a few months before, in which he instituted me as his universal heir.

"I therefore found myself rich, rich beyond my hopes, with two murders on my conscience, of which the memory and the remorse were only to pursue me a long time afterwards.

"Maubel, who had been the instigator of the crime, became odious to me. The singular intoxication in which I had lived since the advent of that woman had dissipated. I saw my infamy clearly then, and I held her responsible for it. She had led me to the abyss, guided herself by an occult power; her role was concluded. I informed her of the abrupt change in my sentiments in her regard and begged her to leave the country as soon as possible. It seemed to me that I would only be veritably happy far away from her. It was her that had murdered my poor friend; I had only been an instrument in her hands.

"From one deduction to another I succeeded thus in exonerating myself, in deluding myself with regard to my sacrilegious past. I also told myself that Jean de Falcaz only having distant heirs like that Ziler—who, in any case, was not in need—I was not cheating anyone. With a little skill and hypocrisy, I could conquer the esteem of honest men, perhaps forget . . . only my companion was an obstacle to my rehabilitation.

"I chased her away pitilessly, knowing full well that she would not talk, her life having been more criminal than mine. She clung on to me with a desperate energy, wept, begged, talked to me about my child, but that maternal plaint, which ought to have moved me, filled my heart with indignation and rage. What would the fruit of that monster be? A being made in her image, a viper who would rear up against me and poison my existence!

"I barricaded myself in the little house where we had been so happy and did not budge while I saw her prowling around the vicinity. She cried and blasphemed for two days, and then disappeared, and I never saw her again."

"But that child, that child that was to be born . . . ?"

"That child," said the wretch, "is Yvaine! Yvaine, who possessed me like her mother, and came to finish the accursed work! Without her, I would have been able to forget . . ."

"What reason do you have for supposing that Yvaine is your daughter?"

"Did she not offer herself to me in order to steal from me at her ease? For a long time, I refused, frightened by the resemblance that existed between her and my former mistress. Then, one evening, in a hallucination of memory, in an invincible intoxication of the senses, I yielded . . . Then, as she was getting dressed, I saw . . . I saw, beneath her breast, the bloody sign that her mother bore, the indelible stain that I had so often covered, once, with my kisses! That strange and pretty mark that no other woman possesses! Yvaine and Maubel are larvae, vampires, who have drunk the blood of my veins and led me to crime!"

Père Lazare was suffocating, and I did not know myself whether everything that I had heard was not a frightful nightmare. Yvaine! Yvaine, my tender Yvaine, the child of that man!

He went on, in a voice that had nothing human about it: "From the day when I encountered the perfect reincarnation of my unworthy mistress, I understood that I was doomed and I abandoned myself to my destiny. If I've told you this story, it's because Maxime and Jean ordered me to do it. Their magnetic force has vanquished mine. There are two of them, to torture me night and day. Their vengeance hovers over me, they pierce my heart with thrusts of pins. Can't you see them by my bedside . . . ?"

Oh, yes, I could see them! My hair was standing up on my head, and the most intense terror held me immobile.

The two white, transparent forms to either side of the bed were accentuated. Leaning over the moribund, they were still swaying with a monotonous activity, sometimes brushing me with a light breath, which penetrated me to the marrow.

"I was rich," Père Lazare went on, "and I enjoyed my fortune until the moment that I encountered that Yvaine. Then my torture commenced: in the midst of noisy orgies, at gaming tables and in the arms of young women, I suddenly felt the influence of the mysterious presence of my victims. They palpitated around me, invisible for everyone, except for my remorse. Under the pressure of a frightful terror, I saw, then, the heads of diners oscillating on the bodies and falling on to the table; my mistresses, extending their lips to me, seemed to be offering themselves to death, and I suddenly perceived that their throat was opened to the carotid, which tore, sending a jet of warm blood into my face.

"I could not, moreover, direct my gaze at another human being without being subject to the same hallucination. Everywhere that I bore my distress, the horrible nightmare was reproduced. In a month, my hair turned white, my shoulders slumped and I had the appearance of an old man.

"A priest whom I consulted, without going into the detail of my crimes, advised me to give my wealth to the poor, to accomplish pious pilgrimages, to burn candles and have masses said. Then I became Père Lazare, the providence of the poor, the respectable and venerable man that you knew! I won the admiration of my quarter, gave to all works of charity, throwing money into the streets to all the wretches in the gutter.

"Every day, on the damp bench of this garden, my eyes gazing into infinity, I thought I was seeing again the execution of Maxime, and when the poor fellow's head fell, I felt warm blood splash my face. My nights, above all, were terrifying; they belonged to Jean, he did not grant me the mercy of a gasp or a convulsion, and just as I had killed him, in a moment of culpable folly, I killed him again, furiously enlarging the wound, until the head was completely detached from the trunk.

"Every night, under the pressure of a rage and a despair for which human language has no expression, I accomplished my crime, and every night I believed that I would die in the excess of my torments.

"Soon, my fortune diminished, shredded by continual gifts and alms. I rose, floor by floor as far as the wretched attic where I'm dying at this moment.

184

"I often thought of denouncing myself in order to escape that vengeance from beyond the tomb, but a leaden seal nailed my lips shut, a hand of ice posed on my heart and I remained trembling and indecisive. Although breathing, acting and suffering, I scarcely belonged to the earth. Since the execrable daughter of my folly offered herself to that monstrous coupling, the sum of my crimes has surpassed measure, and the punishment has come. Jean and Maxime have taken possession of my reason, have populated my mind with unspeakable terrors.

"I've tried to escape their cruel suggestion by suicide, but I've only succeeded in aggravating my woes without attaining the desired goal. I can't die! I can't die! Oh, that blood! Those severed heads! Those teeth, biting me! For pity's sake, you who know everything, finish me! Save me! Kill me! Death! Death!"

The poor wretch was writhing now, convulsed, plunging his fingers into his wounds, enlarging them and raking them as if with claws.

The sight was so hideous—hideous beyond all conception—that I got up to flee. A strange sound was produced, however, that I sought to explain. It was a sort of sharp ripping sound, like the sound a saw makes in biting into wood. That noise was coming from the bed, and mingling with the inarticulate sounds that the dying man was uttering. At the same time, the vengeful shades, the phantoms of Maxime and Jean, which I could see distinctly, leaned over further and further. Soon, the strange vapors met, and were confounded, and I could only see Père Lazare through a fog, as if a cloud had settled over him.

He remained motionless, his respiration became loud and atrocious; then, suddenly, it ceased, and I could no longer hear anything but a sort of gurgling similar to that produced by water escaping through a plug-hole.

The specters had disappeared, and the body was outlined rigidly, the eyes wide-open.

I dared not lean over that breast in order to examine it for a last breath, but I picked up the candle and took a little mirror out of my pocket in order to approach it to Père Lazare's lips. My hand was trembling so much that I bumped into the inert head; then that head—inexpressible horror!—rolled on the pillow and fell heavily at my feet. Maxime and Jean were avenged.

✷

"You don't know," Yvaine said to me, as soon as I opened my eyes, "that Père Lazare died last night."

"Yes, yes, I know."

"How do you know, since you've only just woken up?"

"But I was with him, he told me everything."

"You're mad! You haven't budged, and haven't quit your bed."

"Then you . . . ?"

"It's the concierge who came to tell me that the poor old man has been murdered."

"Murdered?"

"Undoubtedly. The murderers attacked him furiously; his head was completely detached from the body. It's believed that they set fire to the bed then, trying to dissimulate the crime—but what is strange is that nobody saw or heard anything! Theft was the motive for the murder, for it appears that Lazare had a great deal of money in his mattress."

I sat up, uttering a cry.

"I was dreaming! I was dreaming! What a frightful dream!"

Yvaine looked at me with her mysterious smile.

"Yes, certainly, you were dreaming."

I took my mistress in my arms and, abruptly, I parted the lace of her chemise. Then the red mark on her breast appeared to me, seemingly radiant in the whiteness of her flesh . . .

SAPHO

MELCY, in a long robe of orange brocade split down the side, allowing the sight of a turtle-gray leotard and riding boots, whips her wild beasts, scolds them and cajoles them by turns—wild herself, with her thick red mane and the metallic gleam of her eyes. In the efforts that she makes, her shoulders glitter with droplets piercing the velveteen, and when she raises her arms, the golden tufts of her armpits shine with tender gleams under the flamboyance of her yellow corsage.

Sapho, the black panther with the emerald eyes and the long, supple and sinewy body comes to lick her fingers and lie down at her feet.

Sapho is splendid in her languid and voluptuous pose. No patch stars her pelt of darkness; she is as mysterious and disquieting as the night.

Momentarily, Melcy embraces her, places her own head against hers, and, putting her mouth to the contracted muzzle, seems to forget herself in a profound kiss. The panther closes her eyes, tilts her head back, utters a feline purr, and rubs herself against the flesh of the warm and perfumed woman. And they are truly two amorous beasts, as perverse as one another, claws retracted into velvet gloves, gazes lost in the infinity of a dream.

Then, a crack of the whip attains the wild beast, straightens her up, howling and terrible, her maw agape, all her fangs showing, in the regret of the interrupted caress and rancor at the deceptive pleasure.

The woman laughs scornfully, and the humiliated beast gathers herself, ready to fall on her prey and grip her in an unforgiving embrace . . .

The two bodies are about to roll on the ground, to embrace one another, to bite one another in the midst of gasps and roars. A few females screams are heard . . . and a second crack of the whip, a fascinating gaze, a brief order, and Sapho, submissive, comes to crawl at the feet of her mistress, imploring her for a new tender game.

People applaud, with vague discontentment at an overly facile victory: the unconscious desire for murder and bloodshed, the troubled cruelty that haunts the heart of every human being.

There is the ordinary public of menageries: the mixed public composed of socialites, known pleasure-seekers, housemaids and laborers in their work clothes. The monkeys are agitating in their cages, sticking out the crooked hands of old women, seemingly insulting and imploring at the same time, in faint exasperation. Philosophical bears sway gravely, and ironic parrots drop nut-shells on the feathered hats of the female spectators.

In the front row, a tall, pale young man with prominent cheekbones under blond side-whiskers follows all the move-ments of the tamer with the keenest interest, and the panther, who perceives that, roars at him, while standing up furiously against the bars.

"Hop! Hop!"

Melcy has fired two revolver shots at Sapho's ears, and, hold-ing out lit carcel lamps, excites her with her voice savagely. The animal jumps through a blazing hoop, bounds and rebounds, her pelt dolorous, the fur singed, seeming a fantastic beast herself, a monstrous chimera of flame.

The performance is concluded. Melcy bows, shivering, and makes a sign to the pale young man to come and meet her.

Behind the cages, in a kind of corridor hung with green canvas, the tamer is now smiling at the stranger, and questions him:

"You love me? Yes, you love me, since Sapho is jealous and be-coming more malevolent every day. For a month you've been at every performance, and the other evening I was nearly devoured. Are you rich?"

The stranger makes an affirmative sign, and Melcy draws him toward her; lascivious and seductive—as with the panther—she places her painted lips on his.

"Take me away then. I'm afraid of Sapho!"

An indefinable smile distends the visitor's side-whiskers. He does not respond. Melcy, offering an ardent prayer with her entire being, repeats: "Take me away."

"No."

"You don't want to?"

"No."

"We could go far away. I'd like that so much!"

With a strong British accent, he says: "Quit the menagerie . . . never!"

"Why not?"

"I've made a bet that Sapho will eat you!"

"So?" asks Melcy, in an indescribable stupor.

"I'm waiting!"

RED LUST

THE MENAGERIE, empty of spectators, is asleep in a strong mist of respiration and the bitter odor of pelts. The sand, freshly raked, forms slight whirlwinds around crates in which the large reptiles marbled with ocher and cinnabar are torpid. It is the hour when the wild beasts half-veiling their shining eyes, lie down nostalgically, their claws retracted into velvet gloves. One senses, however, that they are armed for defense, ready to bound at the slightest alert, and even in sleep, their fangs glisten menacingly behind the turned-back chops.

After the evening meal, the last performance will take place, the most important one, which will join to the ordinary exhibitions the emotion of the struggle, the dance of the lions in the central cage, where the tamer Stephano will deploy the whip and the revolver, making the terrible beasts pirouette like circus clowns, and redden their bellies with the fire of burning hoops.

Myrta, the black panther, always in revolt, roars dully in anticipation of the imminent visit; her paws clench feverishly and her fur bristles in voluptuous frissons; she is believed to be amorous and jealous. Twice, already, she has thrown herself upon Stephano and, standing up, dominating him with her massive head, she has rubbed her muzzle against his cheek. But the tamer has mastered her with a glance, conquered her with a caress, and, with his boot on her spine, has maintained her there, panting, under the enthusiastic bravos of the public.

It is ten o'clock. The assistants turn up the gas, bring baskets full of meat for the carnivores' meal, distribute fruit to the monkeys and wake up the parrots, living flowers brightening the monotony of the dark pelts, and erecting in the corolla of their open wings the pistils of their irritate crests.

But a young woman has come in, escorted by an ageless and sexless governess, to exchange a few words with the lads, who know her, accustomed to seeing her every evening, since the installation of the menagerie in the suburban quarter. She is Antonia, the daughter of a rich businessman from Madrid, who comes furtively to intoxicate herself on the odor of circuses, in the unacknowledged and almost morbid desire to caress her soul with a little suffering, to see blood flowing and bones breaking.

She experiences the murderous passion that leads señoras to the *plaza del toros* and puts in the puerile heart of virgins the ferocity of inquisitors and torturers. She is, however, as frail as a reed, her voice is soft and her onyx eyes, speckled with gold, crackle in the paschal wax of her skin; she seems a mystical being of grace and bounty. But she comes from the land of the matadors, where amour seems better after the red vision of an arena strewn with spilled entrails, where the troubling perfume of woman mingles with the bitter reek of abattoirs.

For the moment, her *espado* is named Stephano, the superb tamer who juggles with the great lions, and appeases the jealous fury of the black panther with caresses and seductive words.

Antonia has stopped, pensively, before the beast's cage, and her golden gaze, aimed at Myrta's fiery gaze, interrogates it for a long time.

The panther has risen to her feet, her muzzle puckered over sharp teeth, her tail thrashing; then, stretching herself along the bars, her entire body vibrating with a lascivious spasm, she yawns nervously, and is convulsed by a hoarse gasp. The regret of the desert and free amours grips her in the solitude of her prison; her flanks agitate, and her claws scratch the ground in a desire for caresses or murder.

Antonia has slipped her umbrella between the bars, and the beast, twisting the whalebone like flexible stems, is gnawing the ivory sleeve, having passed her head through the zinzoline silk, which makes for her the collar of a female clown.

"Oh, look Gertrude, see how crazy Myrta is today!"

"It's necessary not to excite her," advises the governess. "Something bad might happen to Stephano."

A strange gleam passes through the young woman's eyes. She does not reply, but her heel taps the ground impatiently and her nostrils dilate in an ardent aspiration.

Gradually, the public arrive, the habitual public of fairground marquees, composed of bourgeois, workers, idlers, good-time girls with scented hair, little vagabonds and suspect louts.

The obstinately swaying bears, the hyenas, the foxes and the torpid boas in their crates, and the consumptive or mocking monkeys captivate attention at first; then everyone groups around the central cage for the exercises of Stephano, the handsome tamer whose breast is adorned with flattering plaques and who flexes his harmonious muscles in a bright leotard.

In the front row, Antonia remains motionless, her lips dry, her hands burning. She does not know exactly what she expects, but she senses that something is going to happen, because she wants it to, and because her criminal anguish has communicated itself to the black panther, whose fur is glistening like a velvet robe as her flesh quivers.

Here comes Stephano. Proud, nervous and agile, his whip held high, he has entered the cage and, before the fixed gaze of the women, has made the lions twirl, which come to lie down at his feet, licking his hands, superb and gentle. The pistol shots, the burn of the fiery hoops and the effort of the singular tricks have not been able to irritate them. They crawl in a servile fashion, and the royal fleece of their spine makes a soft seat for the tamer.

Hands applaud furiously, while Antonia's pretty mouth sketches a disdainful moue. Stephano, charmed and surprised by the young woman's assiduity at his exercises, contemplates her with a vainglorious assurance.

She smiles, and her imperious gaze fixes upon that of the tamer, descending into him as if into a mysterious well, and causes all the fibers of his being to vibrate. He goes pale, and the anxious expression of his features reveals that he is conscious of Antonia's tragic desire. His energy is sunk in that of the unknown enemy; he loses the personality of his free and thinking self.

"Stephano," she says, "the black panther is waiting. Only her conquest is worthy of you."

Myrta is now in front of the tamer. She seems to be plunged in a rigid immobility, and, like a cat dazzled by the light, she extinguishes beneath her weary eyelids the double star of her pupils. The young woman standing up in front of the cage is a human panther far more implacable than the captive beast. She utters a scornful laugh at the hesitation of the man, whose instinct is perhaps warning him, and murmurs through clenched teeth: "Coward!"

Stephano puts his arms round the beast for the habitual games; but she resists, roaring, embraces him in her turn and knocks him down. The two bodies roll, bound and twist, in the midst of cries and gasps. Women faint, while the employees, armed with pitchforks and pikes, hasten to the bars, mastering the panther, whose muzzle is red with blood.

Antonia, her eyes capsized with ecstasy, has detached the triple row of pearls that adorns her gracious neck, and she hands it to the vanquished man.

"Thank you," she says, in the slightly guttural voice of a Madrileno virgin. "That was almost as good as the *plaza del toros*!"

THE DREAM OF MYSES

I

IT was the dwelling of Myses in Thebes. The embalmer priest had brought the cadaver of Queen Ahmosis in order to adorn it in accordance with his heart, for he was in love.[1]

The dead, perfectly beautiful, were at risk with regard to habitual Taricheutes, who were sometimes tempted to violate them, so Myses had removed the charming body of his beloved, jealously.

The substitution of an important person was a grave matter, which could be severely punished in the sacerdotal class. That fraud, however, was frequently practiced, thanks to the mystery that surrounded the practices of embalming.

The dead only being shown to their families covered in a mask and enveloped in bandages, it was easy to make them disappear, and the bodies of slaves sometimes occupied princely sarcophagi. No one was authorized to remove the faces of gold or ivory that covered the veritable features, or to unwrap the bandages of the arms and legs, so it sometimes happened that an important dignitary swathed in coarse, crudely stitched fabric, after a more or less prolonged sojourn in natron, came to take his place in the public crypts. The corpses of young women violated by the

---

1 There are now reckoned to have been two important Egyptian queens conventionally given variants of this name: Ahmose-Nefertari, the first queen of the Eighteenth dynasty and wife of the pharaoh Ahmose I, and the principal wife of the third pharaoh of the same dynasty, Thutmose I. We are subsequently told, however, that this one's husband is named "Rhamses" [more commonly rendered Ramses in English, or Rameses] which was a name employed by numerous Nineteenth dynasty pharaohs of the New Kingdom, some two to three hundred years later, so the character is entirely fictitious.

embalmers were delivered to the sacred crocodiles.

Myses had, therefore, taken away the queen's cadaver, substituting for it the remains of a courtesan, similarly of great beauty.

Ahmosis, covered by a thick veil, reposed next to the priest, who, kneeling respectfully, dared not lay a profanatory hand upon her as yet.

"O adorable sovereign," he said, "you who were the joy and the pride of Egypt, goddess with the victorious smile and the long eyes of onyx and nacre, sister of the ibis, the sphinx, the golden lotus and the vermilion rose, pardon the humblest of your servants!

"I would like to give you my life, to conquer for you the glory and splendor of the creator star that warms the world and is reborn more beautiful every day over the earth and the immense sea!"

Slowly, he uncovered the body of the queen, which was still supple, and contemplated it with delight.

The pure, symmetrical features had not been ravaged by death, and the hair, cut above the shoulders in the Egyptian fashion, put a sort of aureole of light plumage around the child-like face. The small teeth were shining like grains of rice between lips coated with tenacious, marvelously scarlet make-up, and the amber, almost luminous skin seemed to be traversed by an interior light.

Myses put his lips upon the slender arm, still rounded in the form of a caress. He traveled all the way to the round and polished shoulder, intoxicated by the perfume emitted by the flesh, rubbed with aromatics, feeling faint with a divine disturbance.

Lying on the priest's wooden bed with the head of a lion, Ahmosis seemed to be smiling, pleased by that supreme homage.

"Wake up!" he sighed. "Let Isis now respond mysteriously to my prayer . . . doubtless she will tame death and render her to my tenderness. Wake up, O my royal lover, and chase away all suffering!

"When you sat on the terrace of your palace, all of nature seemed to collect itself in order to celebrate you and caress your splendor. The breeze brought you the sweetest perfumes, the Nile glided its emerald waves more voluptuously, and the great sphinx gazed at you with admiration!

"Wake up, my beloved!"

But Ahmosis remained motionless beneath the priest's kisses. Her long eyelids hid the onyx of her pupils, her fixed smile had the same mysterious and melancholy charm.

She inspired secret desires, a lascivious dread, a delicious emotion; she was a great flower, dried in balms, a calyx of gold and silk, artificial, sumptuous and disquieting.

II

Amorously, Myses proceeded with the embalming of the queen.

In order to touch the sacred remains, he had put on the symbolic costume of the Paraschites. His head, coiffed with that of a jackal, the emblem of Anubis, the guardian of the interior hemisphere, was completely shaven, and he wore a scarlet schenti fixed to his hip by a golden belt.

In the meantime, members of the royal family were praying in the Mammisium of the temple, evoking the soul of the dead woman and begging her to accept the gifts and prayers of those who had been dear to her, and to enter into communication with the omnipotent Spirit, whose name—Osiris—it is not permitted to pronounce.

Sacred animals had been sacrificed and piously conserved in order to keep the sovereign company, for embalming was not only employed for the remains of human beings; it was also applied to cats, crocodiles, snakes, etc.

Beneath the Egypt irrigated by the Nile there is a subterranean Egypt composed of innumerable mummies accumulated there by the singular piety of a people. Monkeys, jackals and dogs sleep in thousands alongside kings, and the sepulchral grottoes of the double chain that in prolonged from the pyramids of Giza to beyond Philae are filled with cadavers.

At the gates of the Libyan chain there is a mysterious city whose pathways are bordered by urns, caskets and vases containing myriads of birds, with their eggs, and, above all, cats with enamel eyes and phosphorescent fur, and snakes with gilded coils painted in ocher and cinnabar. The vast plain that departs from the foot of the Great Pyramid and extends to the north, the west and the south, is occupied by the catacombs of ancient Egypt, and everywhere, death rubs shoulders with life, the grandiose dream of the past mingling with the spring-like promises of the future.

Passionately, Myses adorned his divine mistress for the eternal slumber. He poured perfumes and balms over her, avoiding wrapping her in the habitual bandages because he had found, in order to keep her close to him, a special preparation that ought to conserve the flesh in all the flower of its splendid youth.

Ahmosis was sheathed in a silver brocade robe patterned with large hieratic flowers. Her hair, lightly curled, strewn with pearls, was raised up over a headband of precious stones, ornamented by the sacred Uraeus; a triple row of lapis lazuli, enamels and cornelians covered her bosom, and an immense gold scarab was clasped on her left breast.

When she was ready, in accordance with his heart's desire, Myses placed the queen in the customary gilded box, ornamented with symbolic figures, which mummies occupy. The lid, only fixed with the aid of a silk cord, could be removed without difficulty. It bore fragments of the *Book of the Dead* and scenes of adoration in the fields of the Amenti, and hieroglyphic inscriptions ran over all the faces.

Myses disposed the coffin of the adored woman next to his bed, in order to be able to make his devotions to her at any hour of the day or night.

The chamber was full of objects that she had loved during

her life: vases of translucent spath enriched with an aquamarine lotus flower, the psalterion or flute of Osiris, a harp with thirteen strings ornamented with the head of a sphinx, a silver mirror, combs of Oriental onyx, turquoise and tortoiseshell, a casket of porphyry and enameled clay, and a scepter with the heads of a hawk, a lion and a baboon.

In the queen's coffin there were also her minuscule flasks of enamel, her cassolettes, her fetishes, her ivory and jade dolls, and, everywhere, fresh blooms of the persea tree: a tree sacred to Isis whose fruits have the form of a heart and its leaves that of a tongue; the tree of all wisdom and all science.

That was because death, in the belief of the servant of the gods, was not at all redoubtable. The funeral retreat of Ahmosis was as cheerful, and as full of futile and familiar ornaments, as her former chamber in her palace.

In the light ewers and the sculpted boxes, amid the perfumes, the balms, the corollas of election and the statuettes of the gods, the double, the faithful, vibrant and passionate astral form of the voluptuous dead woman, would dwell. Her errant phantom would savor amour, and all the intoxications of joyful life, in the calm of that abode.

When the royal mummy was enclosed in its precious sarcophagus, Myses, quite certain that nothing would henceforth trouble his mystical amour, immersed himself in profound prayer.

III

For days, the embalmer priest lived his ecstatic dream in that fashion; then peace settled in his soul and he resumed his habitual occupations.

The defunct friend who never quit him presided from the depths of her golden box, over his labors, his experiments and his invocations of the gods of bounty and forgiveness. That alone could assure him, at present, of the quietude of his being.

Sometimes, he lifted the top of the sarcophagus, and contemplated the royal mummy, scintillating in her robe, florid with lilies and constellated with precious stones. The visage smiled, immutably serene, the eyes filtered amorous gazes through their half-closed eyelids, and Myses prostrated himself before her with delight.

"O sweet fiction," he sighed, "ineffable, ardent and pure dream, what singular trouble is filling my heart? What strange intoxication is augmenting my melancholy? I have never known an emotion so profound! Is it the incense of the voluptuous couch on which you repose, beauty among the most beautiful? Is it the warm breath of the Nile bringing me the odor of jasmines and roses? Is it the silence of this dwelling in which the enchanted corollas of vervain are drying out, with the magical herbs that procure sleep? I don't know, but I feel that I'm dying delectably!"

He ran his feverish hands over the icy body of the queen, pursuing his insensate dream.

"Oh," he said, again, "you cannot die. I seem to see you, all vibrant with amour, on the cushions of your nuptial couch. No veil hides your beauty; you resemble a golden lotus, and nothing in the world can render the charm of your smile. Speak to me, Ahmosis! I love you! I adore you! I would like to feel the caress of your mouth on my lips, in order to melt delectably in your kiss!"

Around the mystical lover, everything was peace and poetry. His dwelling, situated almost outside Thebes, at the limit of the outlying districts, was lost in a nest of verdure. Palm trees extended their leafy fans over the walls; acacias, mimosas and Pharaonic fig trees formed shady arbors propitious to long meditations and fervent prayers.

In the distance, the tips of obelisks, the summits of pylons and immense palaces were outlined beneath the circling flight of vultures.

199

Gusts of harmony came from nearby temples where the priests were celebrating the ceremony of the evening. The music had a strange and mysterious charm; it seemed to float over Myses' garden with the embalmed soul of flowers. Sometimes, a slower note resonated like a peal of bells; then a grave voice intoned a sacred chant, sustained by harps with nine strings and tympanons.

The embalmer priest suddenly remembered that he was due to be on watch in the temple and to recite verses from the *Book of the Dead*, as he did every time the Pharaoh visited the royal hypogeum.

He threw a panther skin over his shoulder, the muzzle of which dangled over his breast. He picked up an acacia-wood staff engraved with hieroglyphic characters and was ready to fulfill his mission.

A woman was sitting in the garden, removing a thorn from her bruised foot. Doubtless she had been walking for a long time through the stones and brambles, for she was covered in dust and her tangled hair fell over her shoulders.

Myses could only see her back, and in his present mental disposition he was scarcely thinking of entering into conversation. So he closed the door of his house again firmly, hoping that the visitor would go away after having rested for a few minutes. But he heard her singing softly, and he recognized the song of the wandering daughters of the night, who collected the herbs and plants that the Taricheutes employed to conserve bodies.

It's Mahdoura, the young man said to himself, *Mahdoura, who comes sometimes to offer me her tenderness. I could doubtless love her if my heart were free. I've often seen the moist gleam of her large eyes, which seem to be imploring me, while the tumultuous beating of her heart makes her virginal breasts tremble. Oh, why am I not like other men, who are content with earthly joys?*

Mahdoura had plunged into a granite basin, where crystalline waves spread out. She washed away the droplets of blood that stained her ankles, made water stream over her amber body, and put clusters of mimosa in her hair.

In the meantime, Myses had prostrated himself again before the queen's sarcophagus, and his lips were stammering words of adoration.

"May one come in?" asked the young woman timidly, knocking on the door. She had brought fateful plants, freshly picked on the river bank.

"Come in," sad Myses, getting up.

With undulating and lascivious movements, the pretty girl dropped a bundle of odorous foliage on the threshold.

"That's for your embalming," she said. "But what a strange idea it is to live like this among the dead, when one has your face and your voluptuous science!"

"The dead unlearn deception. One can adorn them with all the virtues that they did not know during their existence, without fear of ever being disappointed. When one has frequented the living a great deal, one prefers the defunct."

"There are, however, a few good moments on earth," said the child, laughing. "Your mummies won't give you the kiss of two young lips in flower. It's not with them that you can know the pleasure of amour."

Myses shrugged his shoulders. "Days of intoxication have sad tomorrows."

"Why? Because you create chimeras for yourself and search higher than the satisfaction of your desire. When you pick corollas of election, you don't think that they'll be withered tomorrow. You respire them in all the splendor of their terrestrial florescence. It's necessary to respire the breath of smiles in the same way, without thinking about tears to come. Take my mouth on yours and you'll always have the memory of a minute of joy!"

Myses turned away from the pretty young woman who was offering him her lips, irritated.

"No," he said, "for you'd deceive me, because you're as perfidious as all women."

She picked up her plants, and took them one by one to enable him to admire them.

"Look how well I've chosen them. To collect them, I advanced into the giant reeds with dangerous entanglements. The heat was stifling, the atmosphere charged with heavy perfumes, mingled with corruption; but in order to search for these poisonous herbs, I wouldn't have recoiled before any peril."

"Thank you, Mahdoura."

"The King Star was dipping his tresses of radiance in the waves, which he caresses ardently. And I went ever further, in order to find these starry calices with delicate scents, and these slender leaves that wind round them like the coils of snakes."

"It's thanks to these herbs that I embalm the dead prestigiously. I've discovered a marvelous procedure that conserves for the dead the appearance of life, suppresses all the frightful cookery of ordinary preparations, and doesn't necessitate a mask or bandages."

"But is it still necessary to extract the viscera and the intestines by cleaving the belly with an Ethiopian stone? Is it necessary to take out the brain via the nostrils by means of curved pincers?"

Myses smiled disdainfully. "I've suppressed all that."

"What! No more incision with the obsidian stone to take out the heart, the lungs and the liver? No more soaking in myrrh and cinnamon? No more bituminous liquid to harden the flesh? No more baths of natron in the hall of immersion and desiccation?"

"Thanks to my secret, it's not necessary to proceed with those barbaric operations."

"What is your secret, then?"

"I keep it for myself alone," said Myses, jealously.

Mahdoura made an insouciant gesture. "As you please! However, it's by means of my prestigious herbs that you obtain such fine results?"

"I admit it."

"Then you owe me gratitude."

"I don't dispute that."

"Look how I'm made. I deem myself worthy of amour too."

She turned in front of him in order to enable him to admire her, struck hieratic poses, and displayed herself on a pedestal like a voluptuous idol of flesh. Her body, firm and pale, was colored superbly by the light; she had dark eyes through which the glaucous gleam of sacred pools passed at moments; she desired the kisses of the priest with all the passion of her blooming beauty, and all the ardor of her young blood, stirred by long expeditions in the rushes and reeds of the Nile.

"I love you!" she said, kneeling in front of him.

He pushed her away gently. "I don't love you."

"Why not?"

"Because I love someone else."

"Who? No woman ever comes into your garden."

"There's one who lives my life and keeps me company all the time."

Mahdoura opened her eyes wide. "Who is this mysterious lover that no one has ever seen?"

"It's . . ." But the priest stopped, not wanting to confess that he had stolen the body of Queen Ahmosis, for the crime would have been punished by death. He did not value life, but he valued his dream. "It's a familiar soul," he went on. "The double of a being that I cherished . . ."

And he turned toward the sarcophagus.

"A dead woman who is lying in here?" asked the young woman, curiously.

"Yes."

"A mummy you've embalmed?"

"Yes, by my new method."

"Is she beautiful?"

"More beautiful than any terrestrial creature."

"Oh! Show her to me."

"No one must see her face."

Myses thought that Mahdoura might be able to recognize the queen in the extraordinary state of conservation of the body, and he feared his visitor's indiscretion.

"You don't want to!" said the child, chagrined. "I would have been glad, however, to admire your work. And I'm not jealous, you know!"

She uttered a burst of pearly laughter, the laughter of triumphant youth.

"Why would you be jealous? The love I have for that pure fiction can't make you take umbrage."

"Certainly."

"You ought to associate yourself with me in that fervent worship."

"Oh, don't count on that," said Mahdoura, who was still laughing. "I prefer the living. If you like, I'll come to visit you with my friend Aracknis, who is also charming, and whom I love with all my heart."

"I have no desire to know your friend."

"You're wrong. She's knowledgeable in the voluptuous science, and no one knows the art of consolation better than her. So, when Aryes deceived me, it was her who came to dress my wounds and pour me the balm of her caresses."

"Shut up, Mahdoura, you don't know what you're saying."

"Oh, certainly, I'd prefer your kisses to those of Aracknis, but since you're consecrated to the memory of a dead woman, I can no longer hope to conquer you, whatever desire I have."

Mahdoura showed eyes full of tears, and Myses felt sorry for her.

"You really love me, then?"

She raised her eyes toward him, in which a glimmer of hope was shining again.

"Do I love you? How can you doubt it?"

"I don't doubt it any longer."

Mad with joy, she collapsed on his breast.

"Oh," she sighed, "take me. Take all of me!"

He tried to push her away again, but the air was stifling, fully charged with errant perfumes arriving on the wings of the breeze. The heavy branches of the mimosas and pomegranate trees lined up against the walls of the garden were also spreading vehement aromas that intoxicated to the point of dizziness.

Suddenly, he made an energetic resolution, and opened the door wide.

"I have to go."

"Go? Why?"

"I'm a servant of the gods and I have to go to the temple of Osiris for the customary devotions."

"That's true," she said. "You're wearing the sacred emblems."

"I'm already late; let me accomplish my duty, Mahdoura."

"Go, then, if that is your wish, my handsome Myses."

She walked beside him along the flowery pathway of the little garden, seeming a corolla of election, a great blooming and vibrant flower. Outside, the escarpments of the Libyan chain were visible, in spite of the increasing darkness.

Oxherds passed by, driving with guttural cries the admirable beasts with tapering horns like the crescent of Isis.

"Ah," said Mahdoura, "When I was small I took the herds into the sun-bathed plain, and their heavy tread raised long waves of gold, which fell back behind them. Then dusk came, and I rolled in the grass with my favorite heifers. That's how I learned to love natural things . . ."

The huge oxen raised their moist muzzles toward the young couple and contemplated them with their pensive eyes.

"They're destined for the next sacrifice," said Myses, sadly. "They're being taken to the temple of Ammon-Ra to have their throats cut."

Scribes were marking on tablets the number of animals that were to fall under the knife of the sacrificer priests.

A little herder was eating raw onions; a girl was offering dates, figs and durra cakes in a basket.

"Do you want any?" she said. "I'm tired of carrying them."

Thinking that Mahdoura might be hungry, Myses offered her cakes and fruits. She thanked him effusively.

"I daren't ask, but you divined my desire!"

With beautiful teeth she set about biting into the yellow paste of the cakes and the pink flesh of the figs alternately.

They arrived on the bank of the Nile, where canges were traveling idly amid light papyrus skiffs and rafts made of rushes sustained by logs.

"I need to go over to the other shore," said the priest, "so I'll say goodbye, Mahdoura."

"Oh! So soon!"

"What do you want? I'm accomplishing my sacred mission."

She stopped eating the fruits. "But I'll see you tomorrow?"

"No, it's better if we don't see one another again."

"Why?"

"Because I can't love you."

She rebelled, and cried in the night: "Yes, yes, you'll love me! I want you with all my being, all my strength. I've been thinking about you for such a long time!"

"At your age, one forgets."

"No, I won't forget! Aracknis, by means of a thousand charming games, has already tried to detach me from you, because she doesn't believe in the promises of men."

"Aracknis is right. It's necessary to listen to that wise friend. It's only next to her that you'll savor a peaceful and durable happiness."

"Far from you, nothing exists any longer for my heart."

Myses stepped into a cange ornamented by a head of Hathor at its two extremities, and the oarsmen impelled the boat energetically, in spite of the tears and cries of Mahdoura, left behind on the bank.

IV

The pensive priest gazed, without seeing them, at the monuments that were illuminated on the broad brick quays of Thebes. The palace of Rhamses, the husband of Ahmosis, was outlined against the ultramarine sky, with its gigantic pylons, its gilded domes, its formidable walls and its obelisks with white pyramidons.

There was, in any case, only the river to cross in order to reach the Memnonia quarter, where the temple of Osiris stood. That was the domain of the embalmer priests: colchites, paraschites or taricheutes. Day and night, the dense smoke of the natron heaters darkened the air; one respired odors of balms and corruption in the vicinity of those funereal factories of death.

In the mysterious crypts, the servants of the god of wisdom prepared the masks of wood and ivory, and the bandages of fine cloth, covered with hieroglyphics, destined for the cadavers extended on granite slabs.

Myses, having landed, took a path lined by sphinxes with the bodies of lions and the heads of rams, which led to the entrance to the temple.

Waves of harmony rose into the night, for the chants had been resumed with more force in order to celebrate the hours of divine pageantry and sacrifices.

The priest had forgotten Mahdoura's amour. He was no longer thinking about anything except the queen, whose charming remains reposed in his dwelling, and he had no other concern except to return home as quickly as possible. A great breath of passion inflated his chest. Ahmosis was incessantly manifest to him; she appeared behind the great crouching sphinxes, marched lightly in a moonbeam, or seemed a golden lotus swaying in the breeze.

And he smiled at her, extended his arms toward her, calling to her in a caressant voice. Ideas collided in his head, which was on fire, and his heartbeat hammered his breast hectically.

In the temple he joined the other officiants, and then remained alone, to keep vigil and pray until dawn.

A great calm reigned between the solemn walls. Myses had put on a schenti, a sort of loincloth fixed over the hips by a girdle of rope, and a calasiris embroidered with gold. His pectorals, in the form of small naos, enclosed the sacred scarab, the emblem of omnipotence.

Prostrate before the statue of Horus, the son of Isis and Osiris, who had to intercede with regard to his father, he chanted the verses of the *Book of the Dead* ardently. Warm effluvia of incense surrounded him with a blue-tinted cloud; it seemed to him that the priestesses of Isis were shedding roses over him and that divine voices were singing in the shadows. There, again, he pursued the voluptuous vision; a presence floated in the air, the double of the dead woman dissolved within him delectably.

And the temple, with its ceiling and its lateral walls covered in colored sculptures and hieroglyphic inscriptions, suddenly appeared to him as a royal hypogeum. The stone of sacrifices, still stained with the blood of animals immolated the glory of Osiris, took on the appearance of a sarcophagus with precious ornaments. A svelte, diaphanous form escaped from it and came toward him, swirling in the embalmed vapors.

"Ahmosis!" he said, extending his arms toward the charming apparition.

He would have liked to feel, on his eyes and his forehead, the fiery corolla of her mouth.

"Oh," he sighed, "let me drink from the cup of your breasts and taste the honey of your lips . . . Ahmosis . . . Don't go away!"

The tender phantom played with his desire; it was an adorable haunting, an hour of delectable folly.

But the Sam, the high priest of Osiris, came to tap on Myses' shoulder.

"Take care!" he said, in a severe voice. "Your mind is wandering and your prayer is not agreeable to the gods."

The priest shivered, in the dread of having been divined. "What have I done?" he asked, in a low voice.

"You were not exact at the ceremonies of the temple, and you have not been seen for some time in the crypt of the embalmers."

"That's true," said Myses. "I've been ill. In future, I'll accomplish my duties."

He breathed out forcefully. No one knew anything; the theft of the royal remains had not been discovered. That was the only thing that mattered to the culpable priest.

"Take care!" the Sam repeated. "I sense a mystery in you; for the eyes of the god of wisdom have turned away. Your presence is not agreeable to him."

"Should I withdraw?" Myses asked.

"No, remain in order to pray with fervor. I shall consult the hierogrammatic prophets and the horoscopes regarding this strange manifestation."

Myses, disturbed, looked at the statue, and he saw that this time, the eyes of Horus—which were precious stones—were fixed grimly upon him with an expression of anger and hatred.

"Oh!" he said, full of fear and confusion. "I have merited the wrath of the gods!"

And he collapsed at the foot of the idol.

V

When Myses recovered consciousness, dawn was beginning to break. He took off the sacred ornaments and put on the panther skin again, the insignia of the priests of Osiris.

A roseate light was beginning to spread over the valley of the Nile. The immense works carried out by the recent pharaohs were affirmed in all their splendor. Temples with multiple columns displayed the finesse of their bas-reliefs and the majesty of their enormous walls. Under the porticos, slaves withdrew the wicks of dry papyrus that were steeped in vases of moringa oil, which had been burning all night.

Prostitutes were returning to their lodgings, enveloped in veils of yellow and white linen.

"Ah," said one of them, smiling at the priest, "you're too handsome to disdain women."

"Come with me," murmured a girl as slender as a golden tulip. "I'll teach you charming joys."

"Me, I'll love you with submission and tenderness, for your soul must be good."

"Come down to the bank of the Nile," said another, who was plump and jovial, "and we'll make love in the reeds. Then we can fish for carp and pick up stones as polished as agates."

They surrounded him, holding one another by the hand, performing a lascivious dance of which he was the center and extending their lips toward him, still moist with the kisses of the night.

He pushed them aside with disgust, but they came back, more obstinately and more urgently.

"I'm a taricheute priest," he said, "I belong to Osiris. Let me go back to my lodgings."

They hung on to his shoulders, stifling his protests with their kisses.

Finally, he succeeded in getting rid of them, and took his place in the cange that had brought him.

From this side of the Nile the view was even more imposing. Pyres were beginning to be lit before the colossal statues of Ammon and Thoth, for the sacrifices that were agreeable to them. Inside the temples, semi-naked virgins with large eyes burning with fever were shaking amschirs charged with perfumes, and beginning the sacred dances.

Wanting to buy new jewels with which to adorn the mummy of Ahmosis, Myses went into the outlying districts of Thebes. He walked rapidly between low, square houses with walls painted, a meter from the ground, in bright vermilion. From the height of the terraces that crowned those sordid constructions, women displayed their naked breasts beneath necklaces of glass beads and metal, with short hair arranged in stiff locks around their cheeks.

The peel of figs and lemons was crushed beneath his feet; a spicy, acrid and bestial odor assailed his nostrils: the reek of musk and muddy earth, withered flowers and rotten fruits, floating in black water in the middle of the streets.

Merchants were opening their shops and installing themselves like idols in the midst of their jewels, their ivory and nacre caskets, and all the sumptuous items of their displays.

Myses plunged into a narrow corridor, knowing that he would find what he desired at the end of the passage.

A door presented itself, and he rapped three times with his index finger.

A meager brown man opened it immediately, to a scene of wonder.

There were papyrus boxes ornamented with precious stones, terracotta statuettes enameled with green and pink, emerald pectorals, amulets in turquoise, amber and jade, sheaths of green feldspar in the form of stems supporting a lotus flower in sapphire or topaz, solid gold boats, onyx chariots, ivory psalterions, flutes of Osiris with crystalline sounds, harps enriched with lapis lazuli and cornelian, lyres of blond tortoiseshell, canopic jars in alabaster, enameled earthenware, porphyry and oriental onyx whose lids depicted the heads of sphinxes, jackals, hawks and cynocephali.

"What do you want today, my son?" asked the merchant of the dead.

"Show me your bracelets, your fetishes, your rings and your necklaces."

"Have you embalmed some person of note, then?"

"Yes, I want the best you have. It's for the wife of a senior officer in the militia."

"Here are jewels worthy of a queen!"

He did, in fact, set out items of rare and precious workmanship, but nothing seemed beautiful enough to the passionate lover.

"I would like," he said, "a symbolic fetish, a jewel that would be a bond between the husband and the defunct wife. Do you understand my desire?"

"Not very well," said the merchant. "All presents are agreeable to the dead, and all of them attach similarly."

"No, no, the gift of a heart ablaze with amour cannot be similar to that of a vulgar souvenir."

"Take this aquamarine clasp. It's the stone of lovers, the one that assures eternal constancy."

"No, all the dead have similar ones."

"Then choose this golden boat enriched with olivines and peridots; it's the emblem of resurrection."

"No," he said, again. "Give me that malachite serpent; it will repose on the forehead of the beloved and protect her against all jealous attacks."

Myses paid for the jewel and resumed the road to his dwelling. He had almost forgotten the threats of the high priest, and felt joyful.

As far as his modest resources permitted, he made such gifts to the dead woman, imagining that she shivered with pleasure in her gilded box at every ingenious find. She already had beside her delicate amethyst bottles, silver mirrors, dolls of ivory and jade, persea flowers, bracelets, diadems and silky fabrics. He wanted his friend's unknown refuge to be cheerful, as full of futile ornaments as the chamber of her former palace.

In the bottles and the caskets, among the perfumes and the balms, the double of the voluptuous dead woman—her astral form, gentle, light, vibrant and passionate—had to dwell.

Hastily, Myses opened the gate of his garden, glad to find himself alone in his cherished retreat. But a gracious form emerged from the clumps of mimosa and tamarisk and stood in front of the surprised priest.

"Mahdoura!" he said, angrily.

"Yes. I spent the night outside your door. You won't have the courage to send me away?" the young woman murmured, in an imploring voice

"I've told you that any intimacy between us is impossible. Go away, your presence is painful to me."

"Oh, Myses! I'm dying of love for you! I've tried to forget you, but I can't. Don't ask me for a sacrifice beyond my strength."

He tried to push her aside.

"Others will give you what I refuse; you're pretty and seductive. Why be stubborn in pursuing me, since I alone cannot grant you what you require?"

"I'm here," she said, smiling, "because I know you'll end up giving in. Men always give in."

And she placed herself across the threshold with an amorous audacity.

Myses was obliged to remove her in order to go into his house. Supple and feline, she followed him all the way to the queen's sarcophagus.

"That's the obstacle," she said, pointing at the large gilded box set against the wall. "But I shall triumph!"

VI

Every day, Mahdoura came back to the house of the priest, who no longer had the courage to flee from her. She was like a submissive domestic animal with him, accepting his orders and supporting his caprices without ever manifesting any impatience.

Myses felt that he was marching in fatality, in a desolate flight of illusion and hope. All his vain aspirations toward an impossible amour, all his desires, never realized, weighed upon his mind more and more.

The dread of dementia progressed in his soul, and yet, perversely, he sought morbid intoxications, and, further on, plunged into his malaise.

The arteries of his temples beat more feverishly when he returned to the temple or the crypt of the embalmers; it seemed to him that a danger was threatening him in the profound peace of the mysterious abode.

Closing his eyes against the sun's rays, full of dancing dust that filtered between the curtains, he buried himself in a melancholy meditation without seeking to react against the obsession that possessed him despotically.

Mahdoura slid beside him then, applied her lips to his face and pleaded with him for an affectionate word. But he did not respond to those marks of tenderness, which were painful to him.

However, a hot blood was seething in his veins; his flesh summoned the caress, and the obstinate lover, sensing that emotion confusedly, did not despair of arriving at the accomplishment of her desires.

As the day declined she drew him into the garden, beneath the voluptuous breath of the roses, drew water in the palm of her hand and raised that living cup to his lips. He drank, delectably moved, and then looked up at the young woman.

"Poor child!" he said, taking pity on her attentive and persistent affection.

Then she clung to him, begging for a caress, seeking a consent in his gaze.

For a long time she came back like that, without tiring, gaining a little more influence over the young man's heart every day.

"I love you," she repeated. "When you wish, I'll belong to you. We'll be passionate lovers and we'll live happily in this house."

Feebly, he still pushed her away, feeling cowardly against that amour, which solicited him with all the power of its wild energy.

"Oh, how sweet our kisses will be," she said. "For you, I'll invent new games, and you'll never weary of my embraces. Women who love as I do aren't similar to the others!"

One evening, in an oppressive heat, he did not push the young woman away. The heavy branches of the mimosas and the tamarisks, aligned against the walls, sent forth vehement aromas, and Myses closed his eyes, no longer having the strength to resist the carnal temptation. They were very close to one another, hand in hand, voluptuously attracted by an invincible sexual power.

The fluid emitted by Mahdoura's body penetrated the young man, weaned from caresses for such a long time.

Several times, the dark hair had brushed his face, the firm breasts had sought his bosom, in an irresistible offering. The Priest's fingers quivered in the fingers that kept them captive forcefully; his throat contracted in an impetuous desire.

She drew him against her, lascivious and feline, divining that such a moment might not be found again, and that it was necessary, in an audacious coup, to vanquish the priest's final hesitations.

Passionately, with a great sigh, a kind of swooning sob, she applied her lips to his and enveloped him with her arms.

He no longer resisted, transported, succumbing to the sudden maddening of his senses.

She had the profound kisses that enchain energies, bearing away the will in a hectic vertigo. She chained her supple and powerful limbs to the priest's body, adhering to him madly.

He felt her knees, her legs, her loins and her breasts burning his flesh. Her breath, which he drank, ran through him like a jet of flame.

She perceived that she was about to vanquish. Then she played submission, abandoned herself, allowed herself to be carried without resistance to the couch next to the sarcophagus of Queen Ahmosis.

And the royal mummy doubtless quivered with indignation in her gilded prison; the astral double of the forsaken lover fled far from the profaned dwelling in the terror of that murder of amour.

Myses, meanwhile, returned to his senses, tried to drive away the immodest woman, but fell back on his bed, stunned.

He experienced a singular disturbance, a morbid vertigo that rendered him weaker than a child.

That crisis was prolonged, and the priest knew veritable anguish.

Mahdoura heard him speaking in a distant voice, moist with tears. There was a being within him that was gesticulating, imploring and menacing, and a reasonable, mute, gagged being that was witnessing the dementia of the other but could not help him.

During that intense fever, the young woman cared for her lover, surrounding him with solicitude and amour, and when he awoke, cured, in her arms, he did not have the courage to send her away.

VII

At the hour when the three goddesses—Anta, queen of war; Khem, mother of the world; and Seb, sovereign of the waters— were reincarnated in order to pick the herb of eternal life in the reeds of the Nile, the lovers emerged from their dwelling.

Myses and Mahdoura were now perfectly united.

The priest, having tasted the lips of the beautiful young woman, remained in the intoxication of their bite, and forgot even the memory of Queen Ahmosis.

The cherished phantom, the double of the dead woman, no longer accompanied him in all his missions. He no longer saw her melancholy smile, he no longer heard her harmonious voice sighing her passionate cantilena in the nocturnal breeze. The man had returned to the joys of the earth, cruelly unconscious of his divine mission, for his flesh was weak and his spirit fickle.

Mahdoura and Myses wandered, tenderly enlaced, through the eternal city. Pathways bordered by sphinxes, terminated by two obelisks flanking a pylon at the entrance to a temple sometimes opened before them; and they stopped near gigantic granite monuments, pronouncing amorous words whose magnified echo reverberated in the distance, for the priest alone could penetrate into the isolated profundities of sanctuaries. The Sam, the great pontiff, and sovereigns only came there on certain dates to offer prayers and precious vases. The Pharaoh prostrated himself then, in the sumptuousness of his glory, and conversed with the royal dead.

But not all the tombs of Thebes resembled the splendid houses of sovereigns. Sometimes, the sepulcher merely consisted of a little chapel covering a well. The mummy was simply placed in the center of an edifice of pyramidal form, in which a walled cavity had been contrived. In the simplest sepulchers people limited themselves to digging a hole several meters deep, at the bottom of which the coffin reposed, which was covered with earth and stones.

216

Having accompanied the priest in his sacred visits, Mahdoura waited at the exit from the redoubtable enclosure. She sat down on a tomb under construction, near granite colossi backed up against the walls, obelisks and pylons that the last rays of the sun tinted pink.

The immense sphinxes with empty eyelids impressed her vaguely.

Large aquatic birds passed overhead in the dazzling azure, seemingly swimming in dormant water, a dead sea of infinite mildness.

Other distant birds mingled their plaints and melancholy songs; a great desire for amour made the young woman feel faint, and she called to her beloved.

When his priestly duties were accomplished, Myses came to join her in the shadow of the giant stones, under the protection of the mysterious spirits of death.

"I'm yours," she sighed, "my dear lord, my master! Hide behind this rock, for I saw the priests of Osiris passing in the distance." And he collapsed beside her, extracting the violence of her tortuous intoxication, savoring the shiver of reckless tenderness, bound to her by the uninterrupted chain of kisses, melting into her flesh for a joy that was always new.

The moment passed; and, gradually emerging from his carnal pleasure, he sensed an occult presence floating in the air; a form striving to become visible, to draw itself in a space that had become indefinable, and, his gaze dilated, his heart hammering, he remained anxiously motionless.

"What are you thinking about?" Mahdoura asked.

But he, not daring to confess his sudden disturbance, invented a pretext.

"We're culpable," he said, "of loving one another within the enclosure of the dead. Might they not avenge themselves for our audacity?"

"Bah! They've been lovers, like us. Why would they be irritated by a joy that they might perhaps share in their hypogea? Do you not think that the dead are more generous and compassionate than the men with whom we rub shoulders on earth?"

And, in fact, the stone colossi and the crouching sphinxes seemed to be protecting them against the assaults of the living. They were, certainly, beings of good will and pardon, full of strength, glory and silence.

The young couple expected, of their sovereign justice, the support that they needed in order to continue to cherish one another freely before humans.

VIII

However, Myses began to think once again about the dead woman that he had outraged. It was a slow torture, a nagging pain that he could not vanquish. And he closed his eyes in order no longer to see Mahdoura, who followed him like his shadow, obstinate and feline.

In spite of everything, he sensed her there, vibrant with passion, burning with insatiable covetousness. She was seductive in amour and youth, and he saw, through his closed eyelids, the young woman's pronounced cleavage, her shoulders, her loins, and her harmonious and slender legs. She exhaled voluptuous fumes that exasperated his flesh.

"Go away!" he cried. "I need to meditate, to pray in the shadow for the forgetfulness of our sins!"

But she clung to him.

"You would not have the strength, my dear lover, to chase me way after our ardent joys? There is no part of my body that I have not delivered to you; do you not remember them? My forehead, my eyes, my mouth, my breasts, all are yours."

"I have been culpable! I repent!"

"Why repent? We haven't done anyone any harm. Our youth, our bodies and our amour belong to us; we have the right to dispose of them as we please."

"I am the servant of the gods. For you I have betrayed my oaths!"

"Bah! All the priests of Osiris have loved human creatures. And I'm not talking about the orgies that profane the temple of Hapi three times a year. The pallacides deliver themselves to the servants of the gods. The sacrifice of their virginity is made publicly, before the altar of Isis, primordial Nature, the universal womb!"

"I have never participated in those ceremonies of lust."

"Perhaps you were wrong, for you'd be more indulgent to yourself."

"I have consecrated myself to the embalming of the dead, but for many days I've ceased to go to the crypt of the temple of Osiris. The Taricheutes are astonished by my absence. The Paraschites and the Colchites, poorly directed, have damaged the bodies of several dignitaries of the court. It's absolutely necessary that I repair their awkwardness."

"All right," said Mahdoura. "I'll wait for you."

But that was not what Myses desired.

"Go and collect for me the fateful plants that you know so well," he said. "Thanks to them, I'll be able to restore youth to those who are about to appear before the divine tribunal."

"What! You want . . . ?"

"Yes, Mahdoura; I will love you more if you consent to serve me, as in the past, when I had not yet tasted the honey of your lips."

The young woman hesitated. "I'm afraid of losing you."

"Your fears are chimerical. Where could I go?"

"I don't know . . . I'm afraid, that's all."

"You'll always find me again in this dwelling on returning from your distant expeditions, and you'll render me, by virtue of your submission, infinitely more tender and grateful."

"Oh, I'd like to believe you!"

He pointed at the sarcophagus of Ahmosis.

"The woman who is asleep in there is more beautiful than she was during life. It's thanks to the precious plants that you brought me that I was able to accomplish that miracle of embalming."

"Will you show me your masterpiece, then?"

But Myses took on a desolate expression.

"No, I must keep the secret of the death."

"I won't betray it . . . let me gaze just for a moment at the face of the one whom you hide from me so obstinately!"

"No, Mahdoura, don't insist."

"I beg you! Truly, I'm curious to see this supernatural splendor that you never cease to praise. When my eyes have observed what you affirm, I'll associate myself with all my heart with your admirable endeavors. I'll go to visit the distant pools, whose mysterious depths only I know. I'll bring back unknown plants, insects and reptiles for you."

The priest dared not grant his mistress the favor she requested. Mahdoura would certainly recognize Queen Ahmosis, and might betray him in a moment of thoughtlessness or rancor. In that case, it would be death or eternal reclusion for him.

"I can't open the sarcophagus," he said, sadly.

"Then I won't go to search for what you want."

And days passed in that obstinacy, amassing in the heart of the lover thoughts of mistrust and hatred for the unsubmissive woman.

IX

Myses had resumed his occupations in the crypts of the temple of Osiris, in order not to awaken the suspicions of the high priest.

Mahdoura remained in the house, striving to please him when he returned by means of her caresses and adornments.

But he suffered from the constant presence that he could not avoid. Neither his heart nor his imagination drew him any longer toward the young woman who refused to obey him in her blind jealousy.

Human beings, imperfect by nature, march incessantly toward an imagined goal; that goal is equality and equilibrium. In order to attain it, they seek the influences capable of perfecting it, of causing their incessant wandering to cease: hence the irresistible tendency of two beings only any longer to be one, to embrace one another, to fuse with one another in a physical and intellectual communion. Instinct, as much as reasoning, seeks whatever might lead to that enviable state: hence, sympathies are born, attractions, irresistible passions, and, when reciprocity does not exist, despair and folly.

The passions, in any case, all flow from amour, the fundamental law of the world. Thoughts, decisions and actions come in their turn from human passions, and if those passions are hateful, sometimes adopting an umbrageous and aggressive form, it is because they result from secret presentiments that perceive an impediment to the imagined and powerfully desired complementarity.

In the depths of his heart, Myses loved the dead woman.

During her life, Ahmosis had produced an ineffaceable impression in the mind of the servant of the gods. He prostrated himself when she passed by, as she went to the temple of Isis in her gold and silver litter. He had surrounded her with a burning and mute adoration, which she gradually divined, for she smiled at him softly in their chance encounters.

Now he possessed the adorable body of the sovereign, and he cursed the imprudent woman who had slipped into his life of prayer and ecstasy.

The prescience of a mission beyond the tomb haunted his days. Sometimes, rejecting Mahdoura, he knelt before the sarcophagus, and the young woman, trembling and desolate, implored him only to think about her, to go to sleep confident in her tenderness.

She no longer went out; the world no longer existed for her since she had encountered the beloved, and understood the very reason for her existence. She belonged to him, as the leaf belongs to the tree. The leaf falls and dies detached from its stem. Mahdoura did not want to be detached from Myses.

X

When the priest returned that evening, the lamp was extinct and a tremulous voice called to him in the darkness.

He advanced, groping his way, and encountered his mistress, who pressed herself against his bosom.

"What's the matter?"

"I've seen the face of the queen."

He uttered a cry of fright. "Oh! You've dared . . . ?"

"Yes," she said, weeping. "I had such a desire to know your marvelous work that I uncovered the sarcophagus."

"It's a crime! A frightful crime for which you'll be punished! For no one must know the splendor of defunct Pharaohs!"

"Alas," she moaned, "I know the full extent of my sin, and I humbly beg your pardon for it. But hide that august face, which I can no longer contemplate! It seems to me that the cruel gaze of Ahmosis is tearing my heart! Veil its redoubtable glare, I implore you."

Myses lit the lamp and saw that, indeed, the lid of the funereal box had been removed. Ahmosis, in her gold and silver robe, appeared in all the radiance of her august beauty.

Around her, the fateful jewels had not been disturbed. At the place of her heart was the immense scarab, the symbol of transformation and resurrection in a better world.

"She's looking at me! She's cursing me!" said Mahdorua, panic-stricken. "Why didn't you put a mask of wax, metal or wood over her features, as is usually done? You must have thought that a curious desire might brave the secret of the sarcophagus!"

"No, I believed in your obedience."

"Hurry up! My dear Myses, hide the face of the queen, I implore you. Oh, how angry she seems!"

The priest did not seem to hear his mistress. He remained in ecstasy before the divine body that he had stolen such a long time before.

Mahdoura was weeping, at the peak of terror. "Oh, you're not listening to me! I tell you that she'll avenge herself!"

Finally, he took pity on the young woman and replaced the lid of the gilded box.

"Since your fear is so great," he said, "leave this dwelling; return to your family, who must be mourning your absence."

"No," she replied, with a grim expression. "If I go away you'll be entirely under the domination of your obsession. You love the queen, and I'm jealous of her."

"I love her, certainly, but not in the same way as you. It's a mystical and pure passion that can't cause you umbrage."

"I want you to cherish me uniquely. I'm unhappy sharing."

"You're mad, Mahdoura!"

"Yes, since I love you!"

"Well, now that you've been able to satisfy your curiosity, will you still refuse to go and collect the plants that I need?"

"I'll go tomorrow," she said. "You'll forgive me?"

"Yes, but remember that I'm risking my life in keeping the queen's remains with me . . ."

"I won't betray you."

"You swear it?"

"I swear it, my beloved. How can you believe me capable of such a vile action?"

"I don't know . . . I have sad presentiments."

"Me too, dear Myses. A danger is suspended over us, and it makes me shiver all the way to the heart."

XI

The lovers were lying together on their bed, in one another's arms, and in spite of the emotions that had assailed them, sleep came to close their eyelids.

Then Myses shivered. What he saw seemed to him to be the continuation of a nightmare; he sat up amid the cushions and wondered whether he was not drunk or mad.

A phosphorescent glow was emerging from the sarcophagus of Ahmosis; outside, great nocturnal birds were launching their sinister cries, and jackals were howling mortally.

While the room remained in darkness, the coffin was illuminated with increasing brightness, and the queen was distinctly visible.

Myses leapt out of bed, his arms extended.

The dead woman's gaze slowly turned toward his, and fixed itself upon him amorously. Those animate eyes, in that immobile face, troubled him strangely.

Then, with a superhuman effort of will, he begged the queen to reassure him, to prove to him that all human research had not been vain, that a world existed different from the one he knew, that everything did not stop at the threshold of the tomb and that the apparent injustice of life ceased therewith.

He implored her to dictate to him the conduct that he ought to follow, and to assist him in his troubles.

He heard the vibration of a faint echo. As his mind retraced those consoling words for him, a voice that caused all his fibers to quiver delectably repeated them meekly.

He savored that new sensation, that exquisite understanding of the soul, now errant, that he loved, and the voice, whose sonorous waves, perceptible to him alone, troubled him profoundly, murmured:

"You have conserved my body miraculously and you have promised to associate your desire with mine, to summon me to you with all the ardor that I will put into breaking my chains. The moment has come."

Myses prostrated himself before the luminous coffin, and, his eyes ecstatic, his lips extended toward mysterious kisses and all his strength was directed toward a unique goal, he promised to carry out the wishes of Ahmosis.

"If everything must be transformed," he said, "if the progressive phenomena that we have studied must be renewed until complete perfection, if nothing dies, and if humans, initiated into occult powers, can direct at will their various evolutions in life, until the supreme bliss, may my passionate will be accomplished!

"Your soul is linked to mine, Queen of tenderness and amour, and I can no more be deprived of it than I could be deprived of air and sunlight! No, nothing dies! Everything simply changes and is transformed, like the chrysalid that becomes a butterfly, and the immaculate flower a delicious vermilion fruit.

"Can we not, at will, direct the transformation of beings that we have cherished? Can we not, by dint of perseverance and energy, find them and recognize them, fully alive, at our side? Will not the moment come, my adored Queen, of our indissoluble union, in spite of the world and its cruel laws, in spite of the feeble calculations of human science, which believes that it embraces everything, but has never been able to lift the veil of Isis?

"Blood circulates in our bodies like a river returning to its source, and there are lands beyond the sea of darkness covered by other trees than ours and also inhabited by different humans; but no one has yet recognized that all these things that surprise us and trouble us are divine signs. There are signs in the waters, in the redoubtable forests, in the earth, in our muscles, in our bones and in our flesh.

"Nature speaks to us, at every hour of the day, in an immensely sonorous language, compared with which our poor knowledge is no more than a faint whimper.

"The signs of the mysterious world demonstrate to us, in a manner that does not address our failing reason but our instinct, that we cannot disappear without return, that our essence is imperishable and that a divine force guides us, incessantly, toward the eternal light that we will one day see . . ."

Ahmosis, very straight in her robe patterned with flames, kept her eyes open, and her immobile gaze, turned toward Myses, penetrated him with hope and fear.

The priest, consumed by amour, remained on his knees. He believed that he was transported into a different world, freed from his terrestrial bonds, light and immaterial.

Lost in his intoxicating dream, he sensed his soul, projected, so to speak, outside himself, as an imponderable body, an astral form; it seemed to him that the power of his vital fluid, thus liberated, drew Ahmosis, the adorable dead woman, and that she dissolved exquisitely within him. He sensed the being of the most beloved plunge into his own being as into an abyss of amour. Her voice spoke to him ineffably in the great silence, and Mahdoura had disappeared.

He really was alone with the divine, which vibrated within his most secret fibers, stimulating him to the point of vertigo.

Meanwhile, the queen had shifted in her sarcophagus, her breast was rising rhythmically, her complexion taking on a warmer glow.

Myses held out his arms.

"O my sovereign! My divine lotus! My beam of light, reborn for my amour! You are animate already, and I sense your spirit quivering like a beautiful bird of fire! You will live again in all the plenitude of life in order to give yourself to the humble priest who implores you!"

But the mummy had resumed its rigid immobility again.

Then Myses fixed his thought ardently on the goal that he was pursuing; he evoked the palpitating soul of Ahmosis, begged her not to abandon him on the threshold of bliss. Had he hoped thus far, then, only to feel more bitterly the humiliation of defeat? Must he fall back into the miry gulf of his anguish, without being cradled by the happiness of the elect? Was he not worthy of that recompense, after having traveled the rude Calvary of the uncomprehended and the abandoned?

He prostrated himself, his face against the ground, and from all his being, plunged in desolation and tenderness, sprang a profound cry, a supreme prayer.

Immediately, he recovered courage; he felt fortified and sustained. His nerves and his muscles obeyed him, while he stood the heavy sarcophagus against the wall.

226

A few minutes went by in delirious expectation. Then it became evident that Ahmosis' breast was swelling, and that an imperceptible tremor was agitating her limbs.

This time, Myses had certainly seen and heard; the vision imposed itself as an indisputable reality.

"Ahmosis!" he said, in a faint voice. "Ahmosis, my beloved."

And the queen, surging from her gilded box, advanced in a luminous streak, like a detached flower impelled by the breeze.

"Ahmosis!" he said, again.

Then she straightened up, and threw her charming arms around his neck.

"Here I am!"

"Alive?"

"Alive, in order to cherish you!"

She had thrown off her sheath of silver and gold, the jewels of her breast, and the royal scarab that weighed on her heart. And she displayed a slender, polished body, with elastic flesh, harmonious forms, created for the eternal desire of the kiss.

"I love you, Myses! I only wanted to die in order to be yours, for I knew that you would come to take me from the crypt of the temple and that you would take me to your home."

"You knew?"

"Yes, the gods had told me."

She gazed at him, smiling, in a familiar pose, so young and so supple, so full of strength and juvenile ardor that he was bewildered by joy.

"Then you won't leave me again?"

"Never again."

"But you might be recognized?"

"We'll flee, my beloved. We'll quit this land of Egypt, where I was powerful and glorious. We'll go to hide our tenderness in some solitude, obscurely."

"You'll renounce, for me, the pleasures of life?"

"Yours, my dear Myses, will be sufficient for me."

He could not weary of contemplating her.

"Oh, my divinity, everything charms me, intoxicates me, and makes me faint! I've never known a similar emotion! The sad and somber chrysalid has become a vermilion butterfly. Come closer, closer still . . . so that in the adorable whiteness of your veils I can rediscover the reflection of eternal light."

She put her arms around him and glued her mouth to his.

"My Myses! My lover! Take me into the embalmed countryside, to the woods with voluptuous depths. Everything outside is intoxication, perfume, enchantment! Give me your kiss, priest, your embrace, and your pardon. Of all my youth in flower, I make you the offering."

He shuddered under the maddening caress, and rendered the sovereign kiss for kiss.

"Come," he said.

But she escaped, fearfully.

"If some servant of the Pharaoh recognized me, I would be lost to you. You would be taken to a dark cell to await a death that would not be long delayed. Oh, my beloved, I'm afraid!"

"If someone discovers us, it won't do you any harm. You'll resume your place in the palace, as before. You'll be enthroned in the immense halls, as adorable and perfect as an idol. And you'll come on to the terraces of your apartments in order dream amid the flowers . . ."

"But you'd be killed!"

"What does it matter? I no longer value existence. I'd go gladly, knowing that you were happy. Let's go, my beloved!"

"Let's go! Dispose of my destiny in accordance with your desire."

"Yes," he said, "but before then, be mine. I don't know what tomorrow reserves for me and I want to take advantage of the ineffable hour that is passing."

He led Ahmosis to the couch, ransacked by other tendernesses.

She laughed, lightly.

"Mahdoura, your lover, is weeping in the rocks. I've exiled her forever . . . don't you regret her?"

She looked at him anxiously, awaiting his response.

"No," he said. "I didn't love that girl, who came to throw herself between our amour?"

"Truly?"

"How can you still doubt, after all the marks of adoration I've given you?"

She hid her face on the young man's bosom.

"I no longer doubt, for I too have never cherished anyone but you."

XII

Myses contemplated the sovereign, asleep in his arms. Time was flying, and sinister presentiments troubled his happiness.

Nocturnal birds came to beat their wings against his door, uttering their plaintive cry, which is a sign of death.

Death, however, did not present herself to the mind of the priest with its cortege of dolor and fear. Like all men of his caste, he judged it to be beneficent and reparative. The inert mummy, stiff in her bandages, with the fixity of her enamel gaze in her golden mask, did not awaken any dread in him. He took pleasure in the solemnity of sarcophagi, the mystery of granite chambers in which the souls of the dead slumbered.

All of Egyptian architecture, moreover, was the image of human thought, only inspired a funeral dream. The pyramids, the obelisks, the pylons and the immense columns represented a vague human form: that of a cadaver shrouded in its bandages.

The Egyptian only thought about resurrection, and only labored for eternity.

Myses thus enjoyed life in the expectation of death.

With delight, he respired the pure breath of the sovereign, and kissed her closed eyelids, her smooth forehead and the perfumed wave of her hair, devotedly.

And in her sleep, she was still pronouncing words of love.

The priest had never known similar transports; never had the possession of a woman been worth such a complete joy to him.

And Ahmosis, waking up, lifted her mouth within reach of his. She arched her back and pressed herself against the tumultuous bosom of her lover.

He threw her back on the cushions. In the quiver of silks and gauzes, their nerves vibrated divinely. They were no longer the hasty lovers of his first kiss but fervent devotees of a cult, almost divine, those who, having given themselves to one another, savored their happiness delightfully.

"O my glorious Queen," he said, "you know kisses sweeter than honey! Under my lips your body quivers like a vibrant harp; you are reborn more exquisite from every caress!"

And Ahmosis, swooning, sighed in her turn: "I would like, Master of my Days, to repeat the words that fly from your mouth in whirlwinds of flame. I admire your eloquence, but I can no longer find words to express what I feel."

"Yes, don't say anything; stay thus, like an idol of flesh under the lips of the kneeling devotee. I want to animate your slender arms, your shoulders and your throat. I want, after the last frisson, to teach you other frissons, until the annihilation of amour into which we will both sink delectably."

For his royal lover he strung the golden pearls of an amorous science of which he had still been ignorant the day before. Then, intoxicated by embraces and caresses, they rested, exhausted, happy and beyond human strength.

And Death, crouching at the foot of the bed, reached out toward the imprudent couple with her fleshless hand, while the nocturnal birds, even more sinister, wept outside.

Darkness now enveloped beings and things, while passionate and bounding impetuosities went to sleep, while the intoxications that grind the nerves, elevate beings and transport them to mysterious paradises calmed down in reparative slumber.

But Myses uttered a cry.

"It's broad daylight, my beloved, and we're still in this dwelling!"

"Ah!" she said. "I had forgotten everything that was not our amour! Next to you, I quivered to the bone in an unknown ecstasy . . ."

"And I still retain the exquisite perfume of your kisses on my lips. Come, it's dangerous to stay here, for I don't know where to hide you."

"I obey you, my sweet master; here I am."

She stood up, stark naked, in the splendor of her beauty.

"You can't go like that."

With her foot she pushed the precious fabrics heaped up in front of the sarcophagus. "Put my royal ornaments back on."

"But those precious stones, those golden veils and adornments would attract attention to you. No woman in Thebes wears anything similar."

"What can I do then?"

He spotted Mahdoura's garments in a corner. "Take these clothes," he said. "They'll hide your splendor."

In haste, he enveloped her in the coarse fabrics of the daughter of the people, and put a veil over her hair.

Meekly, she let him do it.

"We'll leave Thebes by the fifth water gate, and in our rapid cange, we'll see the terraces, the pylons and the porticos supporting the hanging gardens of your palace fleeing. Like arrows, menacing the sun, we'll see the obelisks covered in fateful inscriptions fly past."

The bestial and peppery reek of the morning of amour was accentuated. There was a heavy heat; it was one of those hours of Egypt in which the air seems to be ferrying sparks, when the Nile is confounded with the land, similarly motionless, beneath a fiery sky.

Myses pushed the queen toward the door.

Before leaving, he had thrown into the sarcophagus the precious sheath, the enamel necklaces and the royal scarab, and he had closed the lid of the large gold and silver box. Nothing in the room revealed the strange scene that had just been played there for the glory of love and death.

"One last kiss," said the queen. "Would you like that, my love?"

He lifted her veil and stuck his mouth to hers.

"Now I can go."

He opened the door and uttered a cry of terror.

Mahdoura was standing on the threshold.

"You shan't leave!" she said. "I'm in my lover's house, and I'm defending my property!"

She seemed magnified, full of wrath and grim hatred.

"Go away!" cried Myses.

"Me go away? Why? I have as much right to your kisses as that woman! You belong to me, for I was able to conquer you; you're as precious to me as my flesh and my blood! Do you think that a love like mine can be extinguished in a minute because your caprice has changed?"

"Not so many words," he said. "Let us pass."

But she had picked up a heavy staff forgotten there by some herdsman, and she threatened the queen with it.

"It's this woman that it's necessary to chase away."

"Are you forgetting who she is?"

"I'm not forgetting anything! I know that your science has resuscitated the royal mummy that was sleeping in your house. I know that the powerful Ahmosis, forgetting the respect due to Pharaohs, has given herself to you, that you want to take her into some solitude in order to savor her incomparable caresses in peace. But that shall not be."

"Go away!" Myses repeated. "I can dispose of my heart as I please, and in any case, I've never loved anyone but the queen. It's to have her charming body with me that I stole her from the crypt of the embalmer priests and brought her here. It's to conserve her luminous beauty eternally that I fabricated prestigious balms and respected the adorable appearance of her flesh. You know that no mask has disfigured her, that no bandage has bruised her, and that I have not deposited her heart in the sinister canopic jar that accompanies the dead. Her heart is beating in her breast and her lungs are inflating voluptuously. She is just as I found her in the crypt of the temple the day after her apparent decease.

"She was only sleeping, and amour has awakened her. It is only just that she should give herself to the man who has respected her mysterious life and surrounded her with vigilant cares. What would she have done if she had opened her eyes in the darkness of the hypogeum, immured in her granite tomb? But the taricheutes would have killed her before then, while I have favored her glorious resurrection. She is mine, truly mine, and I'm taking her away!"

He tried to move Mahdoura aside, but the young woman laughed disdainfully.

"It's possible that you're right. You're defending your amour—but I'm defending mine, and I'm also right . . ."

"But I didn't summon you! You came to surprise me in my retreat. You stunned me with your caresses, your kisses, and I succumbed because the flesh is weak. While I accepted the carnal pleasure that you offered me, my soul was entirely with my divine lover. I've never loved anyone but her. I won't receive the kisses of another woman!"

Mahdoura uttered the plaint of a wounded animal. "Be careful!" she groaned.

"What have I to fear from you? I could break you like a reed if I wanted to."

"You wouldn't dare!"

"It would certainly be repugnant to me to strike a woman; that's why I'm begging you, one last time, to let us pass."

"No," she said, resolutely.

"What do you hope for from me, since I'll never accept your caresses again?"

"Do you hate me, then?"

"Yes, at this moment I'd like to see you chained to the accursed rocks, under the flight of the birds of prey."

"You'd like my eyelids to be furrowed by their avid beaks and my body torn apart by their cruel claws?"

"I'd like that."

"What have I done, Myses, for you to detest me to that degree?"

"You're opposing my amour."

"The amour that you have for another. Understand my frightful torture, then!"

"Understand mine too!"

"Myses, my beloved . . . !"

"I don't know you . . . Time is pressing. Let us pass. Don't oblige me to employ my strength, or I might not be able to master my anger."

"Oh, I don't fear you; it's that woman I want to punish."

She had thrown herself upon Ahmosis, but the young man had seized her wrists abruptly.

"Well, then, break me! For I'll oppose your flight with all the might of my reckless tenderness!"

She clung to him, uttering wild clamors.

Then he put his hands around the young woman's neck, and squeezed until she was no longer making any movement.

When he relaxed the vice of his grip, the body collapsed at his feet like a limp scarf.

It seemed to him then that the trees round him leaned over, gasping, that specters, emerging from hypogea, were howling in a stampede of sacred reptiles eternally rearing up and menacing. Intolerable bites tore his entrails, fiery pincers crushed his bones. Death, now, invaded him slowly, like a frightful caress. The landscape, all the way to the depths of the horizon, was full of open sarcophagi from which laments and sobs rose. He sensed the blood escaping from his veins, drop by drop, and fleeing over the ground in red streams. Then, suddenly, the ground disappeared beneath him, and he tumbled into unknown depths, carried away by an extraordinary, vertiginous fall . . .

With a profound sigh, Myses awoke, utterly anguished by his frightful nightmare.

A bright radiance bathed his bedroom, and Mahdoura was lying beside him, as on the previous evening, but her nostrils were pinched, her eyeballs seemed to have retreated into the depths of their orbits, her flesh was cold and her body rigid.

Myses thought that he was still asleep and continuing, unconsciously, his morbid dream.

He palpated the young woman with a sort of incredulous curiosity . . .

Certainly, he was still dreaming, and reality would soon surge forth from the mists, with its placid monotony, its vague and yet consoling hope. Mahdoura, the jealous lover, was about to open her somber eyes and offer him the vermilion fruit of her lips . . .

He was about to know the burning taste of her kiss again.

"Mahdoura!" he murmured in a whisper. "Don't continue this cruel game! Quickly, smile at me, speak to me, tell me that I'm continuing my strange dream!"

Several times, he repeated the young woman's name, wanting to doubt, even so, and perhaps to prolong his error, in the terror of such a singular event.

He bit his hand and experienced a sharp pain. But no, he was no longer asleep; he was really conscious and alive, alive next to his inanimate mistress.

The emotion was so great that he let himself fall at the foot of the bed, dreading feeling the chill of that inert flesh against him again.

Then his gaze went toward the sarcophagus, which the sun caused to scintillate capriciously. He wanted to see Queen Ahmosis again, so marvelously preserved by the merit of his science

The august presence of his "only beloved" would console him and sustain him in the ordeals of life. Through her, he would be better and stronger.

His heart beating, he opened the large golden box slightly, and recoiled in horror.

A blackened cadaver, with twisted and calcined limbs, sat up therein, in a sinister fashion. Of Ahmosis, the great voluptuous flower conserved in balms, nothing any longer remained. One night had been sufficient to perfect the work of the tomb. The remains of the queen, corroded and hideous, were similar to those that had rested in the earth for a long time, forgotten by human beings.

With a groan, the priest collapsed between what remained of his two amours. He understood then that all happiness was lost for him, for he had outraged the gods by boasting of a vain science and stealing the sacred body of the Pharaoh's wife.

A PARTIAL LIST OF SNUGGLY BOOKS

LÉON BLOY *The Tarantulas' Parlor and Other Unkind Tales*

S. HENRY BERTHOUD *Misanthropic Tales*

FÉLICIEN CHAMPSAUR *The Latin Orgy*

FÉLICIEN CHAMPSAUR *The Emerald Princess and Other Decadent Fantasies*

BRENDAN CONNELL *Jottings from a Far Away Place*

QUENTIN S. CRISP *Blue on Blue*

LADY DILKE *The Outcast Spirit and Other Stories*

BERIT ELLINGSEN *Vessel and Solsvart*

EDMOND AND JULES DE GONCOURT *Manette Salomon*

RHYS HUGHES *Cloud Farming in Wales*

COLIN INSOLE *Valerie and Other Stories*

JUSTIN ISIS *Divorce Procedures for the Hairdressers of a Metallic and Inconstant Goddess*

VICTOR JOLY *The Unknown Collaborator and Other Legendary Tales*

BERNARD LAZARE *The Mirror of Legends*

JEAN LORRAIN *Masks in the Tapestry*

JEAN LORRAIN *Nightmares of an Ether-Drinker*

JEAN LORRAIN *The Soul-Drinker and Other Decadent Fantasies*

ARTHUR MACHEN *N*

ARTHUR MACHEN *Ornaments in Jade*

CAMILLE MAUCLAIR *The Frail Soul and Other Stories*

CATULLE MENDÈS *Bluebirds*

LUIS DE MIRANDA *Who Killed the Poet?*

OCTAVE MIRBEAU *The Death of Balzac*

CHARLES MORICE *Babels, Balloons and Innocent Eyes*

DAMIAN MURPHY *Daughters of Apostasy*

KRISTINE ONG MUSLIM *Butterfly Dream*

YARROW PAISLEY *Mendicant City*

URSULA PFLUG *Down From*

JEAN RICHEPIN *The Bull-Man and the Grasshopper*

DAVID RIX *A Suite in Four Windows*

FREDERICK ROLFE *An Ossuary of the North Lagoon and Other Stories*

JASON ROLFE *An Archive of Human Nonsense*

BRIAN STABLEFORD *Spirits of the Vasty Deep*

TOADHOUSE *Gone Fishing with Samy Rosenstock*

JANE DE LA VAUDÈRE *The Demi-Sexes and The Androgynes*

JANE DE LA VAUDÈRE *The Mystery of Kama and Brahma's Courtesans*

RENÉE VIVIEN *Lilith's Legacy*

CPSIA information can be obtained
at www.ICGtesting.com
Printed in the USA
LVHW032142010119
602325LV00002B/559/P